and the Blood of the Pride series

"Rebecca Desjardin rivals Sue Grafton's Kinsey Millhone as an interesting female PI. Recommended for both fans of the genre and newbies to paranormal romance."
—*Library Journal* on *Claws Bared*

"If you're a fan of strong female characters and mysteries with a paranormal twist, this is a real winner."
—*Reflections on Reading Romance* on *Blood of the Pride*

"Sheryl Nantus' *Blood of the Pride* is a tale of murder mingled with mystery in a secret feline society that will scratch that itch for romance."
—*Love Romances & More* on *Blood of the Pride*

"A really good read that kept me guessing till the end. I loved the romance between Rebecca and Brandon."
—*www.BookLiaison.net* on *Claws Bared*

"Well-written urban fantasy with a strong, appealing heroine."
—Nicole Luiken, author, on *Blood of the Pride*

"This is a shifter series that I will definitely be following."
—*TomeTender.blogspot.com* on *Claws Bared*

Also available from Sheryl Nantus
and Carina Press

Blood of the Pride
Claws Bared
Family Pride

Look for Sheryl Nantus's new series,
coming from Carina Press Spring 2014!

SHERYL NANTUS

BATTLE SCARS

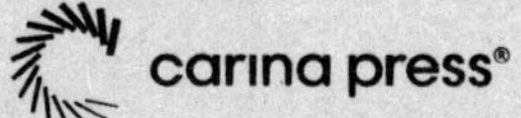

Recycling programs for this product may not exist in your area.

ISBN-13: 978-0-373-00232-0

BATTLE SCARS

This edition published by arrangement with Harlequin Books S.A.

www.CarinaPress.com

Printed in U.S.A.

Dear Reader,

I've always been amazed at how things that have happened in the past can return to the present with a vengeance, usually interfering with the future in some way. You go to a garage sale and trip across an old book—a favorite when you were younger—and it triggers a whole series of memories. Just ask anyone about their high school reunion and you'll get scores of stories about how good and bad it was, depending on the other people who attended.

And old friends and lovers are the best and worst of the lot.

When Brandon entered the reclusive and secretive world of the Felis, he knew he'd always be perceived as second best, but he didn't mind—his love for Rebecca would be more than enough to carry them both through the rocky family seas. But when an old friend resurfaces and wants to become more, he finds himself in a precarious position, caught between keeping the secret of the Felis's existence and paying off an old debt.

I really enjoyed doing a Felis version of *Romeo and Juliet,* with a somewhat different ending. Thank you for coming along on another fun adventure with Bran and Reb!

Sheryl Nantus

To my husband, who has always believed in me,
even when I didn't; AD, who keeps pushing me
to do my best; and Jazz...still missed and loved.
There may be others but you'll always
hold a special place in our hearts.

BATTLE SCARS

ONE

I'd always thought I'd appreciate the sight of a near-naked man scampering around my house in a pair of boxer shorts.

Until now.

I cleared my throat as Jake Middleston glared at me, his back to the kitchen. He had about ten years on me, with skin that had been left out in the sun too long. The jean jacket he wore over a dingy gray T-shirt was ripped along the arms—honest injuries and not for fashion. His short-cropped black hair was turning gray in spots, scattered over the scalp.

His nostrils flared and he frowned.

He could smell Brandon Hanover, my lover and new roommate, as Bran snuck into the kitchen.

He let out something akin to a huff.

Jake was old-school Felis. Tolerated humans when necessary, and even then under duress. He and his kin believed in the doctrine of each to their own and being in the same house as a human was tough, much less knowing said human was mated to me, a fellow Felis. I could see the words on his lips itching to break out, a good old-fashioned racist rant at me for being so involved with human society that I'd consider one of them as my beloved.

I had a snappy retort ready to go, curses included. My home, my rules.

But he was also a client and I had to stay polite in the face of old-fashioned prejudice. I'd done it before for other clients, slimy adulterers who wanted an easy way out of their marriage and itchy-fingered businessmen looking for criminals in their midst who stole paperclips and pencils.

If you had asked me six months ago if I'd have my fellow cat shifters as clients I would have laughed in your face. Being outcast for two decades has that effect on me.

But recent events had brought me back into the family and scored me one hot human mate, so I was prepared to deal with family as possible clients. And keep my mouth shut.

Besides, I needed the cash.

"You said you needed my help," I prompted, trying to draw his attention away from Bran. I couldn't see him but I could smell him, fresh from our bed upstairs.

He hadn't showered yet, making his natural male smell more intense, almost to the point of overpowering—let's just say that we enjoy waking each other up multiple times before we actually get up. I'd managed to get into the shower before my arranged meeting with Middleston but he'd refused, showing his stubborn streak and annoyance at me having anything to do in the morning other than stay in bed.

Bran knew we Felis had an enhanced sense of smell. And I knew he knew my new client would have it, as well.

The older man rubbed the palms of his hands on his

jeans, likely in an attempt to ignore the musky scent drifting across the room. "I have a daughter, Lisa. She's almost eighteen and thinks she knows it all." He gave me a knowing smile. "As you can guess we disagree on a few things."

I nodded. Out of the corner of my eye I spotted Bran tiptoeing toward the stairs cradling a huge bowl of tortilla chips and a bottle of salsa.

He knew I hated crumbs in bed.

He knew I couldn't say anything without making a scene.

I kept my attention on Middleston. It kept me from considering disembowelment.

"She..." He cleared his throat. "She ran away a few days ago. I figured she was just mad at me again, the usual stuff. You know how kids are these days, they get told 'no' once and they fly off the handle." He glanced to one side, a flush coming over his face. "Since her mom passed away a few years ago we haven't been as close as I'd have liked. She's my youngest, a 'happy surprise' as my wife put it. Other two are married and gone off to different Prides, so it's just the two of us." He swallowed hard and drew a deep breath, steadying himself. "Her mom, she raised all of them right, three daughters I love to death. But Lisa and I, we've just sort of been, well, disconnected since Jamie died. I don't do all that great with kits to start with, and little girls, well—"

"Why did you wait so long to come to me?"

He glanced toward the front door. "I called the local cops and they told me to give her a few days, let her think it over. Said most runaways change their minds as soon as they get off the bus down in the city, turn around and come right back." He cleared his throat again. "I wanted to give her that chance, to come home without any questions."

"But she didn't."

"She's down here in Toronto. I know it 'cause she never stopped talking 'bout coming to the city, making her fortune here. She left me a note saying she loved me but she had to strike out on her own and all that. I've heard things, bad things about young women who come to the city." He let out a staggered sigh. "I don't want her to be one of those statistics."

I waited.

He spread his hands. "I don't know nothing about this city, Miss Desjardin. I've been here a handful of times, once to see that *Phantom* thing 'cause Jamie had me buy her tickets for her birthday and a few more times for business. All I know is our town and our Pride. Lisa, she did school trips and all that. It's what made her think of coming here. If I were twenty years younger, even ten, I'd be on her trail. But this, this is beyond my ken. I can't hunt in this city like you can. This is your territory." He bit down on his lower lip before continuing. "I want my daughter back and I think you're my best chance."

"When's her birthday?"

He cleared his throat. "In three days."

"You understand when she turns eighteen she's recognized as an adult by the authorities." I tried not to look toward the stairs. "I can't promise I'll find her by then."

Jake nodded. "I know it's not a lot of time but I want to talk to her one last time. If she wants to go her own way I'll accept that but I don't want us to go our own ways angry at each other. I owe her mother that much." He tucked his chin into his chest. "I just want the chance. Three days, three weeks. Find her and tell her I want to talk, that's all."

"I'll do my best to find her and inform her of your wishes." I'd learned early in the private investigator game to not make promises I couldn't keep.

"Do you—" He paused and I could see him fighting to find the right words. "Do you find a lot of lost kids?"

I wasn't going to lie, not to family. "I don't get a lot of these types of cases. Usually the parents call me in a panic because their darling didn't come home last night and I find the kids a few hours later cowering at a shelter or at the bus station, ready to go home. The glamorous life of a runaway isn't what most kids are prepared for."

"Lisa's a smart kit. Took her kill within the hour on her first hunt." His chest puffed out. "She's a tough little girl. She's a survivor."

"We'll see how it goes. As I said, I can't promise anything but I'll give you my best."

He sat back in the wooden chair and studied me. "Heard you was good and honest." His tone shifted more toward approval than resignation. At least I wouldn't be fighting with Daddy during this job.

I smiled. "I try. Do you have a recent picture?"

"Figured you'd be asking for one." Middleston withdrew a wallet-sized picture from an inside jacket pocket and put it on the desk. The young redhead grinned out at me with youthful optimism. Petite and posing by a fence, Lisa looked like a thousand other young girls on the verge of adulthood.

My hand hovered over it. I paused, wrestling with my conscience. "Forgive me for asking, but why aren't you going through other…resources?"

I didn't want to say it out loud but I knew there were Felis inside the police department along with almost every other area of life—we tended to get around. A single phone call from any Board member and everyone from beat cops up to detectives and beyond would be looking for Lisa Middleston both on and off-duty, backed up by the law since she was still a minor for three more days. I'd seen the system at work and it was frighteningly effective in finding lost or missing children.

I might be throwing away a job but I had to ask why he wasn't using the network.

Middleston stared at the floor. "Don't want people to be knowing our private business. People start talking, start taking things the wrong way."

"Ah," I replied, seeing the light. He wanted to keep his daughter's disappearance as low-key as possible. The gossip mill would be running overtime if he called the Board and asked for an all-points bulletin to be put out on Lisa. By coming to me, Jake was keeping clear of officially calling a hunt—I was family and I was able to access more resources than he could alone but

I was also outcast and the news wouldn't get around about his daughter's indiscretions. His family wouldn't lose face and he wouldn't be bringing in an outsider.

This flexibility was what had brought me back into the family in the first place a few months ago. A blessing and a curse to be part of two worlds and yet not really fully in either.

As if to remind me, my left arm itched, specifically the still-healing skin just below my shoulder courtesy of a stray bullet slamming into me just over a month ago. It'd been a nasty gouge and I'd laughed when the doctors had suggested a referral to a plastic surgeon.

They hadn't seen the old scars on my back, courtesy of my family.

Middleston pulled his wallet from his pocket. The worn leather was bulging with cash, the stress of folding it over splitting the ancient hide at the center. I hoped he wasn't planning to stay in Toronto too long—flashing a wad like that, he was begging to be mugged.

I wasn't worried about Jake.

I was worried about the mugger.

He pulled out five one-hundred-dollar bills. "I assume this'll be enough to start."

I tried to look nonplussed at the generous amount. "Let me draw up the contract and I'll be with you in a minute." I reached for the bottom desk drawer where I kept the standard forms.

One edge of his mouth twitched downward.

"Or," I said, "we can just shake hands."

He was old-school, where a handshake was as good if not better than legal documents.

Not to mention it kept the paper trail invisible. No paperwork, no rumors.

No chance for anyone to connect us.

"Let me know if you need more money." Middleston got to his feet. "How much detail do you need to get started? You already got her picture."

My pencil hovered over the blank yellow legal pad. "Let's start with the basics. Weight, height, eye color." I pointed the pink eraser at the photo. "That's great, but just in case she decides to change her hair color or something."

The older man worked through the list with ease as if he'd been practicing.

I wasn't so sure he hadn't been.

"Is there anyone she was seeing? Some boyfriend, past or present, she might be hanging out with?"

The answering scowl was all I needed.

"No one of note," Jake snarled. "There was a fellow but I told him to shove off."

"His name?"

He shook his head. "No. I'm not giving you that. You go talk to him you'll start this whole thing up again and I told her she's done and over with him." His lips rolled around as if he wanted to spit and couldn't. "No one of note, like I said."

I winced inside. If this was a case of Lisa running off with her boyfriend then this whole thing could get nasty really fast.

"I just want to talk to her," Jake repeated before I could ask anything else.

He slumped in the chair, the flash of anger gone. All that was left was an old man at the point of tears.

Jake looked at me with weary, bloodshot eyes. "If she's going to go her own way I want to say goodbye in a right way, like a father should."

I weighed his words, working both sides of the equation.

"I'll find her and tell her you want to talk to her." I jabbed my index finger in the air. "But I won't let you hurt her."

Jake leaned back as if I'd slapped him. "I wouldn't hurt Lisa. She's all I have now."

My internal judge told me he was telling the truth. There was also the chance she'd run away with a punk and could be looking for a way out of a destructive relationship. I had no way of knowing the truth.

Other than finding Lisa and asking her.

The small voice reminded me that if I didn't take the case Jake Middleston might end up stomping around Toronto looking for her alone and headed for a world of trouble. If he ended up in a street fight it could go badly, with his Felis-enhanced senses giving him the upper hand and someone suffering, either human or Felis.

I couldn't let that happen.

I grumbled inside about a damned conscience that loved to weigh in on my business choices but never showed up when I was pigging out on chocolate donuts to the point of nausea.

"I'll find her and make sure she's safe. And tell her

you want to talk to her." It was a compromise but one I could live with.

"Thank you." He got to his feet and stretched out his hand. "Thank you."

His grip was hard and strong, a typical Felis test of strength.

I made it through without any broken fingers. "I'll call when I have something."

Jake gave me his cell phone number and headed for the front door, walking through my living room. Jazz trilled from where she lay on the couch, rolling onto her back and exposing her tummy for a rub. She looked at him with sad, dark eyes as if she didn't have enough loving and a bowl full of kibble waiting for her in the kitchen.

He stopped for a second to rub the white cat's belly, chuckling as she pawed the air. A few mumbled somethings and he moved on to go outside.

I stayed at my desk and listened to him step through the front yard and onto the sidewalk, his work boots pounding the pavement. A minute later a radio blared incoherent country music and an engine roared before dying down to a low hum. The sound lessened and disappeared as I envisioned the pickup truck pulling away and heading down the street.

I picked up my cell phone and tapped in Jess Hammersmythe's number.

It wasn't that I didn't trust Jake Middleston, but I'd developed a simple mantra over the years of being a private investigator and hearing very different stories from both sides of a divorce case or insurance claim.

Trust but verify.

If there was a missing girl from my old Pride she'd know about it. And as one of the Board members she'd know if there was more to this than just a teenager running off with her true love of the week who, presumably, was another Felis. There was nothing illegal about it but it'd be a note of concern for the Board, who kept a close eye on all of the family—you didn't simply disappear into the crowd. A runaway wasn't enough to call out the troops but there was no way Lisa Middleston was going to stay underground for long.

I'd discovered that when they'd showed up on my doorstep after leaving me alone for decades. The Board always kept track of you no matter where or who you were.

Middleston's sidestepping the Pride's resources sent up red flags and I wasn't about to step in a minefield if I couldn't map it out first.

Jess picked the phone up on the fifth ring.

"Rebecca." She sounded shocked, something I'd rarely seen or heard. "I was about to call you."

I could hear a woman weeping in the background and raised my voice over the wailing. "Is this about the missing girl? Don't get on my case. Her father just left and I haven't had a chance to hit the streets yet so tell her aunt or whoever to give me a few hours—"

"What?" I visualized the tall woman shaking her head. Part of me relished the idea of stumping Jess. The other part was terrified that I had, in fact, stumped Jess, one of the toughest Felis I knew. "No, wait…what? What missing girl?"

"Lisa Middleston," I offered. "She's the missing girl I've been hired to find."

"I'm talking about a missing boy. Evan Chandler." The crying in the background rose and fell like a hockey fan's playoff hopes. "His mother's with me right now."

The pulsing behind my left eye signaled a headache about to start. "Let me guess. This isn't a coincidence."

Jess chuckled. "You think? Let me take care of Mary and I'll call you back within the hour. Don't do anything until we have a chance to talk." The line went dead before I could disconnect.

I put the phone down and pressed my palms against my eyes. This situation had the potential of going bad really fast.

Two country kids running away to find their fortune in the big city might go over well in the movies but the reality was that they'd find themselves out of their depth within minutes of stepping off the bus. Those stories about slavery, prostitution and drug abuse weren't just fluff for the news programs.

I headed for the stairs, determined to get some painkillers into me before Jess called back. This was turning out to be one hell of a morning and I hadn't even done anything yet.

Jazz pattered by me, hopping up the steps and turning toward the bedroom with her tail held high, a spring in her step. I followed her in, scowling at the half-naked man sprawled across the bed.

Tortilla chip crumbs everywhere. A minefield of pointed fried caltrops.

A fat dollop of salsa sat on the quilted bedspread neatly folded at the bottom of the king-sized bed.

Brandon Hanover grinned at me, offering a salsa-loaded chip in one hand. The other nudged the waistband of the boxer shorts down a fraction of an inch, showing more bare flesh.

"Want a snack?"

I sighed. As a lover, the redhead was fantastic. As a roommate, he left a lot to be desired.

"We're going to have to wash that." I pointed at the salsa stain even as I snagged the chip out of his hand and popped it in my mouth.

"No problem." He chomped another chip as Jazz hopped on the bed and began to nibble at the crumbs spread out over the sheets.

"Yes problem. The Laundromat is up on Queen Street and I don't have time to haul the bedspread up there right now."

His eyebrows rose. "Damn. I'd forgotten you don't have a washer and dryer here."

"Remember more often." I swept a handful of crumbs off the bed, annoying the cat, who had already started munching. "Good news is I've got some work. Bring in some cash."

A pained look flashed across his face and I regretted the phrasing. It'd been a month since he'd moved in, forsaking his rich family, and he'd insisted on paying half of everything. He'd begged an advance off his editor for a future article but it'd been barely enough to pay the utilities and phone bills, never mind getting groceries.

Meanwhile I'd been dipping into my own savings to cover my recent unemployed status. We weren't on the verge of losing the house but the private investigation business was either feast or famine.

I really didn't want to go toward the famine side.

I tried to fix the damage. "Got paid in advance. Five hundred dollars."

Bran let out a low whistle. "That'll keep us in cat kibble for a few days." His forehead furrowed. "What's the job?"

"Finding a runaway girl." I took another chip and dipped it in the jar before maneuvering the overloaded chip to my mouth. "And Jess has the other half of the equation. Boy and girl running off together to the big city. Romeo and Juliet with fur and fangs."

A pained look came over his face. I winced, remembering the story that had temporarily propelled him to journalistic stardom.

Brandon had gone native, living the street life with a group of kids who took him in and showed him the seedy underside of Toronto. The article had detailed their struggles as they formed their own family with all the politics and emotions therein. Love, hate, life and death stories happening in a shadow world where being twenty was considered "old."

It'd been a hit, the story rocking the news feeds. So much so that Bran found himself becoming the focus of the attention, the brave rich author gone underground to get the story and so forth. Despite his best efforts to bring attention to the problems street kids suffered, the news became all about him and not about the group and their trials and tribulations; the direct opposite of why he'd undertaken the task in the first place.

Upset, Bran had returned to the streets to find his old family to try and explain what had happened, how his intentions had been twisted and warped into being all about him instead of presenting their stories.

He'd found only two of the group—at the morgue, a pair of lovers who'd overdosed on heroin not long after Bran's leaving. Even though he'd had nothing to do with the deaths it'd cut him deep, deep enough to push him away from legitimate journalism for a few years and sending him into self-imposed exile, bashing out crap for the tabloid *Toronto Inquisitor.*

Until he'd been handed a story about a dead cat-woman.

As they say, the rest is history.

I grabbed the half-empty bag and salsa jar off the bed and headed for the bathroom. "I'm hoping to find them near the bus station, curled up in a donut shop and scared shitless. Country kids don't usually take to the streets that easily, so I've heard. Big difference between small town living and jumping into the big city, Felis or not."

"Might be right there. One can hope they run back home once they hit the streets. Usually the romantic ideal dies a fast death once you're digging in a Dumpster for stale donuts and trying to figure out if the slimy green meat is edible." The response came as I put the chips and dip in the sink and busied myself digging out the bottle of painkillers. The headache wasn't bad, not yet.

A phone call from Jess would make it worse.

The pills went down with a swig of water and a lasting taste of spicy salsa. I stuck my head out of the bedroom, feeling the latest wave of pain begin to wither and die on the drug shore.

Bran lay on his back, his hands tucked behind his head. He stared at the ceiling and let out a low sigh.

I didn't have to be a mind reader to know what he was thinking about.

Time to try and change the mood.

"And could you not wander through the house in your underwear when I'm dealing with a client?" I crossed my arms and tried to sound authoritative. Hard to do with the manflesh on display. "How would you like it if I wore that fuzzed red scrap of cloth you bought me to a meeting with your editor?"

The item in question had been acquired after a late-night crawl through lingerie stores in the Eaton Center, a nightie with wee bits of faux red fur in all the right places.

He grinned.

My reverse psychology was not reversing.

"Ooh." His tongue flicked out, wetting his lips. "Maybe I'd get a better chance at the hot stories if I did take you along." His brown eyes sparkled with glee and more than a little wanton lust. He patted the mattress beside him. "Wanna audition for the job?"

"Jess is going to call back. Within the hour." I let out an exaggerated sigh. Over the last few weeks this had become a welcome work interruption but I never gave in easily. "Not enough time."

Bran put his hands behind his head and looked at the ceiling, making a smacking noise with his lips. "Two, three—"

He leaped off the bed and grabbed me around the waist. "I love a challenge."

I let out an unladylike squeak as his fingers began to pull up my shirt. "Jess—"

"Within the hour. I got it." He nipped my earlobe, the spike of pain disappearing under the burning need, rekindled with his touch. "Just lie back and think of England. Or whatever else you'd like."

"Whatever?" I gasped, the familiar haze clouding my thoughts.

"Well, as long as it's about me." His expert fingers popped the buttons on my blouse with unerring accuracy before moving to the front of my jeans.

I ran my hands along his waistband, tugging at the boxers.

"I think I'm ready for my audition."

Exactly thirty-five minutes later I rolled onto my back, wheezing for air. The cool sheets felt good on my bare skin even with a few wayward crumbs poking at me.

"Dang." My pulse pounded in my ears. "That's never getting old, is it?"

"You're welcome." Bran rolled onto his side with a smug smile. "Never say I don't keep to my schedule." He looked at the digital clock on the night table. "Still some time left. Want to try for a quickie?" He waggled his eyebrows.

As if on cue my cell phone rang.

"Put it on hold, Romeo." I tugged on my blouse, struggling to get my hands through the sleeves. "Unless you want to tell Jess to call back."

It took a concentrated effort to get the buttons lined up. There was no way I was going to talk to Jess naked, even if Bran didn't seem to mind.

He scowled and reached for a half-full bottle of water perched on the side table. The man was daring but not suicidal.

I plucked the cell phone out of my jeans on the floor and propped myself up against the headboard, enjoying his pouty look.

"You've caught this one by the tail, kit." The disapproving tone killed any post-coital mellowness.

Being in my mid-thirties and still being called a kit by someone with twenty-plus years on me wasn't a good way to start the conversation.

"Hi, Jess."

I waited.

The Board member would tell me what I needed to know in her own good time and not a second sooner. I'd learned over the past few months staying quiet often got more answers than opening my yap.

"I'm assuming your newest client is Jake Middleston. Lisa's father," she continued talking without pausing for my input. "I've just had a weepy session with Mary Chandler, Evan Chandler's mother. Seems the two kids were dating and have decided to do that running-away-together thing." She let out a snort. "This is not good."

"Kids run off all the time." Bran pushed himself up

beside me. He'd wrestled his shorts back on, giving me a less distracting view. He tilted his head toward the phone, resting his chin on my shoulder. "Trust me, I've seen it. A few weeks digging in Dumpsters for food and they'll come back home."

"Or be eighteen and out from under their parents' tails," I added. "Let me make this clear—I'm going to look for Lisa no matter what you tell me. I took the job from Middleston and told him I'd find her and at least tell her that her father wants to talk to her. What happens after that is their business, not mine. Or it would have been until now."

I paused, picking my words carefully. Jess was notorious for leaving out details. "But what's the real story here?" I pushed on. "What's so important about these two that one father's calling me in for a private hunt and the mother of the other one's asking you for help? I'm getting some weird vibes on this and it's more than Middleston being pissed off at some young man for chasing his daughter."

"Blood feud," she replied.

I blinked. "What?"

"I should have known there was a problem when Middleston asked about you." Jess said more to herself than to us. "Damned blind fool could have seen that. Should have seen that and told him to stand aside, let the Board deal with this."

I interrupted her pity party without remorse. "The feud. We have those?"

"Yes, we have 'those,'" Jess snapped. "Why

wouldn't we? Every family has brawls and people who don't like each other. Why should we be any different?"

"I guess I missed the memo," I shot back. "Being outcast and all."

Jess sucked in her breath through clenched teeth. The topic of my exile from the Pride for most of my adult life was still a painful topic between us despite six months of working for the family on various jobs.

Bran's hand snaked under my shirt and stroked the scar tissue crisscrossing my back. Most conversations with Jess ended with high blood pressure and a headache.

"We're assuming the kids ran off together. The Middlestons are treating it like just the girl left on her own and the same with the Chandlers, neither one telling me there was more about this. Middleston figured you wouldn't contact me and I'd never figure it out." I could hear the annoyance in her voice. "As if I was born yesterday and couldn't put two and two together. Boy meets girl, boy falls in love with girl. More likely when you're told it's forbidden fruit."

"How could they be dating with their families fighting?" I asked.

"Internet," Jess replied. "Sexting, I believe it's called. Either way they think they're in love and run off to seek their fortune, blah blah blah."

"This feud," Bran said, "how bad is it? We talking a push and shove at the local bar or are we going to start pulling bodies out of Lake Ontario with their throats slashed open?"

We waited for almost a minute in silence. I wasn't

sure if Jess was gauging how much to tell Bran, a human, versus what I needed to know if I had a hope in hell of finding the kids.

"Feuds start over anything in the family, just like in human society. It's usually business-related. Stealing each other clients, undercutting costs on competing bids, that sort of thing. But it's come to brawling a few times when challenges are issued. Broken noses, hurt feelings, lots of cursing and shaking of fists."

I winced, thinking of two Felis facing off against each other over some real or imagined slight. When Changed we manifested claws and fangs along with fur obscuring our features, but a lot of damage could be done with "just" claws and fangs.

Jess had lost an eye over it.

"What started this one?" Bran asked.

"None of your business." The underlying steel in her voice reminded us both that Bran was on the edges of Felis society, as I was—tolerated when necessary. She liked him but he still had a long way to go before being accepted by the family.

As if either of us gave a crap.

"If I find one I'm going to probably find the other." I pushed the conversation back to business. "What are the Chandlers doing to find the boy? Am I going to butt heads with the competition? Are they sending out their own hunter?"

Jess chuckled. "The ironic part is that I was about to refer them to you. Mary Chandler is a widow with one grown adult son and she's not about to send him down to Toronto to start sniffing around for his brother.

She's got friends who are eager to help but I convinced her to keep this as low-key as possible and offered you as an alternative to getting more people involved. The less, the better for all of us."

She wasn't just talking about keeping the feuding members apart. We'd kept our family secret for centuries from human society and it was her job as a Board member to do everything she could to keep our existence off the grid.

Having a major brawl between families in the middle of Toronto wasn't going to happen if she could help it.

She let out an annoyed snort. "Middleston, ass that he is, didn't tell me he needed help finding his daughter. He asked for someone to do a security check on some new farm hands he was thinking of hiring, temporary help and all humans. I figured you needed the work and gave him your number."

"I could use the money but not if I'm going to be walking into the middle of a Felis Hatfield/McCoy feud." I paused before asking the next question. "What's your call on this?"

"My what?" Jess replied.

"What's the Board's position on this?"

Bran gave me a questioning look. I waited, unsure which answer I wanted. The Board controlled and led the Pride in many areas but I wasn't sure where runaway kids fell in their never-ending political games.

"I'm not calling you on behalf of the Board. I'm calling you because Mary Chandler is a good friend who needs help," Jess said. "If you choose to take her case as well I'll get her to transfer the funds into your account today."

"And the Board's position is?"

"We don't have one. We don't choose sides."

I chewed on my bottom lip. "Can't or won't?"

"The Board isn't going to choose which family to support. Haven't in the past and sure won't now, not when it's nothing but a pair of runaway kids who might just as easily turn up at home in the next few hours." She paused and I could hear her choosing her words carefully. "At this point it's nothing that should concern the Board. Personally I'll be happy if you take the second case, but whatever you decide is fine with the Board and with me. You can dump both cases if you want. Jake'll be upset if you turn him down but he'll get over it."

"Give me a minute." I imagined a set of scales in my mind and started tossing weights on each side. Helping was almost mandatory for me as a fellow Felis but I wasn't keen on getting caught between two angry families. I had no doubt people had been burned in the past on both sides and I didn't need the trouble.

The problem, again, was that if I said no I could see Middleston and/or Chandler sending in their own family friends to find the kids and opening a huge can of trouble in my city. It'd be like setting a bull loose in a china shop, or in this case a clumsy lion thrashing around.

I had no doubt if that happened I'd be pulled in either to help clean up the mess or cover up the blood.

At least if I took the case it'd be on my own terms.

"How many runaways have you found over the years?" Bran touched my shoulder, making me jump.

"A few. A handful, to be honest." I tried not to sound defensive, knowing Jess was still listening. "Most of them go home after a week of lying on cold pavement, ready to warm up to their parents again. Usually they leave over a small thing, curfews and crap like that. I usually hit the bus station first and then walk the streets for a few nights until they come up. Get Hank to call the beat cops and put the fear of God into the homeless kids until they run home to mom and dad."

I flinched inside, thinking about Hank Attersley. The police detective and I hadn't spoken since he'd had to take me in for my involvement with the Hanovers and Bran's half-brother. I wasn't sure if I could count on him for help right now.

Bran cleared his throat. "That could take weeks."

"It could," I admitted. "These are kids used to roughing it, not pampered socialites looking to scare their parents because they didn't get a sports car for their birthday."

Bran nodded. "You'll need my help if you want to find them fast. I know it's been a few years but I can help you cut corners, save you wasting time in some areas and maybe use some old contacts." He grinned. "Not to mention two heads are better than one, even when one's mine."

I bit down on my lip, feeling the skin threaten to split.

"Are you going to be okay with this?" Jess asked the question I was thinking.

"I owe you," Bran answered. He wasn't wrong—Jess had been a major factor in finding and saving his baby half-brother a month before. "I always pay my debts. Say the word and I'm with her on this."

Jess chuckled. "As if I could keep you out of her business." Her tone shifted. "Rebecca, are you going to be okay taking him along?"

I hesitated just long enough for Bran to take and squeeze my hand.

"I'll be fine. Besides, the faster we find those two kids the faster this entire thing is over." He smiled and flexed his free arm. "Better. Stronger. Faster." He pointed down at his shorts. "As you know."

"Faster, yes." I turned my attention back to the phone, ignoring his exaggerated wincing, and hoped Jess wasn't getting the joke. "Jess, tell me the truth. Is this going to get nasty?"

She laughed, a low rumbling that both stirred the hunter inside and terrified me at the same time. "It always comes down to blood, Reb. Always down to the blood."

TWO

Within the hour I had all the pertinent information about Evan Chandler on my computer screen courtesy of an email from Jess, including a color photograph my printer screeched out to join the one of Lisa Middleston downstairs.

The young man had dark hair, cropped almost to the scalp, and a wide smile that would have a dozen girls tossing their panties at him on a good day. He cradled a classic guitar with the care and love of a mother for a newborn. It was easy to see how he'd be a dream date for a young Felis girl, especially if he was a bad boy by birth.

Standing at my desk I shoved the two photographs next to each other in a large envelope along with duplicates courtesy of my coughing photocopier. I didn't want to get to the point of plastering their faces on each telephone pole in the city but it never hurt to be prepared to drop off copies. I also scanned the two pictures into my cell phone for backup.

Bran whistled as he came down the stairs wearing jeans and tugging on a light blue T-shirt with the Toronto Maple Leafs logo on it. I winced at seeing the pale pink scars on his chest.

We'd both taken a battering over the past few weeks,

mentally and physically. I hoped this case would be less of both. We could use a little down time.

Bran strolled by me, adding a jaunty strut to his walk. "Enjoying the view?"

I rolled my eyes. "Don't make me regret taking you to the Cat's Meow." Saying the name of the strip club in Penscotta, Pennsylvania, stirred up old memories. That was where he'd gotten the scars and we'd cemented our relationship.

Then he made a less-than-subtle shift of his hips and I forgot what I was remembering.

I resisted slapping his butt as I followed. "It's time for work."

"Your call." He trotted into the kitchen, where the kettle had just started to scream.

"I figure we'll start at the bus station." I threw a handful of cat treats on the floor as Jazz padded down the stairs toward us. She trilled as she dove on the tiny brown nuggets. "They've been in town at least a day or two but I'm hoping someone saw them, maybe pointed them toward a shelter."

"Even if they hit the shelters they'll be trying to get some money for food and maybe a hotel room to stay off the streets. It may be summer but it's still nicer to sleep on a mattress instead of the ground. Whatever cash they brought won't last for long and they'll end up begging on Yonge Street for spare change." Bran poured the hot water into my fat Brown Betty teapot. "That or busking. Any skills between them?"

"Busking?"

"Singing, dancing, whatever brings in the money."

Bran smiled as he prepared two mugs for us, adding a dash of milk to each. “Harder than begging but it has a bit more validity. Actually doing something for the cash and all that.”

I studied my notes. “I just call it panhandling. Evan took his guitar when he split. Not sure about Lisa.”

Bran nodded. “Busking, then. He’ll sing and she’ll either beg for cash or grab a bucket to bang on and supplement his songs.” He picked up the bag of cat treats and opened it. “Working together to survive.”

Jazz did her best impression of a feline ghost, appearing at his feet with a loud trill of starvation despite our previous interaction. I rolled my eyes as Bran dropped another handful of treats into her already-full bowl, ignoring my comment.

“She’s going to get fat.”

“Fatter.” Bran held up a finger. “And I like my women to have a little meat on their bones, thank you very much.”

I placed the file on the counter and busied myself with pouring out the tea into the two mugs. “I’m okay with you sitting out this one. If you’d rather work on your article—”

“I told you I’m fine.” He slammed his hand down on the countertop. The Brown Betty teapot shook and clattered.

Jazz vanished from the room in a white blur.

“I’m fine,” Bran repeated in a lower, softer tone.

I crossed my arms and waited.

“I’m going to be fine.” He lifted the lid off the teapot and peered inside. “I’m not going to sit at home here and let you run out there with the wild dogs. Some of those kids can be nasty and mean and a lot of them have more than just a sharp tongue to defend themselves."

I could smell the sweat gathering on his forehead. Musky, tingling smell speaking of fear.

This was not going well.

"I can take care of myself. I was doing this before you came along, remember." I tried to sound light-hearted, take the edge off. "You can stay here, work the phones. I expect you can run through the list faster than I can physically visit each and every shelter."

He didn't take the bait. "I won't let you put yourself in danger unnecessarily. You don't know the streets like I do."

"Really." The throbbing behind my eye increased ten-fold. I was tired of playing nice. "What the fuck do you think I was doing for years before you came along?" I grabbed the teapot. "Do you think I'm some helpless woman waiting to be saved?"

The pot swung around in my hand, steaming hot liquid shooting out the spout as I aimed for the mugs.

And missed.

I jumped as a splash of hot tea hit my hand. "Fuck." I dropped the teapot back on the counter.

"Damn it." Bran flipped the cold water on and grabbed my wrist. "You've got to be more careful."

My first instinct was to pull away and bare my teeth, snarl at this man trying to dominate me.

His grip tightened. "Don't fight me on this." His jaw tensed up, his lips pulling into a straight line.

He yanked my hand under the flowing water.

I winced at the shock, the light burn now drowned out by freezing water. The tap sputtered for a second, spewing water over us before settling into a thin drizzle.

Bran moved in behind me, pressing his chest against my back. His free hand went around my belly to hold me still against the counter. "Don't try to stop me from taking care of you. It won't work."

I felt his teeth nip at the back of my neck, his tongue running over freshly-healed marks. Marks he'd put there to stake his claim to me, to our relationship.

I growled. "I don't need to be taken care of."

"Of course not." His low voice both soothed and annoyed me, the heated air rolling over my ear. "And I don't need to go out with you on the streets. But here we are and we're both in agreement now."

I squirmed, trying to shake his grip. The iron bar across my belly stayed put.

"I have faith in you being able to handle yourself," he whispered. "But don't blame me for wanting to top you every now and then. It's an alpha male thing."

I huffed and reached for the tap. The light burn had disappeared. "We'll see about the topping."

A soft kiss behind my ear and he released my wrist. "Now I'm hungry for pizza."

"Work now, food and kink later." I finished pouring out the tea into the two mugs, inspecting the teapot for any cracks.

Jazz poked her head around the corner, obviously more hungry than afraid.

Bran added a handful of treats to the overflowing

food bowl as an apology to Jazz. He took his mug, a pensive look on his face. "Been a long time since I thought about the streets."

I didn't push.

Jazz plopped down in front of her bowl. She dipped her paw in and flipped one piece of food out before eating it off the dark blue mat we used to try and keep the kibble contained.

I looked at my watch. "After we finish this, let's head to the bus terminal and see what we can find. If we're lucky we'll trip over the little buggers and have them back to their respective families by sunset."

Bran sipped his drink. "I've finished the first draft on that article about Pennsylvania and need to let it steep for a bit." He chuckled. "It's a piece on small town business revivals. Used the strip club as an example."

"Sounds good." I sipped my tea and watched him.

He threw a saucy wink my way. "I'll be fine." He smiled. "I'm good, Reb. I'm good."

The weariness in his eyes told me otherwise. But I couldn't pass up on a chance to get some help and find these two before any blood got spilled.

Including ours.

I looked down at Jazz. "You stay here and guard the kibble."

The white cat flipped another piece of food onto the floor and ignored us.

The Toronto Bus Terminal is located right at the intersection of Bay and Dundas, a sneeze's distance away from Yonge Street, the main artery for the city. Two terminals—one for arrivals, one for departures and a handful of underground shops offering up food and magazines for the weary travelers too afraid to leave the area and go into downtown proper. Regular travelers bypass the snack shacks and go the extra block to the nearest Starbucks to hook into the free wifi between buses heading out to all points from New York City to the Great White North.

It wasn't hard to pick up the newcomers hopping off the bus with a backpack and a handful of dreams, the wide-eyed visitors staring up at the towers circling around them. And easy to see the predators waiting in the shadows, watching and judging how fast they could pick up the sweet young things and put them to work in one way or another.

We pulled into a lot a half-block from the terminal, squeezing the Jeep between two black Hummers. The parking attendant grinned as he extorted three times the going rate for any other place in the city from me, pocketing the bills and touching the brim of his baseball cap.

I grumbled and led Bran back to the main street. "Highway robbery."

He chuckled. "Just put it on your expense report. You know Jess'll make sure you get reimbursed."

I gave him the stink-eye. "That's not the point. The point is that just because someone owns a piece of real estate that's flat and empty they can ask whatever they want and people have to pay."

"Until they sell it to a construction company so another condo can go up. Free enterprise." Bran laughed again. "Might be a time when you end up buying a condo to park in—it'd be cheaper."

We walked toward the terminals, choking on the amount of diesel fumes swirling around us.

"Place needs better ventilation." He put one hand over his mouth and coughed.

"Place needs a lot more than that." I grabbed his arm as a commuter bus pushed toward us, dangerously close to rolling over our toes as it maneuvered through the narrow street at a snail's pace. "It wasn't ever meant to have this much traffic."

We headed toward a security officer standing to one side, watching the organized chaos. One sniff and I knew he was family, despite the overwhelming stink of urine, gasoline and various heavy body odors swirling around us. His uniform shirt was threadbare in spots, showing me he'd been on the job long enough to know what to look for.

He touched his cap as I introduced myself.

"Morning, folks. What can I help you with?"

"These two kits." I showed him the photographs. "Runaways. Have you seen them come through here?"

He studied Bran standing by my side for a second before answering. "Kits? You mean kids, right?"

I sighed, remembering the first rule. Secrecy. Total secrecy about the Felis. The guard was simply trying to give me a way out of my obvious slip of the lip.

This guy was just following rules.

I hated rules.

I handed him a business card and watched his reaction, his lips moving silently as he read the embossed name and assorted information.

He looked up from the card, the surprise in his eyes weighed with a degree of distaste. Being outcast meant I had to fight for every inch of respect, from being a genetic freak to choosing a human mate.

"Rebecca Desjardin." He said my name like he was spitting out cigarette ashes. "I've heard of you." He bared his teeth. "Got nothing for you today."

I wasn't going to try and justify my existence. Not today.

"I'm working for Jess." It wasn't a total lie. "You can call her if you'd like. I'm sure she'd love to hear from one of our own who's delaying my investigation."

The security officer stood up a little straighter at mention of the Board member. Her reputation far outweighed mine and I wasn't afraid to use it.

He glanced at Bran. I could see the conflict on his face, the fight between helping a fellow Felis and keeping secrets from a human.

I shoved the photos under his nose again, breaking his concentration and forcing an answer. "Have you seen them?"

"I see kids—I mean, kits, come through here every day," he replied. "I could tell you I saw them but I'd be lying. They could have been here or not. I don't keep track of all the foot traffic, I just make sure no one gets run over." His thick eyebrows headed for a collision. "Is there a hunt? I didn't hear anything about a hunt."

The curiosity in his voice was tempered with fear. A hunt wasn't called often but it was the equivalent of an Amber Alert, an all-points bulletin hitting every Felis in the area—potentially thousands of eyes turned toward finding one person. I'd seen it in action and it was full of awesome.

I cursed Middleston silently for not wanting to bring everyone in on this. It would have probably gotten him Lisa back the minute she hit the streets in Toronto, starting with this guard grabbing her right there in the terminal. But I could understand the embarrassment at having to admit losing control of his daughter.

Calling a hunt still would have made things easier.

"No, no hunt."

The flash of relief over his face dissolved into a stoic stare. "Ah." He studied the pictures again. "I don't remember seeing them but there's so many kids coming through these days." He waved a hand at the bright sunlight cutting through the streets. "Summer brings them out of the woodwork. No school and they're all looking for adventure. Come to the big city for a few weeks and see how the wild style works for them." He shook his head. "Usually don't."

"I understand." I handed him a set of the cheap photocopies I'd made and put the good ones back in the envelope. "If you do see them can you call me?"

"Will do." He slipped the photos and my business card into a uniform pocket. "You might want to check out the Spot."

"The what?" I asked.

"The Spot." He paused, seeing my confusion. "The Spot. It's a drop-in place just over on Yonge. Opened up about a year ago—usually there's a volunteer 'round here handing out flyers to whoever needs one."

"Government-run?" Bran broke in.

The officer shrugged. "Don't know, don't care. Place gives out free food and referrals to shelters and safety tips if they want to stay on the street. As long as someone's looking out for those kids it's all good." He glanced over to where a crowd of waiting commuters edged out into a bus lane. "I gotta go corral the animals. Good luck."

He paused for a second. "Name's Bramswell. Tell Jess I helped you out, 'kay?" Without waiting for our response he headed for the mob, waving his hands in the air to get their attention.

"This place, that's new," Bran mused as we edged our way around another long lineup and headed down the sidewalk. "Not too many new outreach programs opening up with the government looking to cut corners. Probably privately-funded, give some of the rich folk some place to drop their tax deductions." The sadness under his words tugged at my heart.

I didn't say anything. Bran's parents had accepted his decision to break off all ties, effectively orphaning him. The single bright light in the dark family cloud hovering over his head was that he'd gotten a chance to spend some time with Liam, his half-brother. The Callendars had invited him over for an evening and he'd been giddy when he got home, babbling his own version of baby talk until I tucked him into bed.

He missed his family's money, of that I had no doubt. Having easy access to obscene amounts of money was addictive and he'd quit cold-turkey, sliding into my lifestyle of tuna casserole and reheated soup without complaint. Bran hadn't said anything but I'd seen him glancing at the meat aisle with envy in the supermarket, checking out the steaks we couldn't afford anymore.

Freedom always came with a price.

It wasn't hard to find the Spot—the huge black period hanging over a small storefront gave it away. We picked our way through the masses of tourists and commuters filling the sidewalk, zigging and zagging as we approached the center.

We passed a set of fast-food restaurants, the doors swinging back and forth as customers flew in and out, getting their sodium fix for the day. I glanced at the middle-aged man sitting almost at the entrance to the restaurant, just close enough to get your attention but far enough away for management not to call the cops on him. He held up a coffee cup in one hand and a small sign with a crayon-lettered plea for help in the other.

Inside I shuddered. This was no way to live.

"Not too far from Second Chance Second Life," Bran said, his voice tinged with sadness. The soup kitchen had stayed open despite the scandal of having one of their employees, a thug on probation, responsible for the death of Bran's father's mistress and the kidnapping of his half-brother. The gossip had died down as of late but it lay there like an open scab on your heel, waiting to be ripped open again at any moment if you turned the wrong way.

I dropped a handful of coins in the man's cup.

Karma and all that. He gave me a nod and a toothless smile before turning his attention to the next passersby.

"There they are." Bran pointed just ahead of us. A cluster of ten teenagers huddled at the entrance to a huge stone building. The fat black period hung over their heads like a Sword of Damocles, swinging back and forth on thick heavy chains.

"I remember this building," Bran said. "Used to be a storefront church. Free sermon with every sandwich. Good food, good times." He chuckled. "As long as you didn't mind hearing you would go to hell on an hourly basis."

We surveyed the pack in front of the church. Lunch had been served not too long ago and cellophane wrappers blew by our feet as the kids munched on prepackaged hard cookies.

"Don't see them here." Bran studied the faces around us. "Damn they're young," he whispered.

"So were we." An unfamiliar voice came from behind us.

I spun around to see a woman smiling at Bran who stood there with his mouth open, catching flies.

She was in her mid-twenties and tall, close to six feet with long blond hair trailing down past her waist in a ponytail. The light gray T-shirt with a giant black spot in the center hugged her form tight enough for me to see she wasn't wearing a bra—and she should have been.

"Been a long time." She flung her arms around him in a deep bear hug that would have squeezed the stuffing out of lesser men. Her hands rubbed up and down his back before resting on his hips, pulling him so close I wondered if Bran would be facing a paternity suit within the year.

This wasn't a friendly glad-to-see-you-old-friend hug.

This was a bloody sexual assault.

My lips curled away from my teeth. I stepped forward and lifted one hand, ready to grab this bitch by the scruff of her neck and toss her into the street where, God willing, she'd be hit by a truck.

A movement to the side caught my eye, disrupting my homicidal thoughts.

A young woman, somewhere between eighteen and a hundred, stood nearly hidden in the shadows of a nearby doorway. She nibbled on a cheese sandwich, watching me. The fading black eye reminded me the woman wrapped around Bran, despite her good taste in men and her apparent death wish, was helping these kids survive.

I stopped still and waited.

"Angie," Bran replied, either not seeing or ignoring my reaction. "My God, how are you?"

The tall woman laughed. "Fine, fine." She waved a hand at the scattered kids. "Working on the other side of the fence now. And you?"

"Still writing." He hadn't let go of her waist.

Her hands stayed on his shoulders, fingers kneading the strong, stiff muscles.

The tea curdled in my belly.

Bran stepped back a safe distance. "Rebecca, this is Angie. Angie Degas." He gave a soft chuckle and turned back to her. "You look exactly like you did the last time I saw you."

"Something every woman wants to hear. Pleased to meet you."

She hadn't even looked at me. Her hands moved down off Bran's shoulder with his retreat, now brushing the front of his shirt with her fingertips.

"Angie here used to be one of the group I worked with and wrote about." There was something in Bran's voice, something I couldn't place. "You were gone when I came back. You all were."

Her hands dropped to her side, releasing him. "The gang, we saw that article—it was all over the streets. The television crews came out looking for us, people wanted to talk to us and we just..." She wriggled her fingers in the air. "We just split. Broke up and went away."

A shadow crossed Bran's face. "You heard about DJ?"

Angie swallowed hard. "Yeah. That was crazy. They should have known better than to buy from Elvis, he never sold straight." She shook her head. "Everyone was pissed. Shouldn't have happened."

"Should have stopped them." The steel in Bran's voice made me flinch.

Angie didn't buckle. "You know it was impossible to stop those two once they got on a binge. They disappeared, they came back. We all did. You remember."

"Yeah, I do." Bran tilted his head to one side. "Where did you go?"

"Don't ask." A shadow crossed her features, vanishing a second later. "I might have to go there again if this deal goes south." Angie took a step back and turned toward me. "So what brings you downtown?"

I took the initiative. "We're looking for two kids. Hit the streets in the last day or so."

"Yours?" Her attention went back to Bran. The single word held a bookful of questions.

"No." He moved to stand beside me. "Pair of lovebirds ran away together. Parents want them home, you know the routine."

"I'm familiar with that tune." She nodded toward the thinning group of young men and women. "Romeo and Juliet. Never goes out of style. You got some pictures?"

I pulled out the two photographs.

Angie studied them for a long minute, her forehead furrowed in thought. Finally she shook her head.

"Can't say they're familiar. Of course we're getting more in every day with the economy crashing and burning..." She waved toward the teenagers already wandering off as the food disappeared. "They might not have even made it here or gotten the word we exist yet. There's other outreach programs they could have tripped into."

"How many times a day do you distribute?" I asked.

"Only once, lunch from eleven until eleven-thirty. We do a clothing exchange from four until five and a street van cruises around with first aid supplies overnight from midnight until three. Front door stays open all day for a drop-in center for free counseling and temporary shelter from bad weather but we don't let them hang out. They come in and go before we end up with a mob scene. Plenty of gangs looking to score new members or expand their territory. I don't let them get a foothold." Angie sighed. "We used to run twenty-four hours a day but across the board government grants have been cut back and we had to do the same. A month ago we started hustling for food donations from the local restaurants with the promise that the kids won't hang out in front of them and beg off their customers."

"Extortion," I said.

She glared at me. "Efficient use of resources. Do you know how much food goes to waste because of silly regulations preventing it from being resold?"

"Tell me." I suddenly realized I'd stepped closer to the tall woman, almost hitting the edge of her running shoes with my own.

Her eyes narrowed. I spotted the steel under the silk, the hardness from living on the streets simmering under the surface. This wasn't some kid playing at being a street tough. This was a woman who, if she'd been born Felis, would be brawling her way to the top of any Pride she belonged to.

Her thin nostrils flared, drawing more oxygen in. I imagined her pulse accelerating, the blood pounding in her ears as she prepared to fight.

"Angie," Bran interrupted, "where's the hot spots to crash at night? Don Heights still good?"

He touched the small of my back, pinching my jacket, and tugged me back an inch, just enough to break the connection.

She turned her attention back to him with a wide smile, dropping her battle stance. "Still the best place to be. Remember how we used to sleep in the trees at night?" The hopeful lilt in her voice sent my blood pressure soaring.

"My back remembers," he replied with a laugh. "Maybe we'll head on over there when it gets dark and see what we can find. The Commons still good?"

She paused and chewed on her lower lip before answering. "Controlled now by the Bloor Street Boys. But it's still safe during daylight hours if you're looking for a place to crash."

He pulled out one of his business cards and handed it to her. "Call us if you see either one of them. Still underage and parents want them home. You know the story."

Angie giggled before stuffing the card into a front pocket. "You got it. Show me the pics one more time."

I handed copies over. "Keep them. Feel free to pass them around, see if anyone's seen them on their travels."

She scrutinized them for a few seconds more before adding them to Bran's card. "I'll call if they show up here or at the overnight shelter down at the church." One hand gestured down the street. "St. Mary's opens a few beds every night down at Church and King. Not too many spots and it fills fast but you never know." She smiled at Bran. "Hot summer nights are great to sleep out under the stars. Remember?"

I resisted the urge to roll my eyes. He wasn't catching what she was pitching, intentionally or unintentionally.

Good for both of them.

Bran took my hand. "Thanks, Angie. We'll be in touch."

She waved as he turned away and led me down the street, maneuvering between clumps of tourists, street kids and locals trying to figure out what to make of the first two groups.

Bran's grip was so tight I feared for my circulation. I tugged lightly and was rewarded with an even more restraining clutch.

I wasn't breaking free without a fight.

"Here." He pushed us toward a coffee shop.

"I'm not thirsty."

"Yes you are. Don't think I didn't see what was going on." He held the door open for me, practically pushing me through.

"What?" I stuffed my hands in my pockets, ignoring my aching fingers. This wasn't the place to throw a tantrum, no matter how tempting it was.

Bran ordered two coffees and turned back to me. "You were greener than green can get."

"Me?"

The squeak in my voice gave me away.

The barista interrupted, sliding the two drinks onto the marble counter. I took the first cardboard cup and headed for a window table. Bran followed after snagging a handful of sugar packets and stir sticks.

He emptied one sugar into his black coffee and dumped the rest in one pocket.

"For later."

I didn't question his money-saving techniques. Instead I stirred my drink and stuck the hot plastic into my mouth.

It gave me a reason to grind my teeth together.

"Don't." This time it was more of a warning than a request. "Don't do this, Rebecca."

The fact that he used my full name made it worse.

I chewed on the black toothpick.

"You want to find these kids, right? Well, we're going to have to deal with Angie at some point. It's better than nothing."

I chomped down on the stir stick. "She tried to mount you right in front of me." My voice rose enough to draw the attention of the other customers. "In front of me."

"Angie—" He licked his lips. "Angie's a handful and a half. She crushed on me the first day I met the gang and propositioned me that night."

The edges of the plastic stick grated against the inside of my cheek. "And?"

He glared at me. "What sort of guy do you think I am? I said no. She was barely sixteen, if that."

I returned the glare with interest. "If I recall correctly you were supposed to be a bit of a horn dog before we met."

Bran snorted. "There's a difference between dating a grown woman and grabbing jailbait." He leaned in, trying to ignore the questioning looks from the spectators. "I told her to knock it off. I'm not a crib robber and I sure as hell was never into taking advantage of any women, no matter her age."

"She's older now."

His shoulders slumped. "And just as annoying. You don't think I knew she was copping a feel? Damned girl practically had her hands down my pants."

"I noticed." I pulled the chewed stick out and sipped the drink.

"Don't be hating." He reached out and tapped the edge of my nose. "I'm yours and you know that."

"Don't mean I gave up the right to be pissed and think about scratching her eyes out."

"As long as you remember whose bed I'm headed for every night." Bran picked up my hand and pressed my palm to his lips. "Only yours."

The soft kiss earned not just a sigh from me but from an assortment of female observers. Bran ignored them and winked at me, sending my pulse soaring again.

I retrieved my hand and focused on finishing the coffee, fighting down the urge to drag him into the washroom for a quickie. "You really slept in a tree?"

He winced. "Bad memories of back spasms." He reached around to the small of his back with a pained expression. "Let's say it was a learning experience and I did it the one time." One eyebrow arched upward. "Just sleeping in the tree." He leaned in. "But I am open to experimenting with different positions if you're game later on."

I pressed my lips together, tamping down my desire. "Later. Right now we've got to find these two before they get into trouble." I paused, my mind running over the possibilities. "More trouble, that is."

"Be able to cover more ground if we split up," Bran said.

I choked on the mouthful of coffee I'd just taken. "What?"

He held up a hand. "Don't get all upset. I'm not going to run off with Angie and drop you a postcard from Sault Ste. Marie."

I glared at him.

"Or anyplace else," he added. "I think it'd be a better use of our resources for us to split up. You take the streets and I'll take the parks, the green patches these kids set up in for the night."

"It's not dark yet."

"No," Bran admitted. "So we're not going to split up right now. But it'll be dark in a few hours. I think our best plan of attack is for me to hit the old places I knew, see if the kids are still using them. You keep working the street, that's your strong point."

"And if you run into Angie? I figure she'll be out and about doing good deeds now that she knows you're on the streets. Waiting to ambush you if and when you show in her sights."

Bran frowned. "I thought you trusted me."

I took a sip of scalding coffee before answering. "I do. I don't trust her."

THREE

I'd hoped it would be as simple as heading for the prime performance spots and tagging the two kids as they asked for cash—twice the fool me. In the next three hours we wandered halfway up Yonge Street, down and across both Queen and King Street and through alleyways that ruined a good pair of running shoes.

There were plenty of performers banging on drums, strumming guitars, offering fast charcoal sketches and a handful playing human robots. One slender girl danced freestyle to her boyfriend's drumming on a set of bongos, waving her see-through silk scarves back and forth. It garnered a few dollars as I watched, mostly from leering businessmen pausing for a break and pretending to like the music.

I couldn't begin to imagine what living like this would be like. I'd gone through my rebellious teenage phase, thought about running away from my foster home and making my way on the street with the usual romantic viewpoint of street life. I'd never followed through with it due to a kind and loving set of surrogate parents keeping me on the straight and narrow despite myself.

Bran squeezed my hand. "I can guess what you're thinking." He lowered his voice. "These young men and women are looking for what we all want—a better life."

"This is a better life?"

"For some of them, yes." He glanced at the girl who now was busy hawking the same scarves she'd been dancing with. "Sexual abuse, mental abuse, physical abuse from their parents, from their family and friends, from their community. This is the only place they can be accepted fully for who and what they are. Gay, straight, transgendered—there's a lot of ways to be pushed into this world."

"Until they get victimized again by drug dealers, pimps and general criminals." I wasn't in a mood to sing the praises of independent living.

He nodded. "For the most part, yep. Some make it, like Angie, and move on into a good life as an adult but a lot don't."

He sighed and dug in his pocket for a dollar coin. "It's not the best option." He flipped the coin into the open bucket, earning a wide smile from the young man working the drums and a wink and grin from his girlfriend. "But for some it's all they have."

"What was Angie's story?"

"You read the article."

"There was nothing in it about her. But did she tell you?" I was walking on shaky ground but couldn't stop rolling. "How did she end up here?"

"I honestly don't know. She refused to tell me and I didn't push." He shrugged. "Push too much and people clam up. I figured she'd tell me in her own good time. She never did. A lot of them never have their stories told." A strangled sigh broke free. "They go to their graves, Jane Does and John Does and no one ever knows. Not even their parents, who keep waiting for that phone call, a visit from the police to say there's some sort of resolution, maybe even a body they can bury." He looked at the growing shadows between the buildings. "Instead there's just silence."

I squeezed his hand. "You okay?"

"Yes." He squeezed back. "You need this done as fast as possible. Whether or not the kids want to go home we have to find them and at least let them know the trouble coming down on their heads. It's one thing to be out here trying to make it on your own, another when you've got people actively hunting for you. And not with your best interests in mind." He let go of my hand and strolled over to the couple, now much friendlier thanks to our donation.

As he showed them the photographs I sniffed the air. It was a long shot that I'd be able to pick any Felis out of the odor soup clogging the street around us but it was worth a shot.

Nothing. A spicy curry from the restaurant nearby, a smattering of perfumes from the pedestrians and bad body odor from a bike courier. The two performers rated above the bike courier, with a hint of soap clinging to the young girl.

Bran returned a minute later. "No dice. They're new here, just came in from Vancouver last week."

"What, they take vacations?"

He chuckled. "Depends on how bad-ass the police are. If there's a clamp-down on street entertainers in one city it's worth it to commute to another until the heat dies down and you can go back. That is, unless it's more profitable where you move to."

I ran a hand through my hair, digging out a blond knot at the edge of the ponytail. "Either way it doesn't help us." I looked at the sun, ducking in and out between the skyscrapers as it headed for the horizon. "Going to be quitting time soon. Streets are going to get busy."

"Evening audience. It'll be good for the entertainers, not so much for the beggars—the commuters won't have time to stop and drop coins into cups but the people hitting the bars and plays and movies might want to enjoy a bit of music before and after the show. The soup kitchens will be handing out meals and then shooing the kids out for the night." Bran glanced at his watch. "As good a time as any to split up."

I couldn't fault his logic.

I didn't have to like it.

"Give me some of those pics." He took the handful I offered and folded them into a tight square before slipping them into a pocket. "Thanks."

"Be careful." I hesitated, unsure of how to word my concerns. "These aren't the same kids you knew from before. We're old enough to be the enemy."

"Don't worry." He kissed my forehead, earning a whoop of approval from the drummer who launched into another crazed rhythmic solo. "I'll be careful. Keep your phone on and I'll see you at home."

I scowled but said nothing.

Bran walked down the street, stopping once to turn and wave at me. I waved back with a forced smile.

The drummer thumped something low and foreboding as I headed in the opposite direction.

Two hours later I stumbled through a tent city under the Gardiner Expressway, an above-ground highway speeding along the edge of Lake Ontario. It'd been built years ago to offer commuters a more direct route into downtown Toronto and now jogged by the fresh skeletons of new condo units springing up along the lakeshore. A second highway under the Gardiner helped, supposedly, with traffic by allowing slower vehicles to pull into dilapidated industrial areas and ancient government buildings waiting for their demolition paperwork.

The dead zones between the condemned warehouses and the fresh, sparkly condos offered a good spot for an impromptu city, the elevated highway offering some protection from the elements with one of the pillars marking the start of the settlement.

I'd gotten here after a few missteps, running on directions given me by one of the older street kids, a young woman who sported a cast on her hand courtesy of a bad fall.

At least that was what she said.

It'd cost me a few dollars to pry the information out of her about shelters out of the way, off the beaten track and off the official radar. Bran might have his spots but they could have shifted and closed in the years since he'd written the article. I also suspected the two lovers might want to shift closer to the lake and as close to the wilderness as they could get, trying to keep in touch with their farm heritage. There was a bit of greenery still within walking range and the few inches of sand that qualified as a "beach" for the tourists foolhardy enough to risk a dip in the lake.

I surveyed the lone barrier to the camp, a rusted and half-down wire fence. Numerous holes cut in the wire let me through to the rest of the camp tucked behind a line of bushes and trees originally planted to try and beautify the area and ending up choking on the carbon monoxide. Now the short bushes and eight-foot trees marched the perimeter in a zombielike state, browned leaves and shredded bark gasping for air.

Cardboard boxes mixed with dark green military surplus tarps with wooden frames to build shelter after shelter, some linked together by necessity. A handful of actual tents were scattered throughout the compound, their bright neon colors dimmed by time and the weather.

No one challenged me but I could smell them, knew they were watching me, assessing if I was a danger or not. This wasn't a kid's camp—adults only. There was no sign, no announcement but I could tell by the inhabitants that teenagers wouldn't be welcome unless they were passing through. No loud music, no room for skateboarding.

I walked through the packed dirt circle I guessed was the center of the camp. Eyes followed my movement but no one said anything.

There was a slowness in everyone's actions, the

weariness of years weighing them down far beyond what would be usual. Men and women looked up at me with blank faces before returning to their small campfires.

I flinched at seeing one woman in my age group, her long black hair tucked into the back of her flannel shirt as she poked at some dying embers. She didn't look at me but kept focused on the small flames, feeding them just enough to stay alive. A tattered flag attached to the lean-to behind her lay limp, the faded colors not enough to identify it.

I turned to go. This wasn't a place to find two young people starting out in the world. This was a place filled with weary, broken souls.

The strong Felis scent rocked me back on my heels, almost physically pushing me back. It was thick and male and definitely nearby.

He'd snuck up on me with the ease of a practiced hunter.

"Don't get too many family here." The low rumble came from behind the dark red pup tent to my left.

I froze.

He laughed and stepped out into the dying sunlight. "Calm down, kit. Ain't no reason to be scared of old Red."

I stared at the elderly Felis. He stood almost as tall as Bran and wore a battered old leather jacket and jeans. His salt-and-pepper beard matched his hair, both neatly trimmed.

Red scratched his chin. "Geez woman. I ain't that ugly." He grinned, showing perfect teeth. "Come on over here and we'll talk a bit. Been a while since I had decent company." His voice rose as he finished the sentence, prompting a shout from another man a few shelters away. The undecipherable reply didn't have any visible effect on the Felis, who motioned me over to the side of the tent.

"Malcolm there been grumpy for days. Says it's the full moon. I say it's the bad meat he pulled out of that Dumpster." Red chuckled. "But here I am, not introducing myself." He extended a hand. "Red."

"Rebecca." My fingers disappeared in the calloused knuckles. He gave a light squeeze, nothing more than a love tap by Felis standards.

He frowned. "Nah. You look like a Susie." He released my hand and jabbed a thick index finger at me. "Susie."

I smiled. "Okay."

Red gestured toward the side of the tent. "I got some tea here. Might be a bit strong."

I followed him to a small clearing where a dark blue coffeepot sat over a small fire.

"Don't want to get the place ablaze." Red sat down on one log. "Get the firefighters here and they'll clean us all out." He looked toward where Malcolm was. "He done got us out of here once by setting fire to his damned tent. Don't like losing everything and having to start from scratch."

I sat down on a tree stump. He busied himself with two metal cups, obviously survivors from an ancient camping set.

The tea was dark and strong, searing my lips both with heat and taste.

Red grinned as I took my second sip. "A bit rough. Been stewing for a bit."

"Nice," I rasped.

"So." He Changed in front of me, so quickly it took my breath away. "Let me see ya."

The red tawny fur on his face offset the black and white in his beard and short hair, giving him a somewhat comical appearance. He smiled, displaying his sharp incisors.

I almost gave myself whiplash looking around to see if anyone had noticed. Malcolm, thank God, stayed in his own little world.

"Well?" Red leaned in.

"I—I can't." I cupped my hands around the metal mug. "I can't Change."

He frowned. "Whattamean?" He tapped his claws on the side of his mug, the clanking sound ripping at my ears. "You're family. You're Felis."

"I can't Change." I tried not to sound bitter. "Haven't been able to for years." I didn't want to even try and explain how I'd managed a Change here and there, usually when my life or Bran's was in danger. Better to let that sleeping cat lie.

"Huh." Red sipped his tea, accepting my disability without comment. "You're an odd one, Susie. But you're family." He Changed back, the fur and claws disappearing within seconds. "Bet you were a looker when you could, eh? Have all the young boys sniffing after ya."

I felt my cheeks burn at the compliment and smiled, despite the situation. "Thank you." I took another drink, letting the acidic tea scorch my throat. "What Pride are you with?"

He frowned. "Now that's a good question." He dug in one pocket of his jacket and came up with a half-eaten energy bar. "You want some?"

"I'm good." I watched as he nibbled on the dark brown square.

Red drank more tea, then took another bite.

I waited.

"I came from the east. By the big water." His forehead furrowed. "I think. Been so long that I forget if it was a dream or not." He tapped his temple with the half-wrapped bar. "Got a bit addled after a car accident. Started walking and ended up here." The energy bar swept across the compound. "Home sweet home."

I wasn't sure what to make of his claim. If he was truly off the grid he was an anomaly, a rogue from his Pride. It was more likely his Pride knew exactly where he was and allowed him to live his life as he wished as long as he didn't risk exposing the family. They should have informed the local Board of his relocation but for all I knew Jess and the others were familiar with Red and just let him be.

I put my mug down, grateful for the chance to avoid scalding the rest of my stomach lining. "I'm looking for two teenagers."

He eyed me, the steady gaze of a hunter sizing up a potential ally or enemy. "You're too young to have kids, Suz."

"Not mine." I withdrew the pictures from my pocket and unfolded them. "These two. Young lovers come to the big city."

Red finished the bar and put the empty wrapper back in his pocket before taking the photographs. His hands moved back and forth as he squinted to focus on the images.

"Hmm." He scratched his chin, sending a flurry of flakes downward. "This boy, he's a Chandler. Bad blood there. Don't know the girl but she's pretty."

"How would you know that?" I almost stood up before realizing it'd be seen as an aggressive move—not recommended considering my possible opponent.

"Got the eyes." Red pointed at his own eyes and then at mine with two fingers. "I met a Chandler once. Never forget his eyes. Nasty stare. Steel under there, hard iron that don't break for nothing."

"What do you know about them?" I stayed still, though my muscles were twitching with anticipation. "The Chandlers, that is."

"He's a young one," Red murmured. "Newest generation." He flipped the photographs, placing Lisa's on top. "He took up with the girl here?" His fingertips ran over the surface of the paper as if he were trying to memorize their features through touch.

"Yes. And she's a Middleston." I watched his forehead crease. "You know about the feud, I guess."

Red let out a low whistle. "Playing with fire, he is. Ain't no way that's gonna end well."

"If you help me find them we can try to help them."

I watched him shuffle the papers back and forth, laying one on top and then the other. First Evan, then Lisa.

The impromptu exercise ended. "You know how this all started? The feud?"

I shook my head. "Before my time."

Red glared at me. "You're hunting 'em and don't know the whole story? Bad form, kit. Bad form. Ain't no one don't know the story of this fight."

"I missed the memo," I offered.

Red snorted and poked the flames with a stick.

"Look, I left the Pride when I was fifteen. Give me a break."

He gave me the stink eye for another minute before answering. "Started off as a challenge like most things do." Red took another sip of tea. "Old Maureen Middleston. When I say old I don't mean old like the museum lions, I mean old like me." He patted his chest. "If she'd lived she'd be my age plus a bit. You understand?"

I nodded, trying to encourage him to keep talking. I had the sense that if he stopped it'd be like trying to pry the lid off an old paint can.

"She challenged Laura Chandler for a spot on the Board. Wasn't anything much to it, just two women wanting the same thing. You know how that goes."

A shiver went down my spine. I flashed back to Jess discussing how she'd lost her eye in just such a fight with my mother. "I know."

"Ended in death." He looked into his near-empty mug. "Death and destruction. Think Shakespeare said something 'bout that."

"I think I remember something along those lines.

The challenge ended up killing one of them? How? It was over a spot on the Board. How did it get to death?"

The mantra I'd been raised with echoed around my mind. Felis didn't kill Felis. The idea of the challenge was to fight to the edge, to get your opponent to submit. When we were young we fought over anything and everything until we got the common sense God gave a newt and figured out to pick and choose our battles.

A few black eyes and bloody noses will do that to you.

"'Twas an accident. Damned hole." Red poked the air with his index finger. "Rabbits' home, exit and entrances. Take a bad step and break an ankle."

My own ankle throbbed, reminding me of my first hunt. I'd waited for hours to be found.

"So one of them fell down and broke her ankle," I said. "She didn't die."

Red grunted. "Ever been in a field? Ain't always as flat and empty as you'd like to think." He rapped his knuckles on the side of his head and made a popping sound with his mouth. "Hit a rock, stop stop stop."

"Hit her head?" I was still wandering in a fog. "And she died? But it was an accident."

In my mind's eye I saw the two women in the field, Changed and fighting each other. One feints with a punch or maybe a kick, the other steps back and falls over. She hits the ground and her head bounces off a rock. Doesn't have to be a boulder, could have been as small as a pebble smacking into her temple but it's enough to do the damage and depending on how far they were away from the farmhouse, too far from immediate medical attention.

She passes out. Her opponent's yelling, screaming for help and it takes the ambulance too long to arrive and the hospital's too far away to make a difference. Wrong place, wrong time and now one's dead.

Red cleared his throat and spat to one side. "'Cuse me."

"So who died? And why would there be bad blood?" I frowned, trying to put the pieces together from Red's erratic speech. "It was a challenge, pure and simple. No funny business, no one pulled a gun or a knife. No one broke the rules."

He put his hand up in the air before letting it drop. "Maureen Middleston. Goes down, doesn't get up." He made a walking motion with two fingers. "Now Laura, she breaks her leg racing to the farmhouse to get help. Doesn't see a dip in the field, bang smash and she's down. Pulled herself close enough to the others to yell for help. Never healed proper, left her with a limp for the rest of her life. Chandlers say it's all a bad accident and just straight-up bad luck."

"And the Middlestons?"

"Family accuses Chandlers of choosing that field on purpose, setting Maureen up to fail. Laura breaking her leg on purpose to make it look like an accident. Only two witnesses—the seconds, standing by to watch what happens. One from each family and each backing their version of the story. One says Middleston's guilty, other says Chandler's at fault."

"That's insane." I drained the last few bitter drops from my cup. "No one could have seen that happening."

"Which is why the Grand Council ignored the Chandlers' complaint and demand for a reckoning. Challenge was fairly offered and fought," Red said. He overturned his mug and watched the last bit of tea dribble onto the ground. "But you know how family is. We never forget." He waved the mug around. "We all heard about it. Good gossip 'bout bad luck. Stuff like that travels fast."

I chewed on my bottom lip, taking in the information. It wasn't really relevant to finding the two kids, not as far as I knew. But it was more than I had an hour ago and that was progress. Of sorts.

The feud was barely a generation old. Didn't make it less important for those involved and I could imagine Mary Chandler and Jake Middleston becoming enraged that the grandchildren of the original warriors running off together. It must have seemed like the ultimate betrayal for their mothers.

"What about the men? Their mates? What did they do?" I asked.

Red tapped his cup against a nearby log, shaking out the last of the tea. "They raised their kids to hate each other. The widower Middleston had no brothers, couldn't risk leaving his kids alone if anything happened to him so he just talked a good brawl. Old man Chandler, he had one sister who moved to another Pride to get away from the entire situation so he was alone as well with his daughters." He smacked his lips. "They talk to friends and soon people's choosing sides. A few fights, some challenges over drinks and now everyone's got a stake in this. Business on both sides split up and start bidding against each other, stealing construction contracts."

"Eventually the two men die." I moved the timeline along. "So it moves down the line to the kids. Jake and Mary. The new family heads."

Red inspected the cup. "Jake's got one younger brother who isn't married yet, still looking for a woman willing to take on the job. Jake got a good wife and she gave him a good family, boys and girls." He squinted. "You know Lisa. Good kits, all of them from what I hear. Now, on the Chandler side you've got Mary and her—" He poked a finger inside the cup. "Darned bugs. Get into everything."

I resisted the urge to look into my own mug.

"Mary and her sister, they're angry. Poisoned by their da from the day their mother, Laura, died. Get married and start raising kits as fast as they can but play it safe and make no direct challenges to any Middlestons or their kin, spreading rumors and doing what they can to screw them over through business deals and getting people to not like them." He smiled. "Ain't hard to hate Jake Middleston after a night of drinking with Mary Chandler, if you get what I mean."

My head began to spin. Too much information and it wasn't getting me any closer to finding the two kids and figuring out what to do.

"How do you know all this?"

He tapped his temple. "I listen. I don't stay here all the time, I get out and walk around. People talk, family talk and some of them give me a dollar here and there to make themselves feel good." Red grinned. "They buy me coffee and want to chat, talk 'bout things they can't tell anyone else, things they don't want others to know their opinions on. I listen."

"Why didn't anyone stop this before now? The Board, the Council—"

Red snorted. "You can't make people like each other. And after a bit of time it's easier to hate than admit someone was wrong."

"This is ridiculous." I shook my head. "Insane."

Red scratched his chin. "To you and me, yes. But how many things have you seen that ain't sensible?"

I swallowed hard, thinking of the many unusual things in my own life. Suddenly a family feud didn't seem so silly.

I stood up and handed him the mug. "Thank you for the drink."

He nodded. "Sorry but this is old folks' camp. Ain't gonna find your kits here. Too quiet for them."

I started to dig out a business card then paused. "Do you have a phone?"

Red's eyebrows rose. "Of course." He pointed to the west. "There's a pay phone over there by the store, one of the last ones in the world. Owner's a good man, lets us pick through the Dumpster after dark as long as we don't make a mess and keep quiet."

I handed over the card. "If you see them please call me. Or if you need something."

"'Something'?" Red cocked his head to one side.

"We're family." I cleared my throat, trying to ignore

the lump that had suddenly come up. "You need help or something, you call me."

He laughed, a nervous chuckle at the end. "Okay, Susie. I'll call you when the aliens attack."

Red took my hand and led me through the makeshift shelters back to the hole in the fence I'd entered by. He patted me on the head and guided me through the gap, pulling the warped wire up so it wouldn't drag on my leather duster.

"You be careful out there." He wagged a finger at me. "Lots of bad blood out there. Splashes on the innocent and the guilty the same."

Then he was gone before I could answer, blending back into the lengthening shadows.

I headed back out onto the street, a little shaken by the encounter. I'd never thought about finding family in a place like this.

It was both terrifying and strangely reassuring to know we could be just like anyone else, choose the path less taken.

A little voice at the back of my mind pointed out this could have been my reality, my day-to-day existence dependent on what I pulled out of the garbage cans or scrounged from strangers. When I'd been sent away from the Pride I'd been cut off from all family help, left to survive on my own. If I hadn't landed on my feet in the foster care system and later on clawed out a place for myself in the human world, I could have ended up like Red.

I wasn't sure I'd be as cheerful as the elderly Felis.

It was just after nine o'clock; my encounter with

Red had taken up more time than I'd realized. There were still alleys to be searched and I moved back toward the center of the city, choosing my steps carefully in the darkness.

Two hours later I was tired and more than a little grumpy. The small packs I'd run into hadn't been much help, either denying all knowledge of any other runaways or splintering into a dozen pairs of running feet, heading away from the bounty hunter looking for their kin.

I couldn't blame them for being suspicious. Anyone representing authority posed a threat to their ecosystem and I definitely was that, wanting to pull two of their own away. Even offering money didn't get me much more than vague references to different parks and shelters where I might trip over the kids. After a few more hours of staggering around green spots masquerading as parks and almost getting run over by more than a few delivery trucks in back alleys making late night/early morning deliveries I was ready to call it quits for one night.

I dialed Bran's number. He answered on the third ring.

"I'm headed home. What's up with you?"

There was a lot of chatter in the background—guitar, drums, maybe a flute or two and a chorus of voices rising and falling in intensity.

"I'm out here at the Point. Kids say they may or may not have seen the boy traveling alone," Bran shouted.

"Think he dumped her already?" I leaned against a light pole, pressing the cool metal against my spine.

It'd turned into a warm summer evening and I was in desperate need of a hot shower and a cold drink.

"Maybe. I don't know. I'm going to hang out for a few more hours until they all crash in case Evan or Lisa show up."

Someone shouted, the phone picking up her garbled giggle.

I recognized it as Angie's.

The little bitch had either followed Bran or tracked him down. Either way she was with him and I was not.

You'll notice, a little hysterical voice in my ear buzzed, *that he's not mentioning her to you. He's keeping a secret from you.*

I kept speaking, using the energy to force my blood pressure down. "Kind of a gamble." I lifted my hand to flag down a taxi. "No luck on my side. I'm headed home for a rest before going back out tomorrow." I chose my words carefully, hoping he'd pick up on what I was putting down. "Going to take a shower and get a bite to eat. Be nice to have some company."

"Okay. I'll catch you there later." Bran cut me off just as Angie's laugh got louder.

Obviously our mental telepathy needed some work.

The cab ride home was quiet, with the driver more focused on the classical music coming out of his radio than chattering to me. Which was good because I didn't feel like talking and/or listening to anyone.

Jazz trilled at me as I stepped out of the shower, a ghost in the middle of the steam filling the room.

I hoped I'd used up all the hot water.

She wound between my legs as I pulled on a nightshirt and crawled into bed. The stained bedspread was in the far corner, waiting to be washed.

I studied the clock. 3:32 a.m.

I wasn't impressed.

Jazz jumped up on the bed and curled into a fat white ball on Bran's pillow with a growly purr. She reached out and grabbed my hand, latching on with her claws. A tug had my fingers tucked under her paws where she licked my skin, still purring.

Cats give the best therapy.

I stroked her soft fur with my free hand and turned out the light.

FOUR

I woke up with a start, my mind cataloguing the noises and giving them names.

Key. Front door.

Bran.

4:47 a.m.

I lay there in the darkness, not moving. Jazz shuffled a little closer and began to lick my hand.

Heavy footsteps on the stairs. A muted curse as he failed to negotiate the corner and banged his arm.

He smelled of smoke—wood and marijuana. A touch of beer.

Angie.

But not of sex.

Just her scent, all over him like a bad overdose of aftershave.

The clothing went into a pile on the floor on his side of the bed, right where he could trip over them getting in and out. He shuffled back and forth for a minute, probably trying to decide whether to shower or not.

Exhaustion won out.

Jazz let out an annoyed trill as he pushed her to one side, grunting at her slow retreat. The fat cat stomped on my leg on the way to the bottom of the mattress where she curled up into a ball and began to snore.

Bran slipped under the sheets and pulled me close with a contented sigh.

I didn't say anything. Instead I closed my eyes and tried to get back to sleep.

"You're awake," he whispered in my ear. "I can tell, you know."

I stayed quiet.

"No luck finding the kids. I stayed until they all passed out or fell asleep. Some of them think they spotted Evan with a group of musicians over on Spadina but they weren't sure. I'll check it out tomorrow."

I said nothing. His arm tightened around my waist.

"Angie was there. She came in with the overnight van."

I stiffened in his grip.

"I know." I turned over, presenting my back to him. "I heard her on the phone when you called."

"I didn't sleep with her."

"I know."

He said nothing and I fell into a dreamless sleep.

I woke up to the smell of fresh coffee and cinnamon rolls. Jazz was still at the foot of the bed and stretched out her long legs as I sat up and tugged on a fresh T-shirt and jeans. She yawned, displaying yellowed teeth, and hopped off to lead me downstairs where my apology brekka waited.

The clock read 7:38 a.m.

My coffee, sugar and milk already added, sat at the small table already. A fat freshly-baked cinnamon roll lay on a plate, holding up a folded piece of paper.

I padded over and sat down.

Rebecca—I decided to head out early because I couldn't sleep. I'll call later on to let you know if I've found the kids.

Don't worry about Angie. I won't see her again.

Bran

I crumpled the note up in one hand and reached for the coffee with the other. Jazz let out a merp as she lay down by her food bowl. I sipped the coffee while dumping a cupful of kibble in her dish.

"Your master's a fool," I told her. "He's getting all tangled up in this and he doesn't have to."

Jazz dunked her face in the bowl and began munching.

"I mean, I appreciate the help. It's not like having two of us looking won't be better than one." I pulled one corner of the cinnamon bun off. It was still warm and doughy. I suspected if I checked the oven there'd be others sitting there, waiting to be devoured.

Jazz licked her lips and moved to the water bowl. She leaned across the dish and began to lap from the far side, dunking her chest in the water.

"Damned bitch is still hot for him." I washed down the sugary bite with a mouthful of coffee. "Goddamn hero worship. Could have looked him up years ago, but she waited until he walked into her lair, walked into her damned house. I should have known better than to let him get involved in this."

Jazz looked up, her chin dripping.

"Bastard." I shoved the rest of the bun into my

mouth. "Cinnamon is good to keep your blood pressure down. He knew I'd need this."

Jazz laid down by the food bowl, exhausted by her efforts.

"It's a good thing you can't talk." I put the empty plate and mug into the sink. "Otherwise you'd have to tell me what a jealous bitch I am and I'd have to kill you."

She rolled onto her back and closed her eyes.

My first stop was over on Queen Street West to a handful of soup kitchens delivering breakfast to street youth. It was a far cry from cinnamon rolls and coffee, but the boxes of cold cereal, cartons of milk and juice boxes offered at least some attempt at a healthy start to the day. The workers shrugged when I showed them the pictures. They saw so many young men and women going through that the faces turned into a never-ending blur.

I thought back to Stacy Hampton, the social worker over at Second Chance, Second Life a few blocks away. There was a chance Bran had already visited her but it wouldn't hurt to check.

I also didn't discount the possibility that Bran intentionally omitted it due to his family's connection.

A short hop on a streetcar brought me back to the renovated storefront. No one was hanging around the door—they didn't open until noon. A hand lettered sign on the front door announced reporters were not welcome and no statements would be made. A lawyer's phone number completed the visual slapdown.

her right. "You may think you know what's best for a person but you have to let them decide in the end. You can't force them into a new life. They have to want to change. And sometimes you have to watch them walk back into the fire and let them go."

"Bran's not that type of guy," I replied, even though my mind was already processing the concept. "He wouldn't get hung up like that."

Stacy nodded. "I stand corrected, then. Let me run these by the staff and I'll let you get back out on the street." She stood up and walked out, taking the photographs.

I closed my eyes and took deep breaths. Not only was I dealing with a Felis family feud, I might be losing my mate to some psychological crisis.

First things first—find these damned kids and figure out what to do with them.

Then I'd deal with Angie Degas.

Stacy came back in. "I've showed them around to the staff. No hits but I told them to call me if they see them."

I stood up. "Do you still have my business card?"

She chuckled. "You bet. Never hurts to have friends in strange places."

"Thank you." I hesitated, trying to find the right phrasing. "About what you said before—is there something I should do or shouldn't do, in your opinion?"

Stacy shook her head. "I can't say. It's his life, his problem. We know about it because he wrote about it and his story was so heartfelt, so honest, which is why it became so famous." She tapped her chest, over her heart. "It hit all of us here, tugged on the right nerves to bring us into that world and let us know their struggles. But he paid a price for it, letting himself get too involved, and he couldn't pull back."

"Too much into the story."

"Exactly. And no matter what you or I say or do we're still on the outside looking in. He's got to come to terms with his choices and their choices, both the living and the dead." She straightened a stack of file folders. "If you need to talk give me a call."

"Thanks." I couldn't think of what else to say so I headed for the door.

The morning commute was starting to ebb, the majority of employees already barricaded behind their glass walls. The streets were emptying out slowly, returning control to the tourists who gawked at the Eaton Centre and cheered at the Hockey Hall of Fame before dumping obscene amounts of money for mediocre food to say they'd eaten at this famous restaurant, paying for the sponsor's name when they'd get just as good food from the hot dog carts.

The kids were out bright and early hustling for their brekka—the squeegee troop perched at almost every major intersection, ready to run out at a red light and clean windshields for spare change. Every once in a while the cops would come around, warn them to be careful and not block traffic. The kids would do their bobblehead impression and allow the police to feel listened to, holding back until the uniforms went out of sight before dodging cars again. The best the police could issue a ticket for was impeding traffic but it'd be

I went around the back and rang the doorbell on the receiving dock. A thick-necked man opened the door and glared at me.

"You ain't no delivery girl."

"Thanks for the update. I'm here to see Stacy. Tell her Rebecca Desjardin is here." I eyed the prison tattoos on his knuckles. "She'll see me."

"She ain't seeing no reporters," the human wall rumbled. "Didn't you see the note on the front door?"

"I'm not a reporter. I'm a private investigator."

"A what?"

"A P.I. Just like you see in the movies. Except I'm shorter." I winked. "And cuter."

His lips curled up into something resembling a smile. "Stay here." The door slammed shut in my face.

I rocked back and forth on my heels, listening to the chatter inside. Felis hearing didn't mean I could listen through walls but it did make it easier to eavesdrop.

One man arguing about the quality of bread dropped off by a local bakery. Another complaining about his probation officer busting his balls for missing an appointment. A series of curses from my original greeter as he approached the door, most of them involving body parts I didn't possess.

It opened all the way this time.

"Stacy says to take you to her office." The large man smiled again. "Follow me, please."

I followed him past the two men working on the dock, busy loading boxes of fresh broccoli onto tables to be sorted.

Stacy's office hadn't changed from the last time

I'd been there, the motivational posters of penguins and kittens still extolling viewers to do their best and never give up.

"Ms. Desjardin. Good to see you." She waved me into the empty chair as she closed the door. "Thanks, John."

The ex-con left us alone.

I sat down. "How are you doing?"

It wasn't an idle question. When the story behind the murder of Molly Callendar and the kidnapping of her newborn son had come out, the media had hammered on the charity's door non-stop, looking for more lurid details about the life and death of Keith Shaw.

Not many organizations could have taken the scrutiny and survived.

I wasn't sure this one had.

She looked exhausted, the dark circles under her eyes poking through the make-up. Her shoulders slumped under the cream-colored blouse.

"Better than can be expected." The blonde nodded toward the docks. "Fellows are on their best behavior since the incident, afraid the place'll shut down if there's another problem and they'll have to go find something else. They've been great."

The elephant in the room sat between us.

"I wasn't sure you'd see me." I sat back, letting the brown envelope holding the photographs flop around. "I wouldn't have blamed you for telling me to screw off."

"You're not to blame for anything. You were looking for a killer and you found him." Stacy let out a weary sigh. "It's just too bad it was one of my boys. We try and we try but you can't save everyone."

I nodded. The fallout over Shaw had gone deep into the charity and the organizations who contributed to it. If the shelter survived another year they'd be out of the headlines but it'd be a hard, rough year for Stacy and her staff.

"But that's in the past." She leaned forward wearing a tired smile, her elbows on the thin brown desk organizer. "What can I do for you?"

"I'm looking for two teenagers." I slid the photographs across the table. "I know you usually only get older folks here but I figured it was worth a shot."

Stacy turned them to face her and studied the cheerful faces. "Can I keep these?"

"Sure." I rattled the envelope. "I've got extras."

"I'll put them up by the serving area so my people can see them. They rotate through serving and cleanup duties but you never know." She paused and I saw the curiosity in her eyes.

I didn't say anything. Sometimes silence is as good as giving permission.

"How is Mr. Hanover doing?"

For a second I thought she was talking about Michael, Bran's father and I wondered why she'd be asking me about a man who'd tried to blackmail me and destroy my life. "Oh you mean Bran. He's doing okay."

"We were shocked by the entire situation. It was just—" She pushed the pictures to one side, shaking her head. "I still can't wrap my mind around it." She drew a deep breath. “Is he helping you look for these runaways?”

“Yes.” I didn’t feel compelled to explain why Bran wasn’t there with me.

“Does he seem, well, obsessed with finding them?”

I took a minute to answer. “He’s been in touch with one of the ‘kids’ from his article. Came across her at another outreach. She got her act together and got a job helping street kids out.”

“Hmm.” Stacy looked over at one of the motivational posters. “Is she doing well?”

“Better than before.” The sarcasm in my tone wasn’t intentional.

Stacy licked her lips before speaking, her eyebrows drawing together. “I may be speaking out of turn but you understand this may be a bit traumatic for him.”

“I know he was quite invested in the street life.” I’d read Bran’s article not long after we’d gotten together. It was intense and vibrant and deserved every accolade it got.

“Then you know about DJ.” Stacy picked up on my blank response. “Dan and Jane. The two doomed lovers and all that.”

I shifted on the cold metal seat. “I know about them.”

“Street kids called them DJ because they hung together all the time, couldn’t pull them apart. Word was that even in death they had their arms around each other.” She looked down at the images. “I always enjoyed that part in the article about Brandon and the two runaways bonding over a couple of joints and a case of beer. Seemed almost too good to be true but I know Brandon wouldn't lie."

She was right, in a way.

It wasn't a total lie.

The real story hadn't gotten into print, hadn't even been a series of pencil scribbles in his notebook.

I'd quizzed Bran on that after reading the article and sensing something was missing, something more than the simple tale he'd woven.

Some of the kids, for a mean laugh, had spiked Bran's drink with a heavy street narcotic. It was a hazing of sorts, a test to see if the smart-ass reporter was worthy of hanging with them.

They figured it'd knock Bran down for the night, have him pissing his pants and acting like a fool.

They were wrong.

Bran, instead of lying down and babbling like a baby, had leaped up and headed for the open street, screaming and yelling. It was rush hour and odds were good he'd have been hit within a few seconds of jumping into the middle of Queen Street.

Dan had tackled him, tossing Bran to the ground and wrestling him into submission before dragging Bran back to the camp. Jane had helped the delirious reporter and kept him safe as he worked through six hours of hallucinations and fever, finally erupting in what Bran recalled as the longest session of projectile vomiting he'd ever suffered through.

It was cliché to say that he owed the kids his life but it was the truth.

He'd put a sanitized version in the article, leaving

out the near-suicide and toning it down to a quiet night of smoking dope and bonding with the two kids.

The truth was the pair had saved his life and he'd never forgotten the debt he owed to them.

He'd also never gotten the chance to pay them back.

Stacy continued. "I don't know Mr. Hanover as well as you do but I don't think I'm reaching to say he might be trying to relive the situation through searching for these two and possibly in his dealings with this other woman."

I felt like I'd been smacked with a two-by-four. "What?"

Stacy tapped the photographs. "From what I understand, Mr. Hanover's biggest regret is not being able to get those two out of danger, the ones from his article. Now he has two new kids to worry about, two young people that could meet the same fate." She turned the photos around to face me. "He wants to save them and by proxy feel that he's redeemed himself, at least in his own mind. Add in the reappearance of one member of the original group and he has a chance to help this survivor as well. He can finally finish up his personal business with his past by dealing with this in the present." She smiled. "I'm not a psychologist, before you ask. But I see this sort of thing a lot and after a while you spot the signs." Her gaze went to the closed door. "We have people cycle through here all the time wanting to help and they slip into that tar pit of emotions—get all caught up in wanting to 'save' people who may not want to be saved in the way someone's thinking." Her fingers ran over the pile of file folders stacked to her right. "You may think you know what's best for a person but you have to let them decide in the end. You can't force them into a new life. They have to want to change. And sometimes you have to watch them walk back into the fire and let them go."

"Bran's not that type of guy," I replied, even though my mind was already processing the concept. "He wouldn't get hung up like that."

Stacy nodded. "I stand corrected, then. Let me run these by the staff and I'll let you get back out on the street." She stood up and walked out, taking the photographs.

I closed my eyes and took deep breaths. Not only was I dealing with a Felis family feud, I might be losing my mate to some psychological crisis.

First things first—find these damned kids and figure out what to do with them.

Then I'd deal with Angie Degas.

Stacy came back in. "I've showed them around to the staff. No hits but I told them to call me if they see them."

I stood up. "Do you still have my business card?"

She chuckled. "You bet. Never hurts to have friends in strange places."

"Thank you." I hesitated, trying to find the right phrasing. "About what you said before—is there something I should do or shouldn't do, in your opinion?"

Stacy shook her head. "I can't say. It's his life, his problem. We know about it because he wrote about it and his story was so heartfelt, so honest, which is why it became so famous." She tapped her chest, over her heart. "It hit all of us here, tugged on the right nerves to bring us into that world and let us know their struggles. But he paid a price for it, letting himself get too involved, and he couldn't pull back."

"Too much into the story."

"Exactly. And no matter what you or I say or do we're still on the outside looking in. He's got to come to terms with his choices and their choices, both the living and the dead." She straightened a stack of file folders. "If you need to talk give me a call."

"Thanks." I couldn't think of what else to say so I headed for the door.

The morning commute was starting to ebb, the majority of employees already barricaded behind their glass walls. The streets were emptying out slowly, returning control to the tourists who gawked at the Eaton Centre and cheered at the Hockey Hall of Fame before dumping obscene amounts of money for mediocre food to say they'd eaten at this famous restaurant, paying for the sponsor's name when they'd get just as good food from the hot dog carts.

The kids were out bright and early hustling for their brekka—the squeegee troop perched at almost every major intersection, ready to run out at a red light and clean windshields for spare change. Every once in a while the cops would come around, warn them to be careful and not block traffic. The kids would do their bobblehead impression and allow the police to feel listened to, holding back until the uniforms went out of sight before dodging cars again. The best the police could issue a ticket for was impeding traffic but it'd be a waste of time between getting a real name from the offenders and believing the ticket would actually get paid. Their time was better spent hunting down real criminals who were doing more than just holding up the occasional car from shooting through the intersection.

It was dangerous work though. An angry commuter, a frightened tourist and a kid could find him- or herself flying into traffic and, at the least, nursing bumps and bruises. Every few months there'd be an article in the paper about an accidental death when a kid didn't move fast enough and bounced the wrong way.

They worked for their money, no doubt about that.

I watched one group at a street corner working their magic, the young women dashing out into traffic while their male counterparts kept close to the sidewalks, unable to get out of the way in time if the light changed before the work was done. It didn't hurt that the two girls wore ripped wet T-shirts that stuck to their slender forms, giving drivers a good reason to slow down and get caught by the red light.

They slapped sloppy wet rags on windshields and followed up with a fast wipe, the chipped rubber leaving more water on the glass than it removed. It was still enough to earn them a handful of change, tossed into a pocket or into a plastic bottle strapped to their belts. The light went to green and they sprinted for the curb to catch their breath and ready for the next red.

They shrugged when I showed them the pictures, watching me warily when I offered cash for any tips and ran into traffic as soon as they could to escape me.

Rebuffed I headed back onto Yonge Street to see if the main artery could cough up anything.

The older man I'd given money to yesterday was back on his stoop, coffee cup at the ready. I gave him a wan smile and nod as I passed him and twisted down one side street where the bike messengers congregated between runs. Maybe the runners could give me something.

I resisted heading for the Spot. If I found Bran there I'd be furious—and if I didn't find him there I'd find Angie and that would lead to a whole lot of teeth-gnashing.

To start.

Mike's Munchies was a small hole-in-the-wall sandwich shop catering almost exclusively to couriers who needed fast, portable food and didn't care if it looked pretty or not. The fat buns wrapped in Mike's signature wax paper were a familiar sight on the streets as the bikers hopped curbs with one hand and ate with the other, dodging cars in a frenzied rush to deliver papers and packages.

The first shift of morning deliveries had just gone out, the business world still demanding print copies despite all the computerized options available. The fellows gathering around the front of the shop were already chowing down on fried egg sandwiches while babbling about bad customers, slow taxi drivers and annoying bike thieves. The smells drifting out of the small shop had me drooling and it wasn't long before I was sitting on the stoop with the rest of the riders, smearing egg yolk on my chin as I devoured one of the best hidden secrets of Toronto.

The couriers eyed me nervously, not willing to share their space with a civilian and a woman to boot. I ignored them and kept on eating, placing my business card down beside me on the step.

The curiosity was too much for one neon-green spandex-wearing young man who peered down at the card, almost falling into my lap.

"A private investigator? You got a gun?"

"Can't afford the bullets." I wiped my chin with a handful of napkins. "Looking for a pair of runaways. Dear old dad's worried about his little girl." I waved toward the street with the half-eaten sandwich. "Any of you boys know where I'd have some luck looking for her?"

Neon fell back to a defensive position and muttered to his buddy who muttered to the one next to him and so on. I watched the discussion spread out like ripples in a pond, some bouncing back close to me before stalling out.

"Over there." An older rider, maybe in his mid-twenties and wearing a bright orange safety vest over his ripped leather jacket, jerked his thumb to the east. He rambled off instructions to find a parking garage off Church Street, where he claimed the street musicians warmed up before hitting the busking areas on Queen. "Ran into a few of them yesterday. Good music, good peeps running their own way."

I nodded, staying silent. The sandwich helped.

"They hook up there, choose who they wanna be

with for the work day, put together new sounds." He pointed at the cars racing by with his sandwich. "You might find someone there."

I handed him a ten and began walking, sandwich in hand. It'd take me a few minutes to walk the distance and I wasn't going to waste good food.

My intention was to go to the parking garage.

My subconscious decided otherwise.

I stopped still and looked down at my feet, scowling through the last of the sandwich. We were nowhere near a parking garage.

I looked up to see the giant black dot swinging over my head.

I mashed up the foil in my hand and swiped at my mouth with my sleeve.

The door was open, a loud electronic blast announcing my entrance. Nothing subtle here.

A threadbare couch sat in the center of the front room with mismatched chairs. Bricks and thin planks against a wall created a bookshelf with tattered and worn volumes of the classics and a few more recent blockbusters waiting for attention.

Angie Degas flew out of a back room. She wore jeans and a tight T-shirt with a fat black spot obscuring most of the front.

I squinted, seeing it as a bull's-eye.

She'd already opened her mouth to speak, probably ready to spew out whatever sales pitch she had to try and keep the kids there and convince them to take advantage of the Spot's resources. I could almost see the wheels in her mind coming to a screeching halt, spokes flying everywhere and gears exploding as she processed who was standing in front of her.

"Oh. Hello." She crossed her arms in front of her. "Rebecca, right?"

I nodded.

"I haven't seen your kids. Put the pictures up on the inside wall for the staff but no takers yet." She pulled a thick strand of blond hair over her shoulder and twirled it around her finger. "Can I do something else for you?"

I studied her before answering, trying to reconcile the mental image I'd been creating overnight with the reality.

She was thin, too thin. Possible result of bad nutrition in her earlier days. Her teeth weren't falling out but they didn't look like they were in great shape. Hair long and lush thanks to the conditioner I smelled. The fruity smell clogged the back of my throat.

An old scar over her left eye, right at the hairline, showed she'd been a brawler. Wasn't that much of a surprise.

"Like what you see?" Angie snapped. She moved into my personal space. "Look, I know Brandon's with you. I'm not stupid."

I stayed silent.

"You think you're so tough, you're a badass detective hunting down kids." She swept her arm around, encompassing the makeshift living room. "You don't know what these kids have gone through, what I went through."

"I read the article."

She shook her head. "You and a lot of other people

who figured they knew us, knew what world we lived in." Her blond locks bounced over her shoulder. "We got so many social workers, do-gooders and flakes wanting to scoop us up and take us home. Problem was, home sucked for us in the first place. That's how we got here."

"You didn't tell Bran how you got here." I kept my tone neutral.

It was hard.

Angie swiped at her nose with her shirt sleeve. "Same old story—I fell in love. He said he loved me, would go anywhere and do anything with me as long as I was faithful." She snorted. "Small town up north near Quebec, you wouldn't know the name. Told me we'd come down here and build a new life, make me into a model and he'd be my manager. We were in town for a week before I caught him trying to pimp me out to some new friends of his, cutting a deal. My ass for a bag of weed. I punched him in the face and never looked back."

I stayed silent.

"Brandon was the first man I met who was nice to me, nice without wanting anything from me." She looked at the front window and out into the street. "I offered to do him a few times. You know, a thank you for being such a good guy." Her lips twisted into a smile. "That didn't make it into the article. I've done the therapy, I know all the medical terms and I know I'm screwed up in the head when it comes to relationships and knowing what's healthy and what's not. I'm still working on it. But when I spotted him last night I just—"

She closed her eyes and shook her head. "I just went back to that time, that place where he was the sane one in an insane world. He was my anchor and I loved him, still love him for being that. The rich little boy who saw past me and got the big picture, who tried to save all of us and not just who was giving him a blow job or a piece of ass." Her eyes shot open and locked with mine. "He didn't save us. But he sure as hell tried to understand us, more than anyone else I've ever met has. And I wouldn't be where I am without him showing me people do care, can care and can change the world."

I swallowed hard, feeling like a piece of gum stuck on the bottom of someone's shoe.

She jerked a thumb toward the back of the room. "You wanna fight we can go out back. But I can tell you he told me 'no' again last night. Figured I'd give it one more shot now that we're older and all that. He still wouldn't go for it." She pulled on the scarlet thread of hair again. "He's a good man."

"Yes. Yes, he is." I leaned in until our noses almost touched. "And I thank God every day that I have him in my life."

I spun around and left, my heartbeat loud in my ears.

It didn't take me long to find the parking lot, tucked in behind a public library. The tiny asphalt square stood three levels high and had already been filled to capacity hours ago, the sole exit and entrance via a small booth with a sleepy, pudgy guard propped up on a stool inside. This was a locals-only lot—if you didn't know where to look or to turn you'd zip on by it and end up paying twice as much at the louder, more vibrantly advertised lots.

I could hear the pounding of drums mixed in with the spirited voices of a make-shift choir and a variety of instruments from flute to guitar to some sort of didgeridoo. Every few minutes the levels would rise and fall, shifting as teams split off. I guessed the musicians ran in shifts, with the late risers coming in to tag team the early birds and keep the corners active.

I spotted a handful sliding out into the greenery beside the library, carrying a set of drums. The wind shifted and brought me a series of scents off the concrete walls, cutting through the motor oil and gasoline fumes.

Family.

One, two—I twisted around, trying to place the odors. Lisa's father gave me some sort of a base scent for the Middleston family line but I couldn't be sure until I met the kit face to face. The other Felis scents were foreign. They could be businessmen and women, street vendors or tourists off the beaten path.

I crept along the ground level until I could see the kids gathered in the far corner in the handful of empty handicapped parking spaces.

Five young men, two women. Drums, guitar and a flute player who kept stamping her feet and demanding something by the way she flung her arms around. Another man, a bit older than her, grabbed her forearm and snapped something in French.

I resisted the urge to charge. This was a street culture I knew nothing about and I had no place in. I reached into my pocket and touched my cell phone, making sure it was on and within easy reach.

I wasn't above calling 911 if it got nasty.

She growled something back and he released her with a laugh, stepping away with his hands raised.

I listened, trying to pick up the speech. It was hard to make out over the thumping and vibrating notes but I got something.

"You don't deserve more than ten percent." This from the drummer, crouched over his bongos. "You just got here."

"But I'm good. All you do is bash away." The guitar player stood up from tinkering with his acoustic guitar, allowing me a clear view of his face. "I pull in the people. You can't deny that."

Evan Chandler. Looking a bit rough around the edges, dark circles under his eyes and a definite strain in his voice. But he was alive and healthy and obviously adapting to his new life.

All good. Now I had to get to him and explain that I wasn't the police, not his enemy and we needed to talk about Lisa and his future plans.

Evan froze in place and turned in a slow circle, taking short puffs.

"What's up?" This from the flute player. "You okay?"

I held my breath instinctively even though it wouldn't make a difference. The wind whipped around us, twisted and warped through the concrete pillars. If I could scent him he sure as hell could scent me.

He snatched up his guitar and bolted, leaping over the low wall dividing the parking lot from the library. He wasn't taking any chances. I was too close to him, too close for comfort.

"Shit." I charged between the cars, not caring if anyone saw me or not. "Evan. Evan!"

The kids scattered as I approached, grabbing their instruments and sprinting out in all directions. I ignored them and focused in on Evan.

I hopped over the barrier and hit the thin line of grass in a crouch, ready to pursue. All I needed to do was get a few minutes with him and I'd be able to—

Something slammed into my right side, a meat wall propelling me into the concrete beside me, the bricks not giving an inch as my head bounced. The freshly-healed skin on my left arm screamed on impact and threatened to split open like an over-ripe peach.

Another Felis scent filled my nose, thick and musky as I fell to the ground.

The fuzzy image flashed over me before disappearing from sight.

Not Evan Chandler.

I hiccupped once before the world went black.

FIVE

I ran through the forest, the full moon sending down a distorted light to show me the path. It was an unfamiliar area and I chose my steps carefully.

The rising and falling howls behind me said it all.

I was being hunted.

I leaped over the fallen log blocking the path. It slowed me down a fraction of a second but it was enough for my pursuers to gain ground.

The shout came from my left, a flanker keeping me on the trail. It was answered by a trio of growls from behind.

A tree root caught my foot and tripped me. I tumbled head over heels, twisting to the right and finding a hill there eager to accelerate my fall.

I landed a few inches from a deep hole. Scrambling to my feet I assessed the size of the pit.

Too deep to jump across.

I couldn't see the bottom.

It spread out to each side, the edges out of sight or obscured by deep brush.

I couldn't get around it.

The roaring behind me intensified. They were going to be on me in seconds.

I took a deep breath and jumped into the darkness.

* * *

"I'm sorry about the inconvenience." The angel's voice chirped behind my eyes. "You were listed as her emergency contact."

"That's all right." A familiar voice growled somewhere down around my feet, pushing away the darkness. "Damned woman's pretty high-maintenance. I'll send the bill to her sweetheart."

My nostrils were stinging from the acrid smell, prompting a throbbing behind my eyes that jutted down through my veins and into every part of my body.

In short, I felt like hell.

I wrestled my eyes open to see Hank Attersley watching me.

The middle-aged cop grunted as he got out of the hospital-issue chair and walked to the top of the bed. "'Bout time you woke up."

"What—" I licked bone-dry lips. "What happened?"

"You got smacked in the head." He pointed to the left side of his balding skull. "Always thought you had a hard head but you didn't need to prove it to me."

I lifted myself up a few inches. The hospital gown fluttered around my shoulders, the thin cloth ties barely holding on.

Hank paused, waiting for me to either give him a free show or settle down.

I stopped moving.

Hank looked relieved. "You were out for a bit. They did an MRI, made sure you didn't crack that eggshell. Nothing there but they're keeping you overnight to make sure there's nothing major wrong."

I lifted my left hand, seeing the thin needle and transparent tube leading back up to the intravenous drip. "Fuck."

Hank wagged a finger at me. "Language, language. Don't be hurting my virgin ears."

I smiled despite the pain. "That might be the only part of you that's left, smart ass."

The detective mimed an arrow hitting his heart. "Such disrespect. I came as soon as they called, left a pile of paperwork on my desk for this." The relief was evident on his face. "I'm just glad you're okay. I figured your luck had finally run out when they told me you'd gotten smacked in the head. A lot of people don't do well after that sort of injury."

I struggled to sit up again, succeeding this time. "I'm sorry, Hank. I didn't mean to cause you any trouble."

He grunted again and touched the controls on the edge of the bed, raising the mattress behind me to support my back.

Our relationship had been rocked in the last few weeks by my involvement in a murder and kidnapping. We hadn't been on opposite sides but it'd been rough, with me falling back on a family lawyer to stay out of jail, putting Hank and me at odds for the first time.

"You feel good enough for a sip?" He poured out a glass of water before I could answer. "Doctor said to take it easy, you got banged up nice. I probably shouldn't even give you this but you look parched."

I leaned in and sipped through the straw sticking

out of the Styrofoam cup. The cool water washed down my dry throat.

"Thanks." I licked my lips, relishing the mouthful of water. Concussions weren't anything to play with and while we Felis were built tough I didn't want to worry about pissing off the medical staff. "Where am I?"

"St. Joe's. And don't worry, your boyfriend's on the way." A scowl appeared on his face. "Bastard's hard to get hold of. Called his cell phone, went to voice mail. Idiot called back an hour ago blasting my eardrums."

I resisted the urge to roll my eyes. Bran had probably gone silent to keep from being interrupted on his one-man hunt and it'd cost him. "What time is it?"

"Just coming up on three o'clock in the afternoon." Hank moved back to his chair. "You remember anything 'bout what happened?" His tone shifted from friendly to official. "Let me find the guy who did this to you. Kick this mugger's ass into next Tuesday and then some."

I went to shake my head but the little miners inside with their pickaxes decided otherwise. "No. I mean, I hit a wall and—" The fuzzy memory of being attacked by another Felis fought through to the surface. "I got mugged?"

"You got banged up," Hank started. "And got lucky. Bunch of street kids saw you go down and came over to help, called 911 and scared the fellow off before he grabbed your wallet or anything else." He smiled. "Guess that horseshoe up your ass is still working."

"Ow." I drew in a deep breath as I sorted through

memories. "I think I remember the ambulance arriving."

I wasn't sure if I was remembering the actual events or a movie.

"Don't sweat it. I've taken worse." He rapped on his head with his knuckles, making a popping noise with his mouth. "You kept drifting in and out, babbling something about kittens."

I flinched inside.

He looked at me with a cop's curiosity. "What were you doing running down there in a parking garage?"

"Got a job."

"I figured that." Hank's bushy eyebrows rose. "Care to share?"

I weighed the pros and cons of letting him in.

"I'm tracking a pair of runaways." I figured I had nothing to lose. And if it helped heal the rift between us I was all for it. "I was hired by the parents to find them. Romeo and Juliet story, you know the tune."

"Think it was one of them that slugged you?" Hank asked.

I paused, weighing the odds. Evan Chandler had enough of a lead that he could have looped back around to clock me. But the fuzzy silhouette and the scent told me otherwise.

Of course I couldn't tell Hank this.

"I'm not sure. I do know they don't want to be found." I touched the side of my head, finding a golf ball-sized lump. "Ooh. That's not nice."

"Do you have any pictures?" Hank pressed onward,

ever the policeman. "Let me put out the word to the street cops. If they're under-age—"

I wouldn't have considered pulling in the police before now but this had taken a twist and not for the better. There was another player in the game, someone who didn't mind beating me like a piñata to get me out of the way.

"They are. At least for a week or so." I pointed at the storage locker in the corner. "There should be a manila envelope in my personal effects bag, next to my clothing. Got pictures of the two of them inside."

I wetted my lips again, taking stock of my body as Hank went to the locker. Toes, good. Ankles, good. Knees, old and aching. Hips sore and I knew if I looked under the sheet and generic hospital gown I'd see bruises that probably matched those on my left shoulder.

In other words, I was a mess.

At least the bullet scar on my arm hadn't re-opened. Logically it was practically impossible for it to have pulled open but emotionally I was always going down the darker path.

"All of your clothing's here, just so you know. Doesn't look like you trashed anything and they didn't have to cut anything off so when you leave don't worry about having to steal any hospital scrubs." Hank put the pictures against the wall, one by one, and took shots with his phone. "I'll send these to the boys and have them distributed to the street cops." His fingers flew over the tiny keyboard. "If we see them we'll take them off the streets." He paused. "I can't promise anything."

"I know. Plenty of other crimes out there, bagging runaways isn't high on the list." I gave him a smile. "But I appreciate it." I fluffed the thin sheets and poked my bare feet out at the bottom. "Feels strange wearing just a hospital gown and having this conversation."

Hank huffed as he put the envelope back in my locker, a light blush on his cheeks. "The doctors might let you go home but not unless you have someone holding your hand for the night. And my wife's got a firm policy against me bringing home strays."

As if on cue the door flew open.

Wide-eyed and panting, Bran looked like something the cat dragged in. His reddened face matched his hair, plastered to his forehead with sweat.

He ignored Hank. "Are you okay?"

Before I could answer he'd stripped off his coat and tossed it over the chair Hank had previously occupied. "What do they have you hooked up to? What's in this?"

Hank put up a hand as Bran came to my side and inspected the IV pole. "It's just fluids. Standard procedure to keep her hydrated. As far as I know no antibiotics, no need for them." He grinned at me. "I'm gonna leave now that your playmate's here. I'll call if we find them."

Bran nodded at the detective, the two men locking eyes for a brief challenging moment. They hadn't seen each other since Hank had dragged the entire Hanover family down to the police station a few weeks ago.

The stalemate broke without incident.

Hank chuckled and walked out the door with a wave. "She's all yours. Might be time to put her on a leash."

My lips drew back in an instinctive snarl at the mental image. I flipped my middle finger up at the closing door.

Bran laughed and bent down for a kiss. "Glad to see you're well enough to be pissy." He played with the transparent tube coming from my arm. "Let's get this out of you and get you into bed."

"I am in bed." I patted the thin mattress. "And, frankly, I'd expected a bit more seduction from you. Just because we're living together doesn't mean you don't have to work for it." The last few words came out a little harsher than I'd intended.

He dropped his chin down, looking like I'd smacked him on the nose with a rolled newspaper. "God, Reb—I'm so sorry I didn't get here faster." He sat on the edge of the bed. "I turned the phone off 'cause I was trucking with some kids and didn't want to be disturbed."

I didn't say anything.

Bran gave me a weary smile. "And you know I was with Angie because you can smell her on me." He rubbed his nose with the palm of his hand. "Damn it's hard to hide anything from you Felis."

My hand wrapped around the back of his neck as I pulled him close enough for me to whisper into his ear.

"Let me tell you a secret."

He drew in a deep breath and held it.

I murmured. "I didn't know until you told me just now."

He made a noise, something between a sigh and a gasp.

I continued. "You might have been in the same room

as her, I can believe that. But I don't scent her all over you like before. She kept her distance, kept her hands off of you." I'd caught a whiff of her hair conditioner, the same gloppy fruity smell but if I hadn't smelled it earlier I wouldn't know or care whose it was. It was also mixed in with a hundred other scents, the usual street traffic picked up from being out in public.

Bran didn't move but I felt the tension ease out of his neck and shoulder muscles. The poor bastard had been terrified to come to me, expecting a tongue lashing.

I felt even worse than before. Bran must have run into Angie after she and I had talked.

She'd kept up her part of the deal. She'd left him alone.

He drew back. "I ran into her while tracking a group of artists. They went to the outreach center for lunch and I went along with them. She didn't do anything, didn't try anything. I left as soon as I confirmed the kids weren't there. I swear." He put his first two fingers of his right hand to his forehead. "Scout's honor."

"I doubt you were ever a Scout." I kissed his forehead. "We're good." I shifted my weight, feeling the bony outlines of the steel frame bed under me. "Why don't you go get me checked out? I'd like to go home to our own bed."

Bran stood up. "I'll get the doctor. Don't see a problem with you signing yourself out as long as you don't do anything silly." He picked up his coat and left before I could answer.

"Men," I whispered to the empty room before closing my eyes. All I wanted right then was my own bed and a cuppa tea.

I drifted, half-awake and wondering what to do about my Felis attacker. There was an outside chance, a thin chance it had nothing to do with my case. Most Felis stayed on the straight and narrow but there could be someone out there who walked on the other side and it'd just been bad luck.

Really bad luck.

I made a mental note to call Jess and see if we had any miscreant relatives on file.

"You're a tough one." The strange voice hit my ears at the same time as the rich earthy Felis scent invaded my nostrils.

Male. Alpha.

Here.

I resisted the urge to open my eyes right away, hoping he'd think I was sleeping. With a tube in my arm and still weak from the concussion I wasn't in any state to jump up and start fighting.

The pounding in my ears increased as I realized Bran could be back any second, with or without other humans.

"I know you're awake. Don't worry, I'm here to talk." A low chuckle followed. "Unlike my associate, I don't knock women around."

I couldn't resist. I opened my eyes.

The large man sat at the bottom of my bed, his bulk filling the hospital-issue chair and then some, muscles spilling over the side. His bare arms were covered with tattoos—lions, tigers and other felines.

Definitely family.

He looked like an ex-boxer, his warped nose barely able to draw a straight line. Short-cropped black hair over dark brown eyes that studied me with the intensity of a hunter. Dressed in jeans, a black T-shirt and leather jacket he waited for me to finish studying him.

“Family,” I said.

He nodded.

“Jess?” I tried not to sound too hopeful. I was in no condition to turn down help if Jess sent it.

A hurt look came over the middle-aged face. “No.” He looked as if he was about to spit on the ground. “I don’t work for the Board.”

“Oh.” A chill ran up my aching spine as I sat up straighter, considering my options. It was hard to resist glancing toward the door.

He held up a meaty hand. “Don’t hurt yourself. I’m here to talk. Nothing else.”

“So let’s talk.”

“Eddie Longstrand.” He didn’t get out of the chair to offer his hand. “I’m here on behalf of the Middleston family.”

I frowned. “I’ve been replaced?”

“I like to think of it as supplemented.” He got to his feet, standing almost as tall as Bran. “You wouldn’t even know about me if that idiot hadn’t slammed you.” He shook his head. “I’d hate to think what would have happened if you’d been really hurt. Wrath of Hammersmythe and all that. As it is he’s going to have a shitload of trouble if and when she catches his ass.”

I pushed myself farther up the bed. “Which idiot?”

"The guy who hit you, Nathan McCallister." Eddie stuck his hands in his pockets. "He works for the Chandlers. We're sort of…competitors. We do stuff for the families." He tapped his chest. "Jake's my cousin, twice-removed."

Felis enforcers.

I tamped down a twinge of panic. I'd never had a good encounter with an enforcer.

"What do you want?" I looked at the IV line. I could pull it out and use the pole as a weapon.

I could also fart and fly if I tried really hard.

"I'd like to offer you an alliance." Eddie pressed his lips together into a tight thin line before continuing. "We're after the same thing—the girl."

"Lisa. Her name is Lisa."

Eddie eyed me. "The girl. Jake asked me to tag along, keep watch on where you went and what you did."

I read between the lines in a burst of belated wisdom.

He pulled out a small notepad and pencil. "You're in no condition to make a big decision right now, I know that. I'm not going to take advantage of a wounded family member to pressure you. I'm going to give you my number. When you're ready to talk, call." The pencil stub scratched across the slip of paper. "Or just wave me in through the front door. I'll be around."

The piece of paper fell on the starched white sheet and he was gone, slipping out the door like a damned sumo ninja.

Bran came back in a few minutes later. "Okay, we've got the paperwork processing to get you out of here.

Doc's on his way to sign off on the discharge. He's not happy but I told him I'd keep you in bed—" His voice trailed off. "What's wrong?"

"Just take me home." I pointed at the note, still sitting on the edge of the bed. "And put that someplace safe. I'll need it later."

Within the hour I was home and in bed, wearing an old nightshirt and tucked in with the stained bedspread up around my shoulders despite my protestations. Bran was downstairs making tea while Jazz padded around my covered feet and trilled her annoyance at my taking back the big pillow before nightfall.

I pushed down the blanket as Bran appeared, balancing a tray.

"Too warm for this." I kicked the bedspread to the bottom of the bed, creating a mountain range for Jazz, who immediately spread herself out to claim as much ground as possible.

"Tea, toast. Lightly buttered and if you feel sick say something." Bran put the tray on the floor and passed me the mug. "Doctor said for you to take it easy. You get any bad headaches, nausea or disorientation and he wants you right back in Emergency."

"Bah." I sipped the tea and sighed. "Heaven."

He crawled in beside me, carrying his own cup. "So what's with the phone number?"

"What number?" I reached down for a slice of toast, delaying the inevitable. My stomach rumbled.

"The phone number I picked up at the hospital." He watched me rip off small bites of toast and chew them until they were mush. "It wasn't lying there on the bed when I left you."

"It seems that I have acquired followers." I chose my words carefully knowing Bran's temper. "The visitor informed me that I got bodyslammed by a Felis enforcer by the name of Nathan McCallister, who works for the Chandlers."

Bran clenched his teeth, his jaw taut. "What the fuck for?"

"Because it seems I need a babysitter. Or to be precise, two." I took another mouthful of tea, studying Bran's face.

He drew in a deep breath, his jaw tightening to the point that I heard his back teeth grinding.

"Again, what the fuck for?" He spat the words out.

I reached down and took another piece of toast. "The two families may be feuding with each other but they've got the same idea—use me to hunt down the kids and then they'll take them whether I agree or not." I nibbled on the lukewarm slice. "Obviously they don't have a lot of faith in me convincing the lovebirds to go home. So I find them and the enforcers grab them."

Jazz trundled over to pick at a crumb on the sheets.

"So what was this all about?" He waved his index finger in a circle. "Trying to kill you was supposed to be an introduction?"

I shook my head. "I'm willing to bet McCallister saw me go after Chandler and wanted to make sure I didn't reach the kid before he did. Get me out of the way before I could interfere with his 'removal.'" I touched the back of my neck and winced, finding nothing but hard, tense muscles. "It worked."

Bran put his mug down and moved closer, pushing my hand away. His fingers began to knead the sensitive skin and break down the tight knots. "Do you think he got Evan?"

"Since I didn't get a call from Jess or Mary Chandler calling me off I'd say no." I sighed as the knots began to unwind. "Eddie's on the opposite side, he's working for the Middlestons. Guess I didn't impress Jake with my sincerity."

"So they're using you like a bloodhound?" The touches became lighter, more gentle.

"Makes sense in a sad, perverted way." I twisted to one side to give him greater access. "Neither side wants to call a hunt and bring attention to their kids running away with each other. Neither side's familiar with Toronto. Their friends and family don't have the knowledge to roam the streets. It'd be like setting a cat loose in a mousetrap factory—they'd end up making so much noise and commotion that either the kids would split town, making it harder to find them or worse, calling attention to themselves through their efforts."

"Threatening to expose the Felis," Bran said.

I nodded, shifting to allow him greater access. "Enough brawling in the streets and threatening will bring in the police and we know where that could go." I tugged my nightshirt up and off, shivering as my damp skin hit the air. "Why not let me do all the hunting and then swoop in at the end to grab the kids? I'll get paid either way. They're figuring I'm all about the money and when they tell me to stop, I'll stop." I tossed the shirt on the floor, trying hard not to obsess over the fresh bruises. I didn't bounce well.

Bran smiled. "I suspect you disagree with that assessment."

"Tells me they didn't talk to Jess a whole lot before deciding to go down this trail." I finished off the toast and reached for my tea. "Those kids deserve the right to choose what to do with their lives outside of this family crap. They might decide to go back but it shouldn't be a forced decision. They're almost adults, after all." I sighed, feeling the heaviness in my arms and legs.

"So what are we going to do about it?" His eyes dragged over my nakedness. "Because I have some ideas."

I finished off the tea and placed the cup on the table before leaning back into his arms. "First, I rest. Then we dump our trackers and find the kids." My eyes wandered over to the digital clock. "Holy…is it really after five in the afternoon?"

The heated chuckle in my ear sent tremors down my spine. "Yep. You did spend quite a bit of time in the hospital. And don't forget you're supposed to be resting." His hands rested on my hips, tugging me closer.

"We have to go find those kids." I felt like I was made of jelly. Melting jelly.

"We'll go out when it's dark," Bran whispered. "You need to give yourself a chance to recover. The kids will still be out there and we'll find them easier at night—they tend to settle down after busking for the evening crowd and stop moving around so much." His fingers danced down my back, bumping over the scars. "Now lie back and let me take care of you."

His teeth nipped the back of my neck, just enough to make me gasp.

"I'm supposed to be resting." It was a weak protest. "I'm not supposed to get over-excited or something like that."

"That's okay," Bran murmured. "Just lie back and let me do all the work."

And he did.

SIX

The water in the shower was lukewarm. Bran shook his head as he stepped in behind me and placed his hands on my waist. I banged on the shower head and cursed as the temperature failed to increase.

Bran ducked over my shoulder, letting the water soak his hair. "Not too bad, but when winter comes—"

"I'll worry about that later." I reached for the soap, trying to shake the lethargy out of my bones. "I'll ask Jess if we've got any plumbing connections. Might be able to barter something for a new heater. We'll need it in a few months."

His hands slicked over my soapy breasts. "I don't mind making our own heat for a bit."

"That's fine when it's warm outside. Wait until there's frost on the windows and you'll be wanting your hot water." I winced as he touched my hip. "Ouch."

"That's going to take a bit of time to go away. Hell of a bruise." He ran his hand along my left arm, stroking the new scar. "At least this healed over."

I shivered and not just from the water temperature. The slash had been the result of an errant bullet fired by Bran's mother in a fit of anger over our interference in her master plan to kidnap a baby and call him her own. The external scars might have healed but I didn't know how well Bran's internal ones were.

Bran leaned past me and twisted the hot water tap full open. "Let's get finished here and see if we can find those two kids before they get into more trouble than we can handle.

Within the hour I'd extracted my Jeep from the tiny parking spot behind the house and we were on the way to Don Heights—Bran's suggested first stop on trying to pry the kids out of the underworld.

"I've never been there before." I resisted leaning on the horn as a pair of drunks staggered through the red light in front of us. "Saw pictures in the paper. Didn't they just renovate it?"

"New playground and all the trimmings. Great place for the kids but at night it goes to the wild side. It's a beautiful park, been there for decades. Plenty of old growth trees that survived everything being built around them," Bran said as we raced along the emptying streets. It was well past eleven and I was invigorated by the cool night air.

The good loving a few hours earlier hadn't hurt either.

"It's not too far from the city core." I zipped around a slow-moving convertible, the driver and passenger more involved in each other than maintaining a decent speed limit. "How many kids go there?"

"Depends on the night. A lot of them go to the Point if they've got extra cash and want to party." Bran shifted in the seat beside me, tugging at the knee of his jeans.

"I figured that out." I pulled up beside a late-night streetcar, the long red torpedo packed with travelers. "And they go to the Heights to sleep?"

"If they can make it. It's a sort of neutral zone—the gangs don't recruit there and they don't allow drugs or booze." Bran looked at the red light holding us in place. "Mutual respect. Makes it a safe haven for everyone."

"Until they step off and then it's open game." I stomped on the gas pedal the second the light changed, jumping ahead of the slow lumbering streetcar.

Bran shrugged. "It's a balancing act for everyone. Détente that keeps everyone going one more day." His attention turned to the dark streets ahead of us. "Sleeping in trees."

"I remember that." I didn't need to mention Angie. "What's that all about?"

"It's a way of keeping safe. If you're in a tree your stuff can't be stolen or pawed through."

I risked a sideways glance. "I thought you said Don Heights was neutral ground."

Bran gave me a sad smile. "For gangs and vices. There's always going to be someone wanting something you've got. Easiest way to keep everything safe is to take it above ground."

I noted a street sign and made a right turn. "We'll park nearby and walk in."

Bran studied my rearview mirror. "Any signs of your adoring fans?"

"If they're good I won't see them." I'd been watching since we left the house. "These two are good."

"So are the kids we're looking for." He pointed at the curb. "Overnight parking available there."

I slid into the empty space. It wasn't hard; the nearest cars were a half block away. "It can't be this easy to get a spot."

"Prime area for theft. These kids aren't usually looking for joyrides but I can't promise they won't consider it," Bran said as he hopped out. "How's your insurance on this thing?"

"Good enough. I hope." I tucked the keys into my coat pocket and moved up beside him. The night air was cool, enough to warrant wearing the duster.

I also viewed it as possible camouflage. These two enforcers were good but now I knew they were there.

My side ached. I couldn't beat them in a fight so I'd have to use my wits.

I could still be outmatched.

A breeze drifted over us. I instinctively raised my face and sniffed, trying to pick up what I could.

Freshly-mowed grass. Turned-over dirt. A scattering of flowers, their sweetness almost intoxicating.

Cigarettes. Sweat. Sex.

Maybe a trace of Felis. I wriggled my nose.

"Anything good?" Bran asked. He'd come to understand my Felis senses could be a blessing and a curse.

"Not sure. There's so much going on. Best way to find out is to do it the old-fashioned way." I waved him onward. "Let's visit fantasyland."

We walked along the sidewalk beside shuttered businesses until we hit a chain of willow trees, their long draping branches brushing the ground. The glossy black lacquered chain-link fence stood no more than a foot high, more of a suggestion at a barrier than an actual impediment.

The entrance started with an opening in the baby fence and a small iron plaque set in the cement announcing we could enter Don Heights here, a park dedicated to the memory of James Hilton the Third.

Whoever that was. I wondered if anyone had considered attaching a small history book to these granite blocks to inform the public who they were supposed to thank. It'd be nice to know why Mr. Hilton was worth having a whole park named after him.

The willow trees parted to show a handful of paved paths wandering in and out of small clusters of bushes with tall, lanky trees scattered throughout the football field-sized park. We followed the path to the center of the park where a small fountain sat, spewing water out the top of a thin spout to fall in a faux rain into the bottom. No statue of a little boy peeing or a horse spouting water out of his mouth—the sculptor had gone simple and plain, probably hoping to reduce the amount of graffiti and defacement public statues tended to attract.

I could smell the soap and detergent.

Bran nodded before I could speak. "Good hygiene." He chuckled. "Kind of hard to go ask for cash when no one can stand being within a mile of you. Wear clean underwear and wash behind your ears like your momma said."

"Good idea." I spotted a rustling in the bushes to our left.

I didn't react.

We weren't going to get anywhere charging around like wild dogs at every twitch and flutter of leaves. I doubted it was either of the Felis enforcers, they wouldn't be so obvious.

Wise hunters don't charge at the first sign. They watch and wait and learn what they can.

Bran sat down on the brim of the fountain and yawned.

I rolled my eyes. "Not my fault. I suggested a nap."

He laughed. "Not my fault. You're irresistible."

I joined him, squirming on the cool concrete edge. "Now what?" I studied the bushes and trees. "Wait for the kids to issue an invitation?"

"Maybe." Bran turned and studied me. "You feeling okay? Not dizzy, shaky or anything?"

The concern in his voice was both wonderful and annoying. I wasn't a frail little kit running home to Mom the first time I skinned my knee.

On the other hand, we could at any second be in the middle of a major brawl.

I drew in a deep breath, enjoying the smells of the scaled-down wilderness. It wasn't a full forest but it was definitely a draw for any Felis in the area. "I'm good."

Not great but good. I wasn't going to push it.

Bran looked around, trying to orient himself. "It's basically the same as it was a few years ago but a bit different." He chuckled. "Now I feel like an old man."

"Given the way you were moving a few hours ago I can testify that you are definitely not an old man." I put my hand on the small of my back and stretched with a magnified sigh. "I might like it when you get older and slower."

"I thought you liked it fast." He gave a sassy wink.

I felt my cheeks burn and looked at the trees. They didn't manage to hide the skyline but did a fine job of obscuring it. If I squinted really hard I could almost imagine being back on the farm or some other forest, away from the scents and sounds of the city.

Bran took my hand and squeezed it. "You like it here." It wasn't a question.

"I do." Another deep breath brought back memories of the farm and the nearby forest. My ankle gave off phantom aches, reminding me of my first hunt.

"We should take a vacation." Another squeeze. "Maybe up to Algonquin Park? Go do a little hiking and camping?"

"You want to go out into the wilderness with me?" I said in a low tone.

He gave a half-hearted shrug. "If you'd like to. We could even go for a run." A pause, long enough to tickle my nerves. "On one of the trails. I could manage a light jog, I think."

I eyed him suspiciously. "What brought this on? You know I haven't heard from Trace. He's given up on me."

Trace Bryson hadn't entered into my thoughts for a good long time. The Felis farmer had taken my rejection well and kept to his part of the bargain, leaving us alone after Bran proved himself worthy of me, in the eyes of the Felis.

It'd been my bad judgment going on a run with Trace that had prompted Brandon and I to re-evaluate our relationship.

I didn't think it was a far stretch to say Angie's re-appearance had brought this back to the surface.

"I just think it'd be a good idea, that's all." His grip on my hand tightened. "I'm willing to try to put up a tent and throw sleeping bags on the ground if it'd make you happy."

Tears blurred my vision. "You make me happy. You don't have to do anything, just be…you."

He leaned in for a kiss, sloppy and heartfelt. "I try. And the offer stands if you want to get out of the city and kick your heels up, run wild for a bit." Bran licked his lips. "But I'll pass on eating raw meat if you catch anything. Got to put my foot down and say we cook it."

The chuckle caught in my throat. "I'll settle for a rare steak at the nearest restaurant instead and a late-night double feature of bad science-fiction movies curled up beside you in bed." I squeezed his hand back. "I'm getting too old for running. I like where I am right now."

Bran looked away, clearing his throat. He pointed at a tree off from the others, the thick trunk signaling the many years the oak tree had managed to survive. "That's the couples tree."

"What?"

"It's full of branches thick enough to put a tarp between, create a sort of hammock for two people to snuggle in and be safe for a few hours. Not a whole lot of privacy and I sure wouldn't recommend wild animal sex that high above the ground but I'd put money on your two lovebirds climbing up there at some point."

I tried to sound casual. "And how would you know about this tree?"

His jaw tightened. "I watched the kids go up there. DJ, for example. They'd scurry up there like they were born to climb trees. Curl up like kittens all tangled 'round each other until sunrise."

I didn't say anything.

He kissed the back of my hand and released it. "It kills me sometimes, thinking about what they could have been. What they should have been."

"It was their decision," I whispered. "You can't save everyone."

"No." He cocked his head to the side and smiled. "But I can sure try."

I looked at the tree. Thick, ancient trunk more than a foot in diameter. The old man of the park, the guardian watching over the willows, the maples and the bushes.

"I'm going to head over there, get up on a branch and wait. If the kids show up, great. If not I'll have a nice view of the park." I stood up and brushed off the back of my coat. "I don't think they'll just wander over to check us out if we keep sitting here."

"Since I have the climbing skills of an elephant I'll pass on that and hang out, do a walk along the paths." Bran dipped his hand in the slow running water. "Maybe see if any of the old crew might still be around. After seeing Angie—"

I flinched inside at the sadness in his voice. I might not have had his experience in dealing with street kids but five years was a lifetime and it'd be a miracle for anyone in his original article to still be around.

I hesitated just long enough to tweak his attention back to me.

"Go." He slapped my butt. "I'll be fine down here. Be careful and if you feel sick or dizzy sing out and I'll be over there in a second."

I strolled toward the tree. The thick bushes on each side were perfect for an ambush. It was a great place to be if you didn't want to be noticed.

I sniffed the air, taking in the deep earthy smells. So different from the usual city scents clogging up my mind.

It took me a few tries to get up the tree and I could have sworn I heard a guffaw or two from Bran but I finally got up onto the first branch. From there it was easy to climb higher and higher, the dense leaves hiding me from anyone casually walking by.

Bran gave me a wave and strolled off.

I stretched out on a long large branch, letting my duster hang down and partially camouflage me. My ears were buzzing and I was pushing myself by being so active after being clocked by the Chandler enforcer.

Still, there were worse ways of spending some time at night.

And better ones. My hand drifted to my left shoulder and dug under the black T-shirt to caress the newest love bite Bran had given me.

I pressed my face against the rough bark, inhaling

the rich smells. It was easy to forget I was in the middle of a city and imagine I was back on the farm enjoying a lazy night out under the full moon.

An hour passed then two. I shifted my legs, straddling the branch as I fought the threatening cramps. I was getting too old to sleep in trees and right now my comfortable mattress called with a siren's voice.

The wind shifted and brought me the scent of Felis.

More than one.

More than two.

More than three.

I resisted the urge to sigh. I hadn't even tried to lose the enforcers knowing it'd waste time I didn't have—not to mention the bastards had way more experience than I did on hiding, prowling and doing whatever their masters asked. The only hope I had was to outwit them.

And in my present state that was going to be a wee bit hard.

The sound of boots scraping below me brought me out of my reverie. I looked down to see a pair of youngsters scrambling up the trunk as if they were born to it, giggling like fools. They reminded me of kits discovering the fun of scaling anything and everything with their claws.

There were a lot of scratched and mangled wooden posts at the farm. Ruth hadn't even tried to replace them, pointing out that Felis babies needed to play and enjoy their claws and she wasn't going to switch out the cribs and staircase railings every time a new baby was dropped off at the daycare.

Ruth died before her time, a victim of Felis politics.

I'd be damned if I wouldn't at least try to get these two free of that particular part of their heritage.

Evan Chandler was being a gentleman, letting Lisa Middleston climb first. It didn't escape me that it also gave him an excellent view of her butt. The dark-haired teenager let out a laugh as his claws extended between his knuckles, allowing him to dig into the tree and get a good grip, better than most humans would be able to get.

He shifted his shoulders, adjusting the backpack. A rolled-up sleeping bag at the bottom of the aluminum frame bounced against his butt. His guitar sat against the pack, tied down with bungee cords.

Lisa's red hair stood out against the leaves as she approached me, her own claws whittling away at the bark. The two of them were focused on each other, whispering and giggling as they sprang up the tree at a faster pace than I had. She wore the backpack's twin a bit better than Evan, the belt around her hips snug enough to avoid the frame smacking against her body.

The pair smelled of soap and a dash of perfume. They were clean and looked good despite the dark circles under their eyes.

I guessed you had to get used to sleeping in a tree.

They passed by me without a glance, headed for higher ground. The Felis in me wanted to smack them hard for not bothering to use their God-given senses and be more aware of their surroundings—if I were one of the enforcers I'd have them bagged and tagged in a few minutes, to say nothing about delivering a strong sermon about displaying their claws in public.

But they were in love and ignoring everything other than each other.

I reached inside my duster to get my cell phone. A quick text message told Bran to come and keep an eye open. I couldn't ask him to cut off their escape route. Two young Felis fleeing would bowl him over and send him flying, not to mention putting him between the enforcers and the kids in a brawl he couldn't win.

He'd dispute this considering he'd bested an adult Felis a few months before in a challenge but Carson had been injured and concussed. And I didn't need to see Bran disemboweled either by the hunters or their prey in a frantic battle in the park. Felis didn't kill each other and tried as hard as possible to avoid hurting or killing humans but I didn't put much stock in the philosophy at the moment, given I still felt like I'd been worked over by a herd of rampaging buffalos.

I didn't wait for Bran's answer before moving to the trunk and pulling myself up, following the trail.

Gritting my teeth I willed my claws to come out. My lack of control over my Felis change hadn't gotten any better, the natural shifting to a full Felis still out of reach. I'd manifested my claws a handful of times under stress and a full change most recently when I'd been shot but I still sat at the level of a newborn kit, stumbling around in the dark.

Nothing shot out from between my knuckles, the hard sharp nails staying silent and hidden.

I sighed and rolled my shoulders, feeling the strained muscles as I grabbed the ragged bark trunk.

By the time I'd gotten up to the same level as the

runaways they'd already begun setting up their sleeping area, oblivious to my arrival.

Another black mark on the kits' record. If I could smell them they sure should have been able to scent me. They were so wrapped up in each other they'd forgotten to be alert and aware of their surroundings.

True love.

A dark blue tarp swung between two branches sprouting close to each other, the fork allowing Evan to tie down the plastic with bungie cords twisted right around the thick wood. Lisa pulled a thin blanket out of her backpack and laid it across to give them some protection from the harsh plastic.

She hummed a familiar hunting song, adding to the warped domesticity around her. Another blanket came out and was neatly folded into a makeshift pillow, wadded into one end of the hammock.

The two hadn't noticed me and I moved around to the other side of the tree and climbed above them. Technically I had them trapped between me and Bran at the bottom of the tree.

I didn't have a lot of faith in technical.

I sat back and studied the pair as they snacked on a small bag of commercial trail mix and passed a water bottle between them. After getting smacked around I deserved to see exactly who I was dealing with.

Now that I had a clear view of him I had to admit Evan Chandler didn't do his picture justice.

The short black hair brought out his blue eyes. He wasn't one of those musicians who sat around all day composing. His biceps were pushing the dark blue T-shirt sleeves to their limit. I could easily imagine him working on a farm, splitting wood and doing chores before retreating to the barn and composing a romantic ode to Lisa.

Lisa Middleston didn't look much like her father, which was probably a blessing. Her long red hair had been pulled back into a ponytail brushing her shoulders, the tight black shirt showing off the same excellent physical condition Evan was in. Her slender fingers seemed more suited for piano keys than working with bungee cords.

These weren't spoiled city kids looking to live on the wild side for a night before going back to their monster mansions. These were two young people who had worked with their hands for almost all of their lives and were prepared to rough it in the big city to be together.

This wasn't necessarily good news. If I'd been able to scare them back to their families offering a hot meal and soft pillows it'd be easier to approach them.

I moved out onto the branch above the pair and waited until they had curled up around each other in the makeshift hammock, cooing to each other.

I cleared my throat, wanting to catch them before I switched from observer to voyeur. "Evan," I whispered. My idea was to approach them as quietly and as calmly as I could. No use causing a scene.

The teenager's head snapped up. He pushed Lisa behind him and leaped onto one of the two branches, Changing as he went. Instead of confronting a young man I found myself facing a full-fledged Felis, his charcoal-black fur taking over his human features. His claws shot out and he snarled at me, his aggressive stance signaling an oncoming attack.

So much for not causing a scene.

Lisa stayed in the hammock but Changed as well, her cream-colored fur a startling contrast to her boyfriend's dark coloring. She pushed herself to her knees with a curse and showed off an impressive set of incisors along with her own claws.

I held up both hands. Even if I could have Changed I wouldn't have, not in this situation.

"You know I'm family," I said as gently as I could. "I'm not here to fight."

Evan's nostrils twitched as he took me in. His baby blue eyes widened before narrowing into a hunter's focused glare. He stayed in a fighting pose but waited for me to make the next move.

"Like I said, I'm not here to fight." I turned my hands so they could see my lack of claws. "I'm here to talk." I couldn't help smiling. "Besides, you kids are too fast for me. Just about broke my neck getting up here, and I might have to call the fire department to get back down."

That earned me a snicker from Evan and a muffled giggle from Lisa. The joke didn't make us fast friends but we'd managed to back away from sworn enemies.

Evan risked a glance over at Lisa. She gave him a nod and Changed back. Evan followed close behind and we were all human again.

"Thank you." I looked at Lisa. "Your dad asked me to find you. He said he wanted to talk to you one last time before you turn eighteen and go on your own way."

She snorted. "Bullshit."

"I know."

Her shocked expression lasted a second before the mask fell. "So why are you here?" She grabbed at the makeshift pillow, rolling and folding the blanket.

"I was also hired by his mother." I looked at Evan. "She didn't have a cover story. Just wanted me to find you and bring you home before you hit your birthday."

"Son of a—"

I cut Evan off before he got to the cursing. "I hear you. The problem is I'm not the only one looking for you." I paused. "But I'm the best chance you have to get out of here together."

Evan growled. "Bastard. I knew he wouldn't let her go without a fight. Goddamn family feud." He looked around. "Send a fucking army after her. How many are there?"

His claws shot out again, gleaming in the dim moonlight.

"One. For each of you." I smiled. "Competing to the very end."

Lisa stuffed the blanket into the backpack, her voice rising slightly. "Then we'll run. Get out of the city. All we need is another two weeks, another couple of days." She tugged at the tarp, climbing up on the branch to release the bungee cords. "As soon as we're old enough they'll leave us alone."

I moved closer, very aware of Evan's claws. "You think your families are going to let you do that? You don't think they'll keep on your trail, keep hunting you down to keep you apart?" I snorted. "I knew you were young, I didn't think you were stupid."

This earned me an angry snarl from Evan. "You don't know what you're talking about." He pointed at me. "I've heard about you. You're that damned misfit, that chick who can't Change."

I held up a finger. "That would be 'that woman.' At least try to be respectful of your elders. And don't think for a second that you're just going to scoot your asses down to the bus station and grab the next Greyhound for Vancouver."

"You gonna stop us?" Evan said, baring his fangs.

"Nope." I pointed down. "The two hunters waiting somewhere in this park will. Not to mention the cops who are on the lookout for you throughout the city." I tilted my head to one side. "You don't look stupid, you do the math. What do you think your odds are of staying free with enforcers from both families following your trail? You think skipping to another city, another province, another country is going to stop them from tracking you down? No Pride's going to take you in without checking with the Board and what do you think they're going to say with both families screaming for your hides?" I looked from one to the other. "You might have gotten away for now but are you really prepared for being on the run forever? Skipping from town to town before the locals get wind of you? What sort of life is that?"

The two didn't answer.

"Exactly. You want to settle down somewhere you'll have to deal with this here and now."

Evan caught Lisa's eyes and stared at her. She shook her head in quiet communication.

His claws retracted, leaving tiny slits between his knuckles. They'd heal soon enough.

"Good." My pulse began to slow. I hadn't been looking forward to a brawl with a kid half my age. "Now we need a plan."

SEVEN

Lisa cocked her head to one side, studying me. "Don't mean to be impolite but why would you want to help us? You're getting paid by our families to find us, like a bounty hunter. You're the bad guy or girl, whatever you want to call it."

"True." A stiff breeze shot through the branches bringing me the scent of the enforcers, down on the ground somewhere. Way too close for comfort. "But they hired me to find you. Not to hand you over to thugs who'll drag you back home and the fact that both sides thought I'd be stupid enough to play their game pisses me off." I gripped the wood, readjusting my balance. "Look, once you're eighteen you can do what you want but I'm willing to bet that if I let your parents get hold of you neither of you will see each other ever again. Call me a hopeless romantic but I figure you two deserve to at least have a chance at true love." I shifted on the branch, trying to feel more secure. "This family feud has got to stop and I think you're the ones to stop it."

"Damned idiots," Evan grumbled. He looked at Lisa. "On both sides." He pulled Lisa up beside him with his hand tight on her waist. "They can all go to hell.

We love each other and no one's going to stop us from being together."

"How much?" I couldn't hold back a frustrated snarl. "How far are you willing to go? I'm willing to go to the wall for you two to have a fair chance at making it work but you're going to have to convince me you're in this for the long haul, not just having a lark playing at being adults or trying to piss off your parents by dating the enemy."

Evan's lips curled away from his teeth. "I love her. If we have to run, then we run."

"I got that. Hell, that's why we're up a tree together." I pointed down at the ground. "But you go with her on the run you're leaving your family. There's no going back home, there's no happy family dinners in the near future. There's no help from anyone, you'll be out on your own." I studied his face. "You ready to say goodbye to your mother forever? You ready to blow off your friends, everyone you ever knew?"

"You left," Evan shot back. "You survived."

"I was pushed out," I snapped. "And you have no idea how hard it was for me to make it." I sliced the air with my hand, talking past the sudden lump in my throat. "We're not talking about me. We're talking about you, the two of you. Are you both ready to write off your families, your friends forever? Everyone you ever knew, everyone you worked and played with? Everyone?"

A panicked look came over Lisa's face. She looked at Evan and I saw the crack in her mental wall.

"Look I get it. You're in love," I said. "Believe me

it's a wonderful feeling. I know that. But we all need family." I said it again, pushing as much emotion as I could into the sentence. "We all need family. Even if we don't like or love them at that moment, we need them in our lives."

I wasn't just being preachy in order to keep the two of them around.

Felis relied on each other and our family ties to keep us strong, supported and secret. Every Felis tithed to their Pride to keep their Board running—they counted on having that support system around for family emergencies and for help if needed. If you lost your job the Pride would help you find one. If you got sick and couldn't pay your bills the Pride would help out. If you needed someone found because of an emergency or crisis you called the Board and they'd declare a hunt.

I hadn't needed the support, hadn't been able to call on it for years. It was only recently that I'd been able to access it and only because I needed the family's help to save a life.

Young Liam Callendar.

They'd come through, my Felis family. They'd helped find him and those responsible for his mother's death and his kidnapping.

It was a debt I'd be a long time paying off, if I ever could.

I knew what I'd lost by being declared outcast. I wasn't sure these kids knew what they were willing to throw away.

"We can go off the grid," Evan said. "No one'll find us. We'll change our names, get fake I.D."

I sighed. "Kit, that only works in the movies. You get a job, you rent a hotel room, you go into the doctor's office for a cut finger you'll be found. You have no idea how deep the family's connections run."

His lips curled away from his teeth. "I'm not a kit." He stood up, balancing on the thick tree limb. "I'm a man."

"Not for a few more days," I shot back. "And being a man means thinking things through, not jumping at the first thing you see like you're on your first hunt. Right now you're up a tree without a way down except through a pair of angry thugs."

"So what do we do?" Lisa asked. She looked at Evan. "I don't want to go home. Not this way."

"First," I held up a finger, "first we get you out of this tree and out of the line of fire. Get you someplace safe where we can sit and think without me getting splinters up my ass. Give me some breathing space and let me see what I can arrange to make everyone happy."

"Why should we trust you?" Evan said.

I spread my hands. "I'm the best one you've got." I locked eyes with the young man. "If you've got a better idea, I'm open to hearing it."

That shut him up for a few minutes as he glared at me.

Evan broke eye contact and turned back to Lisa, who was busy packing up the tarp, folding the dark blue plastic into a fat square and putting it back in her pack along with the bungee cords. It was pretty obvious who the organized one in this couple was.

She let out an annoyed huff. "I can't believe my dad sent someone after me," she said. "Who is it?"

"Eddie Longstrand." I nodded at Evan. "And your peeps sent Nathan McCallister, a fucking thug." I touched the side of my head. "Slammed me into a wall when we were in the parking lot."

"That was you in the parking lot?" His expression turned from surly to sadness. "I'm sorry about that. I scented him and ran, didn't even think about the commotion behind me." He looked at Lisa. "Remember I told you there was some sort of fight in the lot? That must have been her."

"Oh." She turned her attention to me. "Are you okay? Evan said there was an ambulance."

"I'm okay. Head's too thick to know when to crack." I mimicked Hank's earlier joke of knocking on my skull and immediately regretted it when my knuckles hit an egg-sized lump. "Damned hard bodycheck, though."

"Yeah." Evan shook his head. "He's a punk all right. Little weasel's been slithering around my family for years. Married my cousin, widowed a few years later." A puzzled look crossed his face. "At least I think it was my cousin."

I resisted the urge to laugh. Instead I pulled out my cell phone and tapped a text message to Bran, giving him an update on the situation.

The response flew back a few seconds later.

DON'T SEE ANYONE BUT NOT SURPRISED. YOU GONNA ALL RUN?

I hesitated before answering, running through scenarios in my mind. Even on my best day I couldn't hold off two enforcers and I couldn't ask Bran to take them on. The kids were willing and eager to fight but these were two battle-hardened men who wouldn't mind drawing blood if it accomplished their mission to retrieve the kids. Dragging Evan and Lisa back bloody and beaten was a perfectly acceptable option to them.

I'M OPEN TO IDEAS.

Bran's response came back a minute later.

STAY THERE. I HAVE ONE.

I looked down between the leaves and spotted him over near the fountain, strolling casually as if he had nothing better to do than play on his cell phone. I hoped he had a better idea than sitting here until dawn. I wasn't sure how long the enforcers' patience would keep them in the bushes and hidden.

I already had proof McCallister had all the self-control of a whiny brat.

The pair were waiting for everyone around to go to sleep or at least be too tired to take notice of strange things happening in the couple's tree. A little noise, a little growling and anyone still awake would think someone was getting it on with their partner instead of a double kidnapping.

The comforting thing was no one would be killed. Felis didn't kill Felis.

It didn't mean there wasn't a chance of injuries, however. And if it took a broken arm to get Evan back to his family and a twisted ankle to get Lisa back to the Middlestons, I had no doubt they'd do it.

We waited in silence. I stretched out my legs, working out a possible cramp. It'd been a long time since I'd climbed a tree and I didn't miss it a bit.

"So how did the two of you meet?" I asked. "I'm assuming it wasn't over a potluck dinner at the farm."

Lisa giggled and relaxed a bit, leaning into Evan's shoulder as they sat on the branch. "I found him in the dinosaur exhibit. Right by a huge stuffed saber-tooth cat."

"We went to different schools," Evan interrupted. "Never met each other. But one day we ended up going downtown to the Royal Ontario Museum for a field trip. A couple of classes from a bunch of schools all packed onto the same set of buses headed down to the city." He turned and smiled at Lisa. "I saw her hanging out with a few of her friends and knew she was my soul mate. Walked over and introduced myself, wowed her girl posse and they all took off, leaving her with me." His chest puffed out. "She looked at me and I was done for."

I couldn't help smiling.

Lisa took up the tale. "I knew he was family so I figured it'd be okay to talk to him. Didn't even occur to me to ask for his last name. I got his phone number after we had lunch together." She took his hand and squeezed it. "I was all bold and brassy about asking for his number but inside I was all terrified and shaking that he'd say no, that he didn't like me that much after all."

"As if." Evan placed a light kiss on her cheek.

"When did your parents find out?" I asked.

Evan spoke first. "We started texting back and forth

as soon as we got back home trying to arrange a get-together."

Lisa interrupted. "There's a mall in Barrie that my friends go to all the time to hang out. We met there a few times with our school buddies, sort of chaperoning us." She gave me a sheepish smile. "Playing it safe. Can't ever be too careful these days."

Evan took up the story. "So we're running up the phone bills with the texting, as you can guess. My mother looked at the cell phone records and saw me making all these text messages to a number. We were getting close to maxing our calling plan out so she checked out who I was calling." He shook his head. "She freaked when she realized Lisa was a Middleston. Screamed and yelled about how she killed my grandmother."

"Which I didn't," Lisa muttered.

"Wait. Neither of you knew about the feud?" I pointed at each in turn. "No daily roll call of your mortal enemies, no mantra about spilling blood for blood?"

Lisa shrugged. "Sure, Dad talked a lot about it. Told me the Chandlers fixed it all up, picked a field with a rabbit warren nearby to make sure Grandma would be at a disadvantage. She trips, falls and dies and it's all the Chandlers' fault." She squeezed Evan's hand. "I told him it was an accident."

"The story I got told was that Maureen Middleston didn't want to fight but Laura Chandler goaded her on so much that she went into a rage and didn't see where she was going," Evan said. "When Laura ran to get help she broke her leg by tripping over one of those same holes. Be pretty stupid to get caught by your own plan." He looked at me. "I'm not saying my grandmother wasn't partially responsible but that's in the past. I'm not running my life based on old bones."

"You're pretty mature for your age." I winced as I pulled up one leg, tucking it under me. "Most young men would be intimidated by their mother acting that way."

"My older brother, he's the dedicated one." Evan rolled his eyes. "Dale, he thinks we're at war. Mom and he never stop whining about the business, who screwed who and how to screw the Middlestons and their friends. But he's a mama's boy. Gets himself all buffed up, works out and talks tough but I know he's a pussy."

Both Lisa and I winced at the word.

Evan flushed. "Sorry, ladies."

"How aggressive is your mother?" I asked, giving Evan a way out of his faux pas. "Is she likely to send your brother after you or Lisa if her enforcer can't pull it off by himself?"

"Not if she's smart," he snarled. "Michael knows he can't take me in a fight. He might be older but I'm faster."

"And your mother?" I prompted. "Could she get into it beside McCallister, back him up?"

He shook his head. "She's getting older and more tired with every brawl. There's been a few challenges over the years, mostly from family friends who don't want to lose money for what they see as history." He spotted my frown and continued. "She's been nitpicking at the Middlestons for years, undercutting them where she can. My dad ran a construction company, so she tries to poach contracts from the Middlestons. Problem is, now we're running on fumes 'cause she keeps losing money on the deals."

"Wait a minute." I waded through the confusion in my mind. "So Mary Chandler is your mom's married name? She married into the family?"

It wasn't that I didn't trust Red's version of events but I needed verification.

Evan sighed. "Nope. Before Laura Chandler died she made both of her daughters promise to keep the Chandler name even if they got married, continue the bloodline. My dad's name is Farmington and he was the sole one who used it to the day he died."

My head buzzing, I turned to Lisa. "And your dad works in construction. Does he have any brothers?" It wasn't just to make idle conversation. I needed to know the potential number of Felis we could be facing if Jake decided to bring everyone to the party to get his daughter back.

"He's an only child," Lisa said. "He's got plenty of friends, though, and crib brothers." She scrunched up her face. "Like Eddie. He's a nice guy but I know he's done some nasty things in the past for my dad."

I rubbed my face with both palms, keenly aware of maintaining my balance. I'd gotten some information but the cold hard truth was that if we were facing one or one hundred angry Felis it didn't matter—it'd still be too many for me and these kids to handle.

"How passionate is your dad about this feud?"

Lisa shrugged. "Told me and my sisters we weren't ever to talk to a Chandler, be in the same room as a Chandler, the usual babble. I hear him cursing once in awhile, when he's gotten screwed out of a contract from Chandler or her buddies. But he's not as fanatical as Evan's mother, I think."

"Fanatical enough to send Eddie after you." I pointed out.

"That's because he's afraid he'll lose face with the family if he lets me go, especially without putting up a fight."

I had to give it to Lisa. I hadn't even thought of that.

"How did he take it when he figured out who your new boyfriend was?"

Lisa rolled her eyes. "He ranted and raved, stomped around and told me I was to never see him again. As if he could really enforce that."

I didn't think it was the right time to point out her father could, with ease, make it happen.

We fell silent. It wasn't an uneasy silence but the type that goes before a fight when you remember all those old prayers from your youth.

"I know 'bout you," Evan whispered as we crouched low on the branches. "Your mate is a human, right?"

"Yep." I sniffed the air. The hunters were out there but keeping their distance. Bran's scent was louder, stronger as he paced around the base of the tree. The enforcers were waiting for the right time to charge us and that could be soon.

I scented other kids around us, hiding in the trees or huddled in the bushes. Bran was keeping any other couples from attempting to climb into the tree, something I made a mental note to thank him graciously for later. Last thing we needed was more potential victims added into the mix.

"So," Lisa paused, "what's it like with a human?"

I licked my lips before answering. "Fun."

She frowned and looked at Evan before looking back at me. "Fun? But he's not, you know—" She rocked from side to side, suddenly shy. "One of us. Family."

"He is. To me." I put a finger to my lips as a ca horn bleated.

A few minutes later it was answered by a whoo and a yell from nearby.

My cell phone beeped.

CAVALRY COMING BE READY TO FLY GO FOR BLACK SUV AT FRONT OF PARK.

Thank God for texting—with the Felis having enhanced hearing it'd be almost impossible for us to discuss a plan over the phone. As it was I still didn't know his entire plan but it beat hanging out here until daw or the inevitable attack.

"Get ready," I said. "We may have to get down an out of here in a hurry."

Lisa tightened the straps on her pack. Evan looke a little green as he glanced down, the neck of his gu tar smacking the back of his head.

A rush of feet, booted and otherwise, pounded alon the concrete paths. The trees wavered with an invisible wind.

Something was happening. Something big.

"What's going on?" Lisa whispered.

It started as a trickle, a scattering of young people coming in the front gate, the same way Bran and I had entered. They waved bright neon fluorescent tubes in the air, turning the night into a multi-colored spectacle.

It was as if the stars had fallen from the sky and smashed into the park, exploding on contact. The trickle grew as more car doors opened and shut and I swore, even a school bus.

The park burst into a shuddering sea of activity, young people dashing in from all possible entrances in wave after wave of giddy joy. They swept over the fountain, over the empty grass field and spilled out to circle all the trees, including ours.

A chorus of raised voices surrounded us—singing, clapping and yelling. A haze spread out, covering the ground and I caught the smell of alcohol and certain illegal substances.

Lit sparklers passed from hand to hand as the crowd grew and got merrier, the bright lights screwing up my vision and, I was sure, the Felis enforcers as well. I spotted Bran in the middle of the mob, directing the impromptu partiers to put most of their energy around our specific tree.

They were a mixed lot of street kids and young adults, all enjoying the impromptu rave. Music poured out of someone's portable stereo and it wouldn't be long before the cops were called to clean out the park and get the kids to move along.

It was a perfect time to get out.

My phone beeped.

GO GOGOGOGO

I stood up. “Let’s go. Follow me and don’t stop for anyone or anything. Head for a black SUV at the front of the park and don’t look back.”

I dropped from branch to branch without waiting for a response, hoping the kids were following me. I wasn’t in any shape to drag their asses down the tree. My muscles ached and I felt my left leg threatening to cramp up on me.

Bran stood at the base of the tree, glancing around as the mayhem grew. He looked up just as I swung down from the lowest branch and stretched out his arms to catch me.

I fell into his embrace with a huff, feeling my spine complain.

“Hey,” I gasped.

“Hey yourself.” Bran nodded at the two kids, both dropping to the ground in silence. They stood up together and looked around, wide-eyed at the chaos surrounding us.

He pointed at the pair. “It’s go time.” He took my hand and charged through the mob, not hesitating to push a happy reveler out of our way.

The crowd flowed around us, enthusiastic dancers moving with the beat mixed in with laughing teenagers. It was a street party to the nth degree, an organized group of chaos.

It was a perfect storm to escape through.

I looked around trying to find the enforcers. Kidnapping Evan and Lisa in public was exactly what they didn’t want; it’d bring the authorities down on them full force with plenty of witnesses to start the social media tongues a-wagging.

That was the last thing the Pride would want or need. I suspected both enforcers had strict orders to keep this all as quiet as possible.

We went through a tight cluster of partiers, the dancing kids slipping between us and threatening to break our connection. I took hold of Lisa's backpack and saw Evan latch onto her hand, completing the link. We couldn't afford to get split up, not if we wanted to do this successfully.

Out of the corner of my eye I spotted Eddie Longstrand charging from our right on an intercept course. Sweaty and red-faced he shoved one dancing teenager to the ground, her annoyed screech shattering the group bliss. He ignored her and kept heading for us, his lips pulled back in a snarl.

"Get to the black car," Bran shouted. Evan and Lisa didn't falter, picking up the pace and passing us.

"You too." He pushed me ahead. "I'll see you in a second."

I almost stopped moving, my instinct to stay at his side. But I couldn't leave the two kids alone, not right now. I kept running and looked back, cursing under my breath.

Bran roared as he bore down on the surprised enforcer, startling the middle-aged Felis with his ferocity. He slammed sideways into Eddie, his head tucked down like a NFL linebacker.

Eddie flew back and fell to the ground, the shocked

expression on his face saying volumes. He hadn't expected to be stopped by anyone, much less a human.

Bran didn't continue the attack but turned and ran. He'd gotten lucky with Eddie focused on the three of us and ignoring the mere human in his way, figuring no man would be mad enough to meddle with an enforcer on the hunt.

It wouldn't happen twice.

I panted as my feet hit the concrete path, the sudden shift in texture sending shockwaves up my aching legs. We spun around a small group of skateboarders and through the crowd onto the outer sidewalk. A black SUV sat there with the front and back doors open.

Sirens split the air, growing louder with every second.

The party was about to be broken up.

"You waiting for a personal invite?" Angie yelled from the driver's seat. "Get the fuck in."

Evan didn't need to be told twice. He leaped into the back, pulling Lisa in beside him. The backpack frames smacked and cracked against the doorframe as they piled in, his guitar almost shattering as it banged against the roof of the car.

I dove in the front, almost ending up in Angie's lap. Bran slid in beside me with a panted laugh and pulled the door shut.

A fast glance back into the crowd showed Nathan McCallister fighting his way through a belligerent group of young men who didn't appreciate their party being disturbed by an angry thug. He swung at one fellow and landed a full punch on his jaw.

The kid fell like a stone.

Instead of backing off, the rest of his buddies leaped in and McCallister disappeared under a pile of bodies. I doubted he'd get hurt too badly and he wouldn't Change and risk discovery.

Couldn't happen to a nicer guy.

The door locks engaged before we pulled away from the curb with a screech of the tires.

"Fuck yeah," Angie laughed and banged on the steering wheel, her long, blond hair flying around her face. "That was great."

Bran grinned, sandwiched between me and Angie. "Told you I had an idea."

"What was that?" I wheezed, my head spinning from the sprint to the car. I leaned on Bran, hoping he wouldn't pick up on my exhaustion and drag me back to the hospital.

"Party central." Angie turned down one alley and then another, zipping through side streets barely wide enough for the SUV to navigate. "Bran told me you needed a quick mob scene. I supplied the peeps and he paid for the toys. Didn't take too much encouragement to pass the word for a free party in the park."

I scowled at Bran. "How much?"

"Let's just say that your advance from Middleston is pretty well gone," he replied. "But I got you out of there, didn't I?"

I couldn't dispute the results.

"Okay, we're out of the danger zone. Where to?" Angie asked as we spun around a corner and out onto Queen Street.

I looked behind me. It was unlikely either McCallister or Longstrand had been able to get to their cars in time to follow us.

But they didn't have to. I'd eventually pop up somewhere and the chase would start again. I had to figure out a way to take this out of their hands and let me start calling the shots.

"Head for the lake," I said.

Bran frowned. "What's down there?"

I turned and looked at the pair in the backseat. "Sanctuary."

It took a few extra twists and turns to get close to where Red lived, not so much about us being lost than me being sure that no one was following us. I was sure that the enforcers wouldn't be on our tail but I couldn't lay bets they were working alone. I wouldn't put it past Eddie or Nathan to hedge their bets with backup.

Angie didn't say anything as I directed her down and up the streets, doubling back a few times. Angie was smart and fast at the wheel but the less she knew about what we were doing the better. Thankfully she kept her mouth shut and I suspected she figured she'd get the truth out of Bran later.

I wasn't worried about that. I couldn't afford to be worried about that, not right now.

"Trade with me." I tugged at Bran's arm. "I'll need to get out."

He frowned but allowed me to crawl over his lap, copping a gentle feel as I slid down beside him next to the passenger door.

"Okay. This is how it's going to roll," I said to the kids. "We're going to slow down and we're going to hop out—the three of us. Keep an eye on me and move quick."

"Hey." Bran poked my arm. "What about me?"

"You and Angie keep on driving. If anyone's following us, hopefully they'll stay on your tail. Go north, east, whatever for about another hour before heading home."

Angie nodded, her attention moving toward Bran. "Home?" It was a neutral statement without any intent in her voice.

Bran shot me a warning glare, just enough to allay any fears I might have had. "We'll split up when we get near your place. I'll head home on my own via taxi, transit, whatever." He held up his cell. "Text me if you need anything."

I turned my attention to the outside. The fence I'd discovered the hole in ran alongside us, rusted and broken in spots. A fast look behind showed no traffic around us in either direction.

"Let's go."

The car slowed down to a crawl. Without looking to see if Evan and Lisa were following I flung the passenger door open and jumped out.

EIGHT

It wasn't my best landing. I lost my footing, spun around and slammed into the fence, my spine thwacking against the steel diamonds with enough force to rattle my fillings.

I scrambled to my feet and limped toward the hole in the fence. I could sense the two kids behind me, sliding into the darkness to join me in the makeshift camp.

We made it inside before the worst of the pain began. The pounding pressure behind my eyes expanded to shoot down my spine in a series of tiny, painful explosions.

I needed a drink and a massage.

I was definitely in the wrong place for that.

We made our way into the maze of half-constructed shelters and barriers. I didn't have to look back to see the confusion on the kids' faces. We'd fallen down the rabbit hole even farther.

"Suz!" Red sprang out of the shadows to pull me into a deep hug. The tight squeeze choked the air from my lungs and boosted the daggerlike pain shooting up my back. "Good to see you again."

Evan and Lisa jumped back but thankfully didn't Change. They sensed Red was family but weren't sure what to make of him.

I couldn't blame them. I wasn't sure myself.

It took a concentrated effort but I finally disentangled myself from his arms. "Glad you're doing fine." I took a step back, trying to casually grab some fresh air. Red was in desperate need of his own washing fountain. "We need a place to stay."

The two teenagers stepped forward, both with unsure expressions. Evan held out his hand while Lisa hung back just a bit, moving a step behind him.

Red grabbed his hand and pumped it as if trying to draw water from an unseen well. The loose sloppy motion had me smiling despite the pain. "You play guitar? Good, good. I just made some fresh coffee. Come, come." He released Evan's hand and trotted off through the camp without looking back to see if we were following.

Lisa let out a nervous giggle and headed down the trail with Evan close behind her.

I brought up the rear of our little troupe, more out of exhaustion than trying to keep track of them. My left ankle ached and I suspected this was not acceptable behavior for someone with a concussion.

Every once in a while a head would pop out from a tent or from under a tarp or folded cardboard box, check us out and then disappear back inside. As long as we weren't police or an imminent threat I figured we'd be fine.

I kept taking deep breaths for two reasons—first to try and attempt to stifle the screaming pain in my back and second to make sure we were the only family around.

Red led us to his little area. Lisa immediately sat down on the nearest piece of driftwood and reached out to warm her hands at the small campfire. It might be July but we'd just had one hell of an evening.

Evan pulled off his pack, wincing as he inspected his guitar. His fingers danced along the strings, bringing up slightly warped notes. A deep gouge on the back of the guitar neck had him shaking his head.

Putting it down he turned to Lisa and tugged at her knapsack, finally pulling it off and dropping it beside her. He went back to his own pack and dug in a side pocket, coming up with a packet of beef jerky.

Lisa shook her head when he offered it to her. Evan paused before offering it to Red and me. I refused but Red dug in, grabbing a handful of the stringy snack.

"These the ones you were looking for?" Red asked between bites.

"Please allow me to introduce Lisa Middleston and Evan Chandler." I used as formal a tone as I could, racking my brains to remember if there was some vague Pride protocol I'd forgotten.

They nodded at Red in turn, still trying to figure out what was going on. I'd dragged them from sleeping in the trees to digging in the dirt within an hour and they were still in shock.

Red, for his part, looked as if he took in strays every day.

"Ah. The lost souls." He ripped at the burgundy-colored stick. "So you're the ones causing all this trouble, eh?"

Evan puffed his chest out. "We're not doing anything. We just want to be left alone."

Red waved his hand around. "So do I. So do all these people. But it don't work that way all the time." He took another bite, talking around the dried beef. "We need each other. Dave over there forgets sometimes to eat and his blood sugar goes all haywire. Steven is pretty good at scavenging food. He's good looking and the ladies love to give him stale bread and rolls." He eyed the couple. "Figure you're going to avoid all the bad blood by getting married and turning your back on it all? You think they won't care about you when you're married, hmm?"

"I don't care about my family." Lisa's tone said otherwise.

"Sure you do," Red replied. "We all care 'bout family. You there." He gestured at Evan, who now sat next to Lisa, one arm protectively draped across her shoulders. "Your grandma was responsible for her grandma dying. How do you feel about it?"

Evan shrugged. "Means nothing to me. Doesn't affect my life."

Red reached over and rapped the end of the beef stick on Evan's nose. The kid jerked back, almost falling off the log.

I forced myself not to laugh.

"Everything affects your life, kit. Every day in every way affects who you are and what you are." He pointed the stick at Lisa. "What if she wakes up one day and gets all pissy 'cause you forgot to make the bed and throws the frying pan at your head 'cause you got Chandler blood in your veins?"

"I wouldn't do that," Lisa answered, almost too quickly. "I love him."

Red put the rest of the jerky in his mouth. He picked up one of the steel cups on the ground and blew in it, dislodging dust before reaching for the coffeepot. "You sure 'bout that? Sure enough to turn your back on your heritage? Say goodbye to your family and friends, everyone you knew up there?"

She nodded slowly.

Red smiled. "Good. It's hard enough to love yourself some days, much less love someone else. If you can do that, you're halfway to winning in this life." He filled the cup halfway and passed it to me before turning to Evan. "Drink?"

"Yes please," Evan answered, as polite as could be. He was still trying to figure out what Red was all about.

Red passed a mug to Evan and another to Lisa without asking. They both grimaced, sniffing the strong coffee, but said nothing.

"So what's your plan?" Red looked at me. "I'm thinking you didn't bring 'em here for me to tell stories to." He winked at Lisa. "Not that I don't got a few, mostly dealing with fishing and hunting."

"I need them to stay safe while I work out something." I sipped the coffee, thankful for the caffeinated rush through my system. "I don't want them dragged off by their family enforcers. That's not what I agreed to do."

"You're a funny one, Suz." Red turned his head to the side and spat. "Most people would take the money and run, flip these kits for the cash." He studied my face. "You're trying to stop something that's been going on long before you got birthed."

"I'm not trying to stop it. I'm just trying to save these two from being caught up in it for another generation." I handed him the half-empty cup. "Please keep them safe until I get back." A smile tweaked my lips. "Maybe teach them a little about living off the grid here. If they want to stay on the streets they'll need to know how to survive."

Red gave me a knowing look. It was one thing for these kids to swing in the trees and play at being runaways, another to deal with the harsh truth. They'd done well for the few days so far but I wasn't sure they were built for doing this long-term, staying under the radar and away from their hunters.

"You two. Please don't leave this area." I stood up. "Stay here until I come for you."

"What about the enforcers?" Lisa got to her feet as well, rubbing her forearms. "Won't they find us here?"

Red chuckled. "Little chance of that. No one comes here but old men. It's an old man's camp." He eyed the couple. "You got cell phones?"

I mentally smacked myself in the forehead. If they had and they were GPS capable it'd be like sending up flares to announce our location.

Red had more smarts than he was letting on.

"No sir," Evan answered. "Left all that at home when we split. Knew it'd be too tempting to call someone and tip our hand as to where we were. Made a clean break."

The kid had smarts.

"Good. I hate those damned ringtones. If I wanna sing, I just sing." Red gestured toward the tent set up to one side. "Girl gets the tent, you and I sit out here and enjoy the night air." He took a deep breath. "Smell those diesel fumes."

It was time for me to go and let them figure out the arrangements, although I was tempted to wait until he explained where the bathroom was.

"Don't leave," I repeated. "If I don't come back in three days get to a phone and contact Jess Hammersmythe. Tell her everything that's happened. She'll know what to do."

Lisa drew a sharp breath. It was reassuring in a way to see their reaction—Jess's reputation as a hard-nosed woman still had clout.

The unspoken assumption that I'd be dead or too injured to return hung in the air.

I turned and made my way back through the camp. A few sets of eyes followed me but no one said anything. It was obvious that Red had their respect and they wouldn't be poking around his newest visitors.

It took me two hours to get back to the park, most of which was taken up doubling back on my tracks and making sure I wasn't being followed. The cab drivers must have thought I was a little crazy, taking the ride for a block or two before hopping out. I wasn't worried as much for myself as for the kids and Red—if Longstrand or McCallister backtracked my route they'd find the camp, and I had no doubt they'd plow through it to get to their charges, despite the possible consequences.

My Jeep sat where we'd parked it, ignored and alone on the street. I checked the car for any obvious tracking devices before getting in. The park was deserted and empty, the party dissolved away in the early morning leaving no sign anything had happened other than a few discarded streamers blowing down the street.

I made a mental note to give Hank a call and see if they'd actually arrested anyone or just chased them all out of the park. I'd feel guilty if a kid ended up in lockup because he'd gotten an invite to a wild party to inadvertently provide us with a diversion.

The Jeep grumbled but turned over on the second try, coughing as I yanked the wheels away from the curb. She and I weren't morning folk.

I was delaying the inevitable confrontation. If the enforcers wanted to find me all they had to do was wait at my front door—it wasn't like I had a secret Felis cave I worked out of. Since Bran had given up his condo there was no place for me to hide unless I went onto the streets the same as Evan and Lisa.

Besides, I'd never run from a fight in my life.

Heart of a warrior, mind of a fool.

Within the hour I pulled into the narrow driveway and parked behind my house, sliding the Jeep into the empty slot with practiced ease. The skyline was streaked with light blues and pinks and I felt quite old, which I put down to the aches and pains running through me.

Not to mention the growling in my belly. I should have taken the beef jerky.

With visions of tea and toast I walked around the rose bushes and opened the gate to my front yard.

Two angry Felis enforcers stared at each other, each man standing on opposite sides of my lawn.

Neither man spoke at first, too busy focused on each other in a classic macho standoff. I wondered for a brief second if I retraced my steps if they'd even notice my leaving.

Eddie's head snapped to the side even as I pondered my chances. His eyes locked with mine and I knew I didn't have a chance if I ran.

Instead I strolled up to the front door and worked the key in the lock, concentrating on not letting them see my hands shake.

At least the bastards hadn't broken in.

"Can I offer you boys some tea?"

I didn't turn around, knowing they'd follow.

McCallister slipped in behind me without saying a word, taking up a spot on the couch where he could watch the entire room.

I walked by him and tossed my coat on my desk chair. Jazz was nowhere in sight. She'd probably picked up on the negative vibes and was upstairs under the bed.

I considered joining her. Instead I decided to follow through with my original plan of tea and toast, letting the routine carry me along.

I couldn't think of anything else to do.

Eddie followed me into the kitchen and watched

while I filled the kettle halfway with water and plugged it in.

"Been waiting long?" I asked.

"A bit," he answered. "Nathan figured this would be the best place to find you after that little stunt." The restrained anger in his voice sent shivers down my aching back. "That human bastard of yours, he can hit hard. I'm luckier than Nathan—he got a black eye from one of those little punks."

I turned and leaned against the counter, pressing my hands against the cool linoleum to keep them from shaking. Even if I could Change there was very little chance I could hold my own against two enforcers.

Felis didn't kill Felis.

But we could beat up on each other something bad.

The scars on my back began to throb.

"Where are the kids?" Eddie asked. The unspoken threat lay under the surface of his words.

I smiled.

It was either that or scream and I didn't have the energy for that. My legs were shaky enough, I couldn't withstand a prolonged run or chase.

"Where are they?" Eddie repeated.

I said nothing.

He spread his hands with an answering grin. "Plenty of time for us to talk. We ain't going nowhere."

The kettle whistled for attention. I went back to making tea, filling the Brown Betty teapot to the top before adding three mugs and a small pourer of milk to the tray.

Common courtesy told me to be a good hostess and at least provide tea for my visitors.

I wasn't making the bastards toast.

Nathan watched me as I brought the tray out and placed it on the table. My eyes strayed to the discolored patch of hardwood floor. I hadn't gotten a throw rug to hide the bloodstains.

I went to the old wooden chair reserved for clients, placed in front of my desk. It took a second to turn it around and sit down but it gave my back some support and allowed me to view the two men with the wall behind me. I wasn't going to give them a chance to get behind me if possible.

Eddie positioned himself in the cushioned chair opposite Nathan on the couch—both of them between me and the front door.

As if I was going to be chased out of my own house.

"I assume you both drink tea?" The strength in my voice surprised me.

It was my first full view of Nathan McCallister, other than the shadow that smashed into me. He was thin and tall, a man who probably used a safety line in the shower to avoid slipping down the drain. His dark hair was neatly pulled back in a ponytail and his eyes darted everywhere, constantly updating himself on what was around him. He wore a black T-shirt and black jeans, muscles taut and tight. A large bruise on the left side of his face showed he hadn't walked away from the park unscathed.

He smelled of trouble. This was a man you did not

bring home to mother, unless your mother was a major-league badass biker mama.

Eddie was wearing the same outfit from the hospital. I guessed he hadn't slept much either.

He crossed his legs as I poured tea out into the three mugs. "You're being very polite, given the circumstances."

"My mom raised me properly." I passed him a cup. "And it's been a long night."

"Got that right," Nathan growled. He didn't take the mug.

I put it on the table facing him.

Eddie sat back in his chair, cradling his mug in both hands without fearing the heat. "Let me spell this out. You know where the kids are. We know where you are. Just tell us where the kids are or bring them in and we're all done here."

I waggled my hand at the two men. "Since when do you two play with each other?" I allowed myself a smirk. "And do you let others watch?"

Nathan crossed his arms and glared at Eddie. "I want Evan. He wants Lisa. You've got them both. Simple enough. Double the trouble."

Eddie gave a half-hearted shrug. "It's the nature of the business. Enemy of my enemy and all that."

"I'm not your enemy." The left side of my body started to ache, the fresh skin from the scar on my arm burning. "We're all family here."

Nathan let out something between a snort and a cough.

"We is and we aren't," Eddie said. He leaned forward. "Look, this is something beyond what you signed on for. This is why I came to you in the hospital, trying to let you know this wasn't going to work out. We want to take it off your hands before it becomes something you can't handle."

I sipped tea before responding. "Seems I'm handling it quite well, considering where we stand right now. Or do you not want to go back to your bosses with your tails between your legs?"

The two hunters exchanged glances and Nathan's lips curled away from his teeth. He wasn't used to verbally jousting with anyone.

Eddie put his mug down on the table. "Look, just hand over the kids and no one needs to get hurt." He glanced at Nathan, a smile tugging at the edges of his mouth. "Well, any more hurt."

Nathan snorted. "I'm not apologizing for doing my job."

"Well maybe if you hadn't slammed her into the wall we wouldn't be sitting here," Eddie responded.

Nathan uncrossed his arms. "At least I'm not playing nice guy waiting to screw her over if given the chance." His eyes narrowed. "Don't tell me you wouldn't be putting the moves on her if she weren't outcast. Get into her bed and get what you want without throwing a punch." He leered at me. "Unless that's how she likes it."

Someone cleared his throat.

It wasn't either of the enforcers.

Bran stood in the doorway. He looked more tired and pissed-off than I'd ever seen him, his flushed face almost matching his hair. His right hand was tucked behind him, hiding something.

"Oh look—it's the boy toy." Nathan snorted. "About time you got here."

Bran's hand appeared. The baseball bat was worn and stained in places.

I had no idea where it'd come from.

"Get. Out," Bran rasped.

"We're not finished talking to your girlfriend. When we're done we'll leave." Nathan turned back to me, ignoring Bran. "We were talking about you handing the kids over to us." He smiled. "Before anyone gets hurt again."

Eddie shifted in his chair. He studied Bran for a minute then looked away, speaking to me. "Look, the kids are going to turn eighteen in a few days. Best thing for them is to go home and figure out what they want with family. Let us take them back and we'll all be done."

Bran began to walk over, his lips pressed into a tight, thin line. Neither Felis paid much attention to him, focusing on forcing me to give up the two runaways.

That was about to be a big, big mistake.

"Kind of odd, isn't it—these two having birthdays so close to each other. Reaching the age of maturity within the same short period." I threw out the small talk trying not to stare at Bran. "Sort of a cosmic coincidence."

Nathan shrugged. "What of it?"

I shifted in my seat. "Maybe it's a sign of some sort.

Like they're supposed to be healing the families instead of continuing this silly feud."

Eddie's nostrils flared. "It's not silly." His voice dropped an octave. "Death is never silly."

Bran strolled behind me and stopped at my desk. He placed the bat on the cluttered surface and opened a drawer, making quite the noise as he rummaged around.

"You still got munchies stashed in here? I'm starved."

Both men wasted a second watching and assessing him before turning their attention back to me.

"Anyone want a candy?" He unwrapped and popped a hard caramel in his mouth from my stash, making a big deal of fussing with the thin plastic wrapper.

The two men ignored him.

"A woman smacks her head during a challenge and now you've got people beating each other senseless for generations?" I shook my head. "Madness."

A snarl worked its way up from Eddie's throat. "The Chandlers chose the field. They knew Laura would have a better chance of winning 'cause she knew it was full of holes."

Nathan shook his head and grunted. "Bullshit."

I held up both hands. "I'm not going to debate the events. One woman died, one woman was crippled and I'm sorry for that. But this feud can't continue."

Bran picked up the bat and walked away from the desk.

Nathan chuckled, a low menacing sound that set the hairs on the back of my neck on edge. "What are you going to do about it?" He turned a fraction of an inch to glare at Bran, who had moved behind the couch. "And don't think you can get the jump on me, kid." He motioned at Eddie. "I'm a hell of a lot faster than that fat bastard."

"Let's see." Bran swung the bat toward him with one hand, a surprisingly half-hearted attack given the way he'd been glaring at the enforcers.

Nathan twisted around with frightening speed, even for a Felis, and blocked it with his forearms. The bat stopped still, hanging between them.

Nathan's hands curled around the varnished wood as he prepared to wrestle it from Bran's grip.

"Boom," Bran whispered.

He spat the candy into Nathan's face, startling the Felis.

Before he could react Bran jabbed the stun gun into the side of Nathan's exposed neck, a perfect counter-attack.

I couldn't see his face but I could imagine the look of surprise as he realized he'd been bluffed, thinking my mate was nothing to worry about.

I'd been bluffed, as well. I'd forgotten about the weapon stashed in my desk, lying dormant since our trip to Pennsylvania. Bran had taken it when he'd gone for the candy, keeping it hidden until needed.

Eddie didn't move as the Felis enforcer shook and twitched, the electrical charge short-circuiting his body functions for a brief time. Instead of going to help Nathan he watched Bran like a predator studying his next prey, studying every move.

He was remembering Bran bodychecking him in the park.

There'd be a reckoning for that but this wasn't the time or place. He'd already been surprised once by Bran—he wasn't going to risk getting taken again.

Bran pulled the gun away after a few seconds and watched Nathan collapse against the cushions.

Bran's left hand came up, still clutching the baseball bat, and pointed the rounded end at Eddie.

"Time for you to go. You've worn out your welcome." He gestured at the still-twitching body on the couch. "Take him and get out of our house."

Eddie got to his feet slowly. "He ain't no kin of mine."

I stood up as well. "Kin enough for you to drag him off my property. Dump him in the street, I don't care. But I'm done talking about this. You tell your master I won't be answering to his lapdogs. If he wants to talk to me he'll have to do it in person."

Eddie crossed to the other side of the coffee table and picked up Nathan like a rag doll, hefting the semiconscious Felis's body with ease. He eyed Bran who stood there, taser in one hand and baseball bat in the other.

I held my breath. If Eddie Changed, if he shifted to full Felis and attacked, I wouldn't be able to stop him from tearing Bran apart. I doubted Bran could hold him off, having used up his one surprise attack on Nathan.

Felis weren't supposed to kill humans.

Didn't mean it didn't happen.

"He misjudged you. I won't." Without waiting for

a response Eddie turned and walked out of the house, dragging Nathan along.

Bran strode to the front door and kicked it shut.

I sat down again, slumping into the cushions in a controlled fall. The room spun for a minute before settling into place.

Bran vanished from sight and materialized on the couch beside me, his arms cradling me. The stun gun and bat were nowhere in sight.

"This is finished," he murmured. "We are done."

I didn't struggle against him. "Not over." My arms felt heavy, my eyes closing of their own accord. "It's not over. Not yet."

I'd hit the wall. Between the concussion, tree-climbing and scrambling to deal with two angry enforcers I had nothing left.

"Sleep. I'll take it from here." Bran's voice came from a distance. "I'll take care of you."

I felt him lay me down on the couch, carefully stretching my aching legs out. Jazz let out a trill from somewhere and brushed against my hand as I slipped away into a dreamless sleep.

NINE

The couch was bumpy and moving and I was sitting up again, my head bouncing against a pillow. My back was twisted and bent and my feet vibrating to a steady rhythm.

This was not right.

I forced my eyes open to find myself propped up in the passenger seat of my Jeep as we roared down the highway, a pillow offering scant neck support.

Bran risked a glance over before returning his attention to the traffic around us. "There's a soda in the cup holder. Figured you'd need the caffeine and I know you hate cold tea."

I fumbled for the cool can and pressed it to my forehead before pulling the tab and taking a sip.

The scenery was familiar, rolling farmland spotted with housing developments every once in a while, breaking up the wilderness.

We were headed north, out of the city.

Bran kept his eyes on the road. "I called Jess and told her we were on our way." Before I could speak he put up one hand. "Don't even try and argue this one with me. Those bastards came into our home, invaded our space. If I hadn't come home when I did

God knows what would have happened, what those two could have done to you there, alone."

I started to say something but didn't get past a peep before he continued.

"You've got those kids someplace safe but we are not going to sit around and wait for them to attack you again. I got lucky but that's not going to happen again."

I couldn't dispute his findings. He'd gotten the jump on Nathan once and that'd been a fluke. He'd slammed Eddie in the middle of a scuffle when the enforcer hadn't been prepared to fight a human.

They wouldn't let him do it again. They weren't going to stop until they got the kids.

I closed my eyes and ran through my options, fighting the urge to fall asleep again. There weren't many and none that included me being at half-strength.

"Okay. What did Jess say?" I sat up straighter and sipped the drink, feeling a bit more alive as the caffeine started to kick in.

"She asked where you were, what was going on and then berated me for taking so long to call." Bran chuckled. "She said she'd have some brekka for us when we arrived."

I rubbed my eyes and looked at the dashboard clock. It was approaching noon—I'd lost a few hours of straight sleep somewhere between the couch and the Jeep.

"I took a bit of a roundabout route," Bran said, almost apologetic. The average drive to the farm took two hours and if we'd left not long after dealing with the Felis enforcers we'd have been there a good hour ago. "Ducked down along the Lakeshore and headed west to Oakville before circling back. It may not stop them from tracking us but at least they'll have to work for it." He tapped the dashboard. "Good gas mileage as well. They're more likely to run out before we will."

"Good idea." I took another deep drink and burped a very un-feminine burp.

Bran chuckled. "How are you feeling?" He risked another glance.

"I ache all over. And not in a good way." I patted his thigh. "You done good, partner. That was fucking amazing."

Bran grinned. "Owed the bastard for what he did to you. It's not even but it's a good start in my book." He pointed at a green and white sign on the side of the road, rapidly growing larger as we approached it. The fork and knife images signaled the possibility of hot food. "Want to stop for a rest and a bite to eat?"

"No. Keep on going." I finished the drink and tossed the empty can in the back, ignoring the small pile of discarded candy wrappers and drink containers. "Jess'll have kittens if we don't show up when she expects us."

"The kids are safe, right?" His attention flickered briefly to the rearview mirror, checking for any possible followers.

"As safe as they can be." I told him briefly about meeting Red. "I suspect they'll have a whole new appreciation of street living after spending some time with him. It's a whole different thing when there's no bathrooms and they'll be sleeping under a tarp."

"Your idea of shock therapy?" Bran switched lanes as we neared the exit. "Not to be nasty but I figured the Felis had that living natural thing down pat. Street living should be a breeze." He skipped the car over again, narrowly missing a Hummer who bleated his annoyance at us. "They had the park figured out and I'm sure the other kids were giving them enough hints on how to do well."

"Maybe, maybe not." I rubbed the back of my neck. "It's one thing to meet their buddies for a free breakfast at the shelter, another for them to be digging in Dumpsters when the resources run out. They may have gone on a few runs on the farm and gone on a hunt but that doesn't necessarily prepare them for full-time living on the street." I allowed myself a chuckle. "I did read your article, you know. Right now I'm willing to bet it's like a sleepover, a slumber party that hasn't ended yet with lots of new friends and experiences to keep them from thinking about what they want and where they're headed."

"What do they want to do?"

"End the feud."

Bran whistled. "Sure. Why not go for world peace while we're doing the impossible?"

I squeezed his thigh, causing him to bump onto the shoulder for a brief second. "Some people would say our relationship is impossible."

He held up a finger. "Improbable, maybe. Impossible, no." His cheeks went red as he pried my hand free. "And keep doing that and we'll be making a pit stop before we get to the farm."

I looked in the back. “Sorry, not enough room.”

“Not planning to lie down.”

I cleared my throat. “Not enough time.”

He shot me a wicked grin. “I can do fast.”

“I just woke up.” At the back of my mind I wondered at the warped turn this conversation had taken.

Bran chuckled. “Calm down. I’m just kidding. You’re right about the time and I wouldn’t want Jess to get all grumpy.” He took my hand and brought it to his lips for a wet kiss. “Although I’d love to take you back to that couple’s tree sometime.”

“Only if you schedule the chiropractor appointment beforehand.” I reluctantly pulled my hand free. “Keep an eye out. I wouldn’t put it past the jackholes to put an ambush up here to get us before we contact Jess.”

“Roger that.” His attention returned to scanning the rearview mirror every few seconds.

I studied the road as we turned off and turned off again onto a dirt road, weaving our way out to the Pride’s farm, set far away from the main roads and providing as much privacy as possible. A sanctuary for Felis looking for a place to rest and enjoy ourselves, the farm was also the headquarters for the Board which made most major decisions for their members.

It was also considered neutral ground.

Jess’s name was still on the weather-beaten mailbox at the entrance, the barn still standing and now painted a lovely shade of bright yellow—some kit’s punishment for a rules infraction. I stifled a yawn as we pulled into the large gravel-covered parking lot beside a handful of battered SUVs and pickup trucks.

The farm was never empty. Between offering child-care and a safe place for Felis to run wild it was also an active working farm, making enough to support the Board members who called it home.

Jess stood on the porch, using one hand to shade her good eye. The angry scar on her left cheek was pale against her tanned skin and she didn't move to meet us.

I sniffed the air. A small pack of kits hunting in the forest, chasing down squirrels and unlucky rabbits. Apple pie cooling in the kitchen and fresh coffee waiting to be drunk.

Sanctuary.

Jess watched us come up the path and onto the porch. I held on to Bran's arm as if I were recovering from an all-night drunk, still weak in the knees and feeling like a very old, old woman.

"How is she?" This was directed to Bran, not me.

"Fine. Just needs a bit more rest."

"I am here, you know." I poked Bran in the ribs with my free hand. "And very much able to speak for myself."

"I know." Jess spun around and led us into the house, holding the door open for Bran to half-carry me through. "That's why we're in such a clusterfuck."

I bit back my snappy retort. It wasn't the time or place for it.

The inside of the farmhouse had changed since the last time I'd visited, the nursery that once occupied the main living room replaced with couches and chairs, a large ebony black circular coffee table in the center reminding me of the mythological Round Table.

With Bran's help I sank into the burgundy-colored cushions, letting out a pained sigh. Bran headed for the kitchen where Jess was.

"Are the kids okay?" Jess called out. I heard the clink of metal on ceramic and smelled cinnamon, the spicy scent landing on my tongue and starting my mouth watering. The harsh coffee also spanked my senses, encouraging me to wake up even more.

"Yes." I swallowed a mouthful of saliva, wanting them to hurry up.

"Are they safe?"

"Yes."

"Are you out of your goddamn mind?"

"Probably." I watched her exit the kitchen with two mugs of coffee. Bran followed behind with a tray containing three pieces of apple pie and his own mug.

"I thought this wasn't going to be a problem. I thought all you had to do is find the kids and convince them to go on home like good little kits. I thought it was going to be a simple little job, a quick way for you to earn a few bucks." Jess placed my coffee on the table and took her place opposite me. "Now I've got all hell breaking loose and the Board wants it dealt with pronto before the Grand Council gets involved. As it is, the Council's demanding updates left and right and I'm right in their sights." She blew a wayward strand of pale white hair out of her face. "Because I started the whole shitstorm bringing you into this, it's my problem as well."

I reached for the mug. Strong and creamy—none of that fake powdered milk crap here on the farm. Honest-to-goodness cream churned from the nearby herd. I resisted the urge to smack my lips. "What do you want me to say?"

Jess took an offered piece of pie from Bran. "Tell me you have some master plan to get everyone out of this without anyone getting hurt." She paused. "Anyone else."

There was enough anger in her voice to keep me quiet through my piece of pie. Hot, flaky apples with just enough spice to give that snap in your mouth. I hadn't known how hungry I was until I caught myself licking the empty plate.

Jess raised an eyebrow but said nothing, daintily cutting bite-sized pieces with her fork and popping them into her mouth.

Bran grinned and finished off his own slice before taking my plate and Jess's and stacking them on the tray.

I took another mouthful of coffee, savoring the rich caffeinated rush. We didn't grow the coffee beans here but the farm always stocked the best.

"Now that you've been fed and watered," Jess said, dabbing at her mouth with a paper napkin, "can I get some sort of briefing here?" She held up a hand before I started. "Do not tell me where they are. If I know that then I'll have to act on that and I don't want to go there." Her eyes narrowed. "Pick and choose your words carefully, Reb."

"The two families involved got pissy and sent in enforcers to grab the kids when and if I found them." I figured it wasn't time to mince words. "One thug clocked me when I was close to finding Evan Chandler, putting me in the hospital. I went back out and we tracked Evan and Lisa to a park. They agreed to leave with me because the two enforcers were near, waiting for the right time to make their move. We avoided the punks and I took the kids to a safe place before I went home." I drew a deep breath. "Then the two enforcers showed up at the house to try and intimidate me into telling them where the kids were." I couldn't resist grinning. "Bran made them leave."

Jess's eyebrows rose. She looked at Bran. He shrugged.

"And then we came here." I brushed crumbs off my lap. "How's that?"

"Better than the rambling diatribe I got from your mate." She crossed her legs. "Let's cut to the chase. What do you need to make this right? Not just for you but for everyone since you look bound and determined to save the world."

"I need everyone to leave these kids alone." I took another sip of coffee. "They're both turning eighteen soon enough and legal adults get to make their own mistakes."

"Well, that's not going to happen," Jess replied. "You were hired to find them, not become their life coach." She rapped the side of her mug with her knuckles. "The enforcers might have been a bit of overkill but that's because the feud is still very much alive and well in their minds. It's something bigger than just two kids who think they're in love running away." She sat back. "They can't disappear anyway, go underground and vanish. The Board won't let them. I assume you made that clear to them."

I nodded, not wanting to start a discussion about how much control the family had over our lives. I had my own views but this wasn't the time or place for it.

"Is there any wiggle room? Something between locking the kids up and letting them go?" Bran asked.

"Not from where I'm sitting. When they're returned to their families they'll be separated forever." Jess took a sip. "They'll be sent as far apart as they can, probably to family friends on opposite sides of the country until they get over each other. As long as it takes to break them up for good."

"But when they turn eighteen they can leave," I protested. "Walk out of wherever they're being kept and do what they want."

She peered at me over the edge of her mug. "Hitting a magic birthday number doesn't give you the power to do anything you want. These are teenagers raised within the family, within their own family. It's one thing to say you're going to go against what you've been raised to believe in, another to actually act on those thoughts." She shook her head. "I don't know if they have the willpower to do it. True love or whatever, do they have the guts to break with tradition?"

"This isn't tradition," I replied. "This is cruel and inhuman."

Jess cocked her head to one side, a sad smile on her lips. "We're not human, Rebecca. We may play in their world, work their jobs, even love their men but we're not human."

She didn't look at Bran.

I flashed back to Lisa's confusion in Red's camp. It all sounded very romantic until reality came to call. Despite their affirmations to me while we sat in the tree I wasn't sure they were ready to turn their backs on their mutual families and go it alone with only each other for support.

"And they can't go rogue." Jess put her mug down. "Before you even contemplate that option. You know they can go to another Pride, they can go anywhere they want as long as they stay registered. But they can't disappear, they've got to stay on our radar."

"Which allows their families to know where they are at all times," Bran added. "Which sort of makes it pointless because they'll be grabbed anyway and their new Pride will probably let it go because they don't want to be involved with the politics."

Jess nodded. "Yes."

Bran sat back, crossing his arms with a smug smile. "See. I can be taught."

Jess chuckled.

I rolled my head around, hearing various pops and snaps. "I'm getting him a new leash for Christmas."

"Good. Just remember to use a safe word," she answered without missing a beat.

"What makes you think we don't have one already?" Bran smirked.

"Duly noted," Jess said dryly. "And before you toss the idea out of getting the Council involved, we all know the feud isn't official and that the Grand Council ruled it an accident. Doesn't mean the families involved don't think it's as real as the pie we just ate. They won't kill anyone but you know now how far they'll go to do what they think is right."

"Duly noted," I repeated. "But I have an idea."

Jess motioned me onward. "Go ahead."

"I want a meeting with the leaders of the two families. Here, neutral ground. I want to get this settled and settled now." I touched my skull, wincing as my fingers ran over the invisible bruise. "This can't go on."

"I can have them here within a few hours." Jess moved her mug to the tray, now holding the empty plates. "Let me make the calls. You two rest here—she's safe now. There's a bedroom upstairs that you can use."

Her last two sentences were directed at Bran, who had shifted closer to me and who now pulled me into his lap, my head resting on his shoulder.

As Jess left the room with the dishes I let out a sigh. "I don't know if I can fix this."

"Then why try?" Bran mumbled. "It's not your life. They're not going to kill Evan and Lisa. They'll just separate them."

"If they're really in love, pulling them apart isn't going to work. They'll find a way to communicate and run away again." I sighed and closed my eyes. "Good pie."

"Excellent pie. Now let's go to bed."

"No, no." I stifled a yawn. "I'm going to just lie here and think until they arrive. 'Kay?"

Bran didn't say anything. His arm tightened on my waist, keeping me close and warm.

I closed my eyes and tried to think.

I woke up in a strange bed, my feet tangled in an ancient-looking quilt. For a second I panicked before my senses took in the familiar scents and sounds.

The farm.

Safety.

The pillow under my head gave a rumbled noise, rising and falling with a familiar rhythm. I stirred, then realized I'd drooled on Bran's shirt.

He chuckled as I brushed at the damp fabric. "Won't be the first time you leave me with the wet spot."

I poked him with my index finger and sat up, yawning.

The mattress sagged in the middle and I'd ended up almost atop Bran, rolled against his side with my arm draped over his waist.

"How long was I out?"

Bran glanced at his watch. "About two hours. Which obviously you needed badly, given your cute snoring." He winced as I pushed his shoulder to give myself enough leverage to swing my legs out over the side of the bed.

"Cute snoring?"

"Cute snoring. Snoring that's cute. Actually, totally adorable." He paused as the sound of car engines roared up the stairs. Multiple vehicles spun wheels on gravel and skidded to a stop.

"They're here." I spotted a bathroom through an

adjoining door. It took two bounces to get off the bed and stagger toward the sink.

I wasn't going to face down two angry family leaders with sleep in my eyes.

Bran rolled onto his side and watched me as I gave myself the once-over, splashing the cool water on my face and attempting to tame the wild mess of blond hair.

A come-hither beauty I wasn't. The best I could do was pull my hair back into a ponytail and hope the dark circles under my eyes didn't have people mistaking me for a raccoon.

"What's the worst that can happen?" he asked. "I mean, how pushy can they get? We're on neutral ground, sanctuary for Felis—right?"

I paused and studied myself in the mirror. "Possible scenario. They demand I tell them where the kids are. I say no, they issue me a challenge. I win, I get to stay quiet. I lose, I tell them where the kids are."

Bran bounced off the bed and stood up. "You can't Change. You can't accept a challenge."

"I wouldn't have a choice." I swiped at the edges of my mouth. "It's not a voluntary thing. You don't refuse challenges. If I do I risk being declared outcast again."

"And that's different from what?" he snapped. "It's not like they've embraced you as of late." He shook his head. "You don't owe them anything."

"I have to answer." I waved a hand over the sink. "Any credibility I have left, any status I have gained over the past few months will be gone if I don't respond."

"How much status are they going to get for beating up a cripple?"

I looked at Bran.

He stood there, his mouth hanging open and shock on his face.

I swallowed hard and felt the invisible door slam shut between us.

"I'm sorry," he whispered. "You know I don't think of you like that, I'd never think of you like that."

"I know." I turned back to the mirror and lifted a finger to trace my reflection. "But it doesn't matter. It didn't matter decades ago when Jess challenged me and it doesn't matter now."

Bran shook his head. "Then I'll fight for you. You allow proxies, right?" His voice rose a note. "You allowed it in Penscotta."

"No. Not here." I walked back out to where he stood. "You're challenged, you fight. No switching, no tag teams."

"But they can't force you to talk. They can't force you to tell them where the kids are." The words came out faster and faster, a runaway train as he fought for control.

"No, they can't. The question is how many challenges I can survive before giving them what they want."

Bran's face went scarlet as he understood what I was saying. His lips moved without sound, the rage building inside him.

"This, this is how Felis society works." I didn't try to make apologies for what I didn't agree with. "It's not right and it's not perfect but it's how it's worked for decades, centuries."

"Will Jess just stand there and let them beat you down? Because I sure as hell won't." His fists were clenched at his sides, his breath coming out in pants. "I beat one of your kind once and I'll do it again."

I touched his cheek, feeling the tension under my fingers. "We're not going to let it get to that point. It's not going to go that far." The truth was he'd gotten lucky and had beaten Carson because the corrupt police chief had been concussed and out of shape.

It was hard to keep my hands from trembling. My options were limited and while Jess wouldn't let them kill me, it wasn't a guarantee I'd walk out unscathed.

The scars on my back were testament to that.

Bran grabbed my hand and pressed it between his own, lowering his forehead to touch mine. "You know I'll do anything for you, right? Anything."

The voices grew in intensity downstairs.

Bran continued. "Say the word and I'll call Hank. Hell, I'll call the entire police force, the *National Inquisitor* and the CBC. Bring in the SWAT teams and blow this place wide open, bring the media down on their heads with God's vengeance."

"You can't do that," I whispered.

"To save you—yes. And a whole lot more I haven't thought of yet. I'll be damned if I let your family destroy who you are." The steel in his voice strengthened me, replenished my flagging resolve.

I kissed him, drawing strength from his strong heart and soul. "Let's give this a try first."

I drew a deep breath and headed for the stairs, trying to calm myself. Bran followed close behind, his body heat trying to wrap around me like a security blanket.

Showtime.

As we descended the stairs I caught the different scents and automatically catalogued them into sides—Middleston, Chandler and other.

Jess stood at the bottom of the staircase, firmly in the other category. Arms crossed, she surveyed the group now filling the room. Her stern expression set the tone for the meeting.

The muttering and muted voices stopped at my appearance. All eyes turned to me and not a friendly pair among them.

Jake Middleston stood up from his chair, watching me approach. Behind him Eddie nodded at me, an unknown man standing beside him. Another enforcer or family friend, I couldn't tell.

Mary Chandler stayed seated in the opposite chair and glared at me. Nathan McAllister allowed himself a snicker as I drew closer, his beady little eyes flicking to Bran every few seconds. There was still a reckoning between these two waiting to happen.

I didn't need it to be here.

This was the first time I'd seen Mary Chandler. A thin woman in her thirties, there was nothing outstanding about her other than her long black hair flying loose over her shoulders. Her eyes were red and swollen and she gave me the stink-eye of all stink-eyes as I moved closer. The man standing beside Nathan was barely an adult, his hands jammed in his pockets and wearing a rock band T-shirt. The similarities between Mary and Evan and the mystery man were evident.

Evan's older brother. Second-in-charge of the family, in theory.

Given the commanding posture his mother took I figured it'd be a long, long wait for his ascension to the throne. He shuffled his feet, the grating against the wooden floor scratching at my ears.

I felt Bran behind me, his low measured breathing brushing against the back of my neck.

Jess didn't look at me as I stepped down beside her.

"This is Rebecca Desjardin." Her eyes traveled around the room, finding and locking with each Felis in a display of command. "You will hear her out and give her your respect."

Bran stayed behind me. I was sure he noticed he hadn't been introduced.

Thankfully he stayed silent.

I stepped forward. "Jake, you hired me to find your daughter. I've found Lisa—she's a smart and beautiful young woman." This earned me a natural smile, a father's love for his daughter clear.

I turned toward Mary. "Mary, you hired me to find your son. He's a strong and mature young man, a proud future leader of your family."

Her face didn't change, a stoic mask hiding her feelings.

"The two of them are safe and adapting well to their new situation. I spoke to them regarding their relationship and they told me they're in love."

That earned a few snickers from both sides.

I spread my hands, putting a sheepish smile on my face. "Hey, I know how it goes. One day you're madly in love with this guy or girl and a week later you can't remember his or her name. But you all have to admit that it's a powerful, strong force of nature that can't be denied. Once you're bitten by the bug you'll do anything for the one you care about, anything and everything."

Behind me Bran cleared his throat.

Jake shifted in his chair. I suspected he had a few of his own stories hidden away.

"Evan and Lisa love each other. If they return here, willingly or not, you will separate them and they'll never see each other again. Now I'm not psychic but I can guess those two are going to move heaven and earth to get to each other no matter where you put them." I drew a breath, hoping they wouldn't hear the shakiness in my voice. "They want to be together and soon enough they're both going to be legal adults. This could be the best chance for you both to heal the rift between your families, close this gap keeping both sides apart. We are Felis, we are one family. Your children deserve better than to be shackled by the past. Let's make it so that they can come home to a united front and a future together, if that's what they choose."

The words were thick in my mouth. Felis ceremony dictated more formal conversation but I wasn't sure what applied here.

Jess's lack of interference told me I was doing fine. So far.

Jake looked over at Mary and gave a slight nod of

the head, offering her the first chance to reply out of politeness.

She narrowed her eyes and glared at him.

No one moved.

Jess placed her hands on her hips. “If someone doesn’t say something I will. And you don’t want to know what I’m going to say.”

TEN

Jake got to his feet and cleared his throat. "You're the one who referred me to her." He pointed at me. "You told me she was a good tracker, she'd find my girl and bring her home." Spittle flew from his lips as his voice rose. "All you had to do is find her and bring her back. Is that too hard for you to comprehend? Was that too hard for your simple mind to get? Even a freak like you should have been able to do that."

I felt rather than heard Bran's huff behind me.

Jess waited a second, making sure Jake had finished saying his piece before she gestured at Mary.

She stood up and brushed her hands over her black jeans before speaking. "I went to you for help, for advice on how to find my runaway boy. Jess told me she had faith in your abilities to find Evan and deliver him back here safely, back to the bosom of our family. You've failed to do so." She glanced over her shoulder at Nathan. "I took other measures to ensure my wishes were being followed because I didn't believe an outcast could do the job and do it right. You still haven't done what I asked and brought my boy home."

The thin Felis enforcer sneered, his lips twisting up into a warped grin.

My turn.

"You didn't give me much time before setting your dog on me. I had your son under observation and was about to make contact. Then your pup hit me and not only revealed himself to me but also caused a major incident involving the police." That changed Nathan's grin into a snarl, exposing teeth. "He put me in the hospital and missed his chance to get your kit. I wouldn't be giving him any gold stars."

Mary pressed her lips into a straight line. I suspected Nathan hadn't been as honest as she expected about his actions.

"And as for your daughter—" I turned to Jake. "She's going to be an adult in a few days and has the right to make her own decisions, be they right or wrong. I promised to find her but I never promised to drag her back to you in chains. She's alive and well and still cares for her family." I glanced over at Mary. "As does your son."

"Do not speak of them in the same breath," she whispered. "Evan is a good boy obviously enticed into this folly by his slut of a daughter."

I winced inside as Jake bunched up his fists, his face flaming scarlet. There weren't many words that could push a father's buttons but that was one of them.

Jess threw up her hands just as Jake took a step around the circular table, his enforcers moving with him.

"We are not going to do this," she warned. Her piercing stare hit Mary. "Apologize. Now."

Mary squirmed for a second under her inspection before muttering something under her breath. It was enough to stop Jake's approach and allow him a respectful retreat back to his chair.

Jess looked at me.

I steadied myself and continued.

"Let me get this straight. This, all of this, this feud is all over one woman dying because of an accident." It probably wasn't the most sensitive way of saying it but I'd worn out my reserve.

Jake scowled. "Maureen Middleston was a good woman. She deserved better than to die through deceit and treachery from Laura Chandler." He shot an angry look over the table. "It was murder, plain and simple."

Mary began to speak but I shot my hand up, stopping her. "The Grand Council ruled it was an accident. Why didn't both families accept the ruling at the time? Why has this gone on for two more generations of hatred and mistrust?"

This got me mumblings and mutterings, the enforcers shuffling their feet and looking to their respective leaders for a response.

Jess looked at me and raised an eyebrow.

"Anyone? Anyone?" I prompted them.

"It's not like Laura walked away unscathed," Mary said quietly. "She was crippled, limped for the rest of her life. She never got over it until the day she died." She glanced at Jess. "Long before her time. And you took her place."

Jess said nothing.

"She got over it enough to take the spot on the Board," Jake said. He turned his head to one side as if to spit before catching Jess's glare and stopping.

"Better she take it than leave it empty for someone else to fight over," Mary replied. "She would have won the next challenge, if there'd been one, anyway."

I put my hand up again. "What's done is done. Once the kill's been picked clean there's no use in fighting over dry bones."

That earned me an approving look from Jess. I hadn't forgotten everything from being on the farm.

"Your mother chose that field 'cause she knew it was full of rabbit holes." This came from the unidentified Middleston Felis standing beside Eddie. My guess was another enforcer, another family associate standing by in case Eddie couldn't close the deal. "She knew it gave her the advantage in the fight."

"And what if she did?" Mary replied, a definite edge to her words. "The old woman should have watched where she stepped. She wasn't a kit out for her first challenge. Not our fault if she was blind as well as dumb."

Jake jumped to his feet, his mouth opening and closing in a series of silent curses. The two men behind him surged forward, pressing against the back of Jake's chair.

Mary rose as well, her son moving around to stand beside her. Nathan stayed where he was, watching and assessing his potential targets.

"I love diplomacy," Bran muttered behind me.

The two camps ignored him and glared at each other. I could smell the challenges about to be tossed out, the blood boiling on both sides.

Jess didn't say anything. She stood there with her arms crossed and watched.

I cleared my throat loudly before raising my voice. "No offense, folks—but this isn't about you," I said.

Both parties turned and studied me as if I was covered in raw meat. I resisted the urge to take a step back.

"You want to beat each other senseless through challenges and screwing each other out of business deals, that's your right as a family and as Felis. But we're talking about the lives of two young adults who don't want to play your game anymore." I pointed at Nathan who continued to wear his smirk proudly. "And neither do I. Next time either of your enforcers come at me I won't be as nice about it."

Nathan chuckled and tucked his thumbs under his thick leather belt. "Easy enough to knock you on your ass." He looked around the room at the others. "She's a lightweight. All talk and no go."

"Wasn't no go when I put you down." Bran stepped forward. "Still got that mark on you, kit?"

I resisted the urge to roll my eyes. This was the last place for Bran's machismo display.

Part of me couldn't blame him however—we had to draw the line somewhere and Bran'd stepped up and thrown the proverbial gauntlet in their faces.

I hoped it wasn't going to come back at us with lethal force.

One edge of Nathan's mouth curled up. "You've got no place here, human. The only reason you're even present is because you're hooked up with her." He spat the last word out like a curse.

From the heads bobbing in agreement it was one of the few things they could all agree about.

"Good thing we're not a democracy here," I replied. "He's got as much of a right to be here as I do."

"Outcast." This came from the Chandler son. "I'm not sure if you have the right to be here among us." He ignored Jess's warning glare. "Freaks got no place in our family."

I sized up the pup. He had black hair like his younger brother, the disorganized mop hanging over his ears. The black T-shirt advertised some heavy metal rock band while his jeans were headed southward, allowing me to see his Fruit of the Looms.

I motioned him on with one hand. "Is that a challenge?"

Bran let out a low growl. I ignored him.

Jess shifted her weight from one foot to the other. She bit down on her lower lip but said nothing.

"I guess it is." He smiled at his mother as he approached me, his cocky walk showing major attitude. He stopped in front of me and tucked his hands into his pockets, turning his head back toward the waiting Felis to give them a wide grin. "Yep, I think it is."

"Good."

My right knee slammed up into his groin. I followed up with an elbow jab to his nose, now that he'd dropped his head to the right angle.

The kid dropped to the ground, mewing. His hands flew back and forth between cradling his balls and trying to stifle the blood flowing from his nose.

I took a step back, almost unable to stand. It'd taken the last of my strength and I was done.

Jess put her hand up to her mouth, something akin to a chuckle escaping.

Jake let out some sort of cough.

Mary didn't move toward her son but the clenched fists told me I was a whisper away from dealing with her.

"Challenge—" the young man groaned from between his hands.

"Well challenged and met," Jess said. She glanced at me before turning her attention to the young man curled up in a ball. "When you challenge, the game is on. You don't pose, you don't vogue for your buddies." Her gaze went to Mary. "I thought you'd been trained properly."

I nudged the moaning boy with my foot. "You'll survive. Next time don't underestimate your opponent. Felis, human or outcast."

Mary locked eyes with Jess, silently appealing the outcome.

Jess shrugged.

The young man pulled himself back to his mother's side, coughing and snorting blood out his nose. Nathan pulled out a handkerchief and dropped it next to the injured Chandler without comment.

"Now that we're done with that." I paused for another few seconds to let Mary console her son. "Let's get back to the issue at hand. What's best for these two young people?"

Jake looked at Jess before turning his attention to

me, picking his words carefully. "I want my daughter home. She wants her son. I'm not seeing what the problem is here."

"The problem is that they're not coming home unless you let them be together," I said. "Simple as that. End the feud or you'll never see them again."

Jake's eyes narrowed. "You'd keep me from my kin?"

"I'll keep your daughter free to make her own decisions. And mistakes." I caught Mary's attention. "And your son. I'm appealing to you both to let bygones be bygones and put this feud behind you. I won't tell you where they are and I won't deliver them to you like lambs to the slaughter. If you want them you'll have to go to Toronto and start ripping the city up."

This brought a low cough from Jess, signaling her disapproval of the option.

"They're ready to go rogue. Are you ready to let them do this if you truly love them?" I looked at her son, busy trying to casually check his family jewels without shoving his hands down his baggy jeans. "Let that be the last of blood spilled for this feud."

Jake rolled his tongue around his mouth before wetting his lips. "I need some time to think about this. What you're suggesting, well—I can't give a decision right now." He gestured toward the Chandlers. "I'm thinking you've got the same thought. It's a big thing, what she's asking and I ain't going to jump without thinking it through."

Mary nodded. Her son had managed to stand up and now resumed his spot beside her, wobbling a bit. His nose was red and swollen but I didn't think it was broken. He held the handkerchief to his mouth as if sucking on a lollipop. "We agree. Let's take some time to consider all our options."

"I want both parties back here by—" Jess checked her watch. "It's more or less one o'clock now. Let's be back by eight. That's more than enough time for everyone to get dinner and make up their minds." She paused and looked at each family leader in turn. "This is going to be finished tonight, one way or another. So don't come back without a solution you can live with."

The two groups filed out of the living room, one after another alternating between families. Mary Chandler linked her arm with her son's, helping him leave with as much dignity as he could. Jake Middleston didn't look at me but muttered at Eddie, who bobbed his head up and down.

Jess waited until the screen door had slammed behind the last person before letting out her breath in a long, measured gasp.

"Woman, you know how to flip people on their heads. I was shitting nickels trying to figure out how to get you out of that one."

"Tell me about it." Bran spun me around and hugged me, his arms tight around mine. "Especially when that little punk came up to you. I'm assuming that's not how you usually handle challenges."

Jess let out a snort. "Not by a long shot. Ceremony says you declare the challenge and then choose an arena and so forth but those are just the bells and whistles. He should have realized we didn't have the time for that and Reb was full in her rights to take him on right there." She chuckled. "Full of piss and vinegar and wanted to show off in front of his mother and the Middlestons. He'll think twice about doing that again."

"If his balls ever drop again," I said, leaning into Bran. "Damn, I need a drink."

"Sit down and I'll get something." Jess headed for the kitchen. "First let me make sure they all got out of the parking lot without killing each other."

As she left the room Bran helped me to the couch, urging me to stretch out with my legs across his lap. "You scared me something awful. Thought we were going to get into it right here with the fighting."

I sighed as he rubbed my bare feet, his hands rubbing over the skin. "Close call there. If the little shit had Changed I probably wouldn't have gotten the drop on him." I winced as he hit a sensitive spot.

"Whiskey times three." Jess came back with the same tray that had previously carried the pie, now carrying three glasses with a whisper of booze at the bottom. She handed me a glass and let Bran pick his own before settling into the chair so recently vacated by Jake Middleston. "Well played." She lifted the glass in a toast. "You might want to consider a Board position if you ever come back to the Pride full-time."

I sniffed the amber liquid. The good stuff. It tasted as smooth as silk and burned all the way down to start a fire in my belly.

I sighed, feeling the warmth rush through my aching bones and muscles. "I'm not sure if the doctor at the hospital would approve of me drinking."

Bran tossed his back in one shot. "He wouldn't have approved you getting into a full-fledged fight." He put his glass down on the tray. "How 'bout I whip us up some lunch?"

Jess gave him an approving look. "Help yourself to anything in the kitchen. We try to keep it pretty well-stocked."

"I'm thinking pasta. Fast energy and doesn't take too long to cook." He untangled himself from my legs and went into the kitchen.

Jess smiled. "Dang, you got one that's trained to cook? Give me some DNA and I'll get to cloning him."

I almost choked on the drink.

"The kids are safe, right?" Jess asked. "No chance they're going to get nabbed while you're here."

"Yes. I've got them tucked away with a friend." I didn't think it was the right time to mention Red.

"Hmm." Jess held her glass up and peered at the whiskey. "Good stuff." She rested the glass in her lap, caressing the cool smooth surface. "I hope you know what you're doing, Rebecca. I can only do so much and then it's beyond me."

I nodded. "You've done enough. Thanks for having us here."

She sniffed the air. "Oh, he's raiding the cupboard. Canned tomatoes and the man knows his seasonings." Her attention returned to the drink, dipping her index finger in to stir an invisible ice cube. "For the record I've already warned both families that farther sneak attacks on your person will not be tolerated. Felis may not kill Felis but that doesn't give them carte blanche to beat the crap out of you by broadsiding you in an alley. McCallister was way out of line for slamming you like that." She took another sip. "Damned idiots."

I didn't dispute her opinion.

We sat in silence, a comfortable quiet, for a good half hour. The alcohol sent a warm buzz through me and I felt fine, refreshed and ready to deal with anything.

It wouldn't last but I didn't want to think about that right now.

"Come eat." Bran appeared in the doorway, brandishing a ladle. "Now."

Jess chuckled as she pushed herself up, letting out a grunt. I rolled off the couch and headed for the kitchen with my stomach already growling for food.

Bran whipped up a spaghetti dinner, salad on the side with giant slices of homemade bread hanging off the edges of the plates. He'd cooked for me before but this tasted extra good this time, the delicate spices dissolving on my tongue as I spun the thin pasta around my fork.

We ate in silence, a mismatched family enjoying the calm before the inevitable storm.

"Whoa." Jess pushed the empty plate away and dabbed at one side of her mouth with a paper napkin. "I'll have to add in an extra run tonight to make sure this doesn't stay on my hips. Thank you."

Bran gave me a saucy wink, and started to clear the table. He'd been the perfect host and I couldn't have loved him more for it.

She patted her stomach. "That's a meal that demands a round of applause." Jess looked at her watch and sighed. "They're going to be back in an hour. Anything you need me to do?"

"Stay around and make sure they don't kill her," Bran murmured from the kitchen counter.

"I was planning to do that anyway." She got up from the table and carried the near-empty salad bowl to the refrigerator. "Got too much invested in you two." After sticking the wooden bowl inside and closing the door Jess turned and rested her hands on the counter behind her. "What's your plan?"

I mopped up the last of the sauce with a bit of crusty bread. "Same as before. Negotiate for the kids to come home and be allowed to continue dating each other. If they fall out of love or not is their decision, not their families'."

Jess shook her head. "You are a hopeless romantic." She picked up the electric kettle and nudged Bran aside to turn on the water in the sink. "And if they don't give in? You're fighting a feud that's been going on for two generations." She stuck the kettle under the stream of water. "You're asking a lot of them. Jake and Mary were raised to believe their mothers were right in their actions and that the other side was wrong. It's going to be hard, if not impossible for them to let that go."

I chewed on the bread for a minute before answering. "I'm asking them to do what's right for their children. The blood's already been spilled and gone dry, there's no point in continuing this insanity for another generation. Neither family will benefit in the long run and it won't help the Pride." I licked my lips, tasting the last of the tart sauce. "They can't make me tell them where the kids are."

"No they can't." Jess busied herself making tea. "But you know they can make you pay for your silence with more challenges and you won't get away with that sneak attack again." She studied my face. "Are you ready to take them on to protect two teenagers?"

"Yes."

She shook her head and pulled down three mugs from the cupboard.

"Wait," Bran interrupted. "You're warning the idiots not to attack her again with one breath and in the other authorizing more challenges? What the fuck is that?"

Jess frowned and I knew she was trying to figure out how to explain something inherently Felis to him.

"It's a matter of customs," I started.

Jess held up her hand and stopped me. "Bran, it's a case of procedure. When you were down in Penscotta and met those two enforcers you knew they'd do anything Carson asked, right?"

"They destroyed evidence that could have helped us find the killer faster. Redneck punks."

"I agree. But they didn't know that at the time, they were working for Carson. They were there to give Carson and the Board a private security force, someone they could trust to be there when needed." She paused and I could see her trying to put words to something she hadn't had to explain before. "What McCallister did was wrong. Enforcers aren't allowed to attack other Felis unless necessary to protect the family."

"Your own police force."

She tilted her head. "In a way. Imagine them as sort of bodyguards with the ultimate goal of helping keep the Felis hidden."

"But this has nothing to do with keeping your secret, chasing down two runaway kids. And they're not working for the Board here. Carson at least justified his thugs by being the police chief."

"Usually enforcers work for the Board. Some work for individual families, like in this case." She frowned, her thin eyebrows drawing together as she searched for the words. "Enforcers do more than just punch and threaten. They help out when and where a strong man is needed, when a father's been lost and a child needs help. They build barns and homes for those who need them. They help the elderly get around and deliver supplies if necessary. Think of them as a sort of Peace Corps with claws. We call them enforcers because they enforce our way of life, our code. It's not an easy job and not every man wants the title. It's a necessary part of our support system. I'm sorry you've only seen the negative side of it."

Bran paused for a minute before nodding. "I get it. But what I don't get is them beating on Reb and hunting down those kids. That can't fall under helping the Pride."

"It's not. They're not supposed to be active without approval from the Board and we sure as hell wouldn't approve of smashing someone into a wall so hard she needed hospitalization." Her left hand rose, waving away invisible flies. "A challenge, that's different. That's a traditional way of settling matters for the Felis.

Family leadership, Board positions, it's our way of settling matters in a definitive matter. Once it's done, it's done. No going back, no appeal process."

"Might over right? Survival of the fittest?" Bran growled.

A flash of anger in Jess's eyes signaled her impatience with him. "Look, you may not like it but it's what we do. It's how we survive, how we handle things. If you don't like it—" She bit back the response.

Bran's problem with the Felis was my problem and Lord knew I had more than one gripe with the system.

Bran took a deep breath, trying to steady himself. "So they can challenge her again. And keep challenging until she either tells them or what, dies?"

"I won't let that happen to her," Jess said. "But I can't deny them the right to try."

Bran turned the hot water on and busied himself with the dishes. I knew he was dying to say something but it'd be pointless. This was a fight he couldn't take on for me and he desperately wanted to.

The tea was ready by the time the last wet dish hit the drying tray. Bran sat down next to me. Jess brought over the Brown Betty teapot and put it in the center of the scarred wooden tabletop. She waved Bran down as he started to rise and got three mugs, adding a dash of milk to all of them before placing them in front of each of us.

Bran picked up the teapot and began pouring with a steady hand.

"When they come back you need to stay quiet." Jess warned Bran. "They're tolerating you being in the same room and that's because I'm here. But I can only do so much."

"I knocked out Carson," Bran said with a touch of pride. "I can hold my own against them."

"And they know that. Trust me, everyone knows that." Jess smiled. "Which is why they'd love to take you on. But this isn't the time or place for that, it's Reb's game and she's got to play it out." She poured out the tea and passed him the first mug.

"I won't let them hurt her," he said quietly, steel underlying the softness.

"Wasn't asking you to." Jess pushed the second cup at me. "Just asking that you think about the bigger picture before you act. Listen to your head before acting on your heart."

I heard the spin of rubber on gravel.

It was time.

Jess got up and strolled out. Bran didn't move other than to drain the last of his tea and study the invisible tea leaves in the bottom.

I stayed in the kitchen, listening to the Chandlers and Middlestons file back up on the porch and march through the front door. There was some mutterings but I couldn't make them out even with my Felis hearing.

I probably didn't want to.

By the time I'd finished my tea the two groups were back in the living room in their assigned seats.

Jess appeared in the doorway. "It's time."

I stood up. My legs were steady and I waved off Bran's attempt to help me walk.

I couldn't afford to be seen as anything other than at full strength.

I strode from the kitchen with a jaunt in my step and teeth clenched to the point of almost shattering.

It was a rerun of the previous meeting with everyone in the same place. Jake Middleston on one side, Mary Chandler on the other. Nathan McCallister glared at Eddie Longstrand from across the circular table but he didn't say anything.

The Chandler kit's nose was swollen but not broken. He whistled through it as I strode to the bottom of the stairs, Bran at my side.

Jess took up her position. Both family heads watched her like a hawk, waiting for her to make the first move. I suspected if she'd been a lesser woman one or both families would have challenged her position on the Board already.

But they knew Jess and her reputation.

Jake cleared his throat. "I think we're ready to begin."

I glanced at Mary. She sat there with her legs crossed and a prissy grin. That couldn't be good.

"I'm prepared to discuss Evan and Lisa returning to their families under certain conditions," I started.

Mary put up her hand, stopping me.

"I'd like to bring another option to the table."

Nathan stood beside her pale and wheezing son, grinning like a Cheshire Cat.

My stomach churned.

"You bring my boy home to me, right now." She didn't look at Jake other than to nod in his general direction. "This is between you and me. What he arranges with you is his business. I just want my Evan safe and sound and out of that bitch's arms."

Jake sucked in his breath hard but stayed seated. Jess gave him an approving nod of her head.

"I'm negotiating for both of them. A package deal."

"No," she said, the underlying growls sending a shiver up my spine. "Only my son. Only Evan and you're going to bring him back to me."

"And I would do this because—" I said.

"Because of this." She reached up behind her, eyes locking with mine. Nathan put a photograph into her hand, a glossy eight-by-eleven sized page.

She pulled her arm back and tossed it onto the table in front of her, not breaking eye contact.

ELEVEN

I blinked first, pulling away to look down at the image.

Angie.

Gagged and tied to a chair. A copy of the *Toronto Star*, today's edition, in her lap. Her eyes wide and scared, reminding me of a deer caught in the headlights.

Bran, God bless him, didn't react. His breath stuttered but he didn't move.

Jess did.

She flew toward the table with almost unnatural speed, snatched up the black-and-white picture and waved it in Mary's face. "What the fuck is this? What the fuck is this all about?"

Mary stood her ground, staying seated as Jess hovered over her. Her angelic look increased Jess's fury, her face shifting from pale white to an angry red, the scar on her left cheek becoming more visible with each second.

Bran shifted beside me, the floorboards creaking under his movement.

Mary turned her gaze on Jess. "This is no longer the Board's business." She spoke slowly, as if to a child.

I thought I could hear Jess's blood pressure rise.

"The Board deals with Felis business. This—" Mary

tapped a finger against the photo in her face, "—is no Felis. This is a human. For whom we will bargain with another human, leaving the Felis out of the equation." Her eyes narrowed. "Therefore your presence, and your interference, is unnecessary." She smiled. "We've just decided to change the battlefield."

"By kidnapping a human," Jess whispered.

"Not just any human." Mary looked past Jess to Bran. "Your friend. Your very good friend, from what she told us. You get her back when we get Evan back."

"I don't believe you. I think you're full of shit." Bran poked a finger at the photograph. "That could be all faked, Photoshopped. I know the business and it'd be damned easy to fake all this."

Mary smiled and looked over her shoulder at her bloodied son.

The punk stepped out to stand beside his mother. He pulled out his cell phone and tapped in a number before placing it on the table.

"Yeah?" The rough voice shot out of the tiny speaker.

"Give her the phone," the young man said.

I allowed myself an inside smile at hearing the squeak in his voice.

"Hello? Hello?" Angie screamed. "Who's there? Police? Is this the police?"

Jess looked at Bran and nodded.

Mary tilted her head to one side and grinned at me.

"Angie," Bran spoke first, careful to speak slowly and clearly. "Listen to me. It's okay. You're going to be fine."

"Bran?" She sobbed. "Bran, what's going on? They said they're going to hurt me if you don't do something, something—" The words drifted off into more sobs. "They said they're going to cut me, cut my face."

A cold ball of fear curdled the remaining food in my belly. I'd seen what Felis claws could do to bare skin.

Bran had as well.

I couldn't help looking over at Jess and the scar on her face. Delivered by my mother, the deep gash had taken Jess's eye and marked her forever.

It took a lot to survive that.

I wasn't sure I wanted to find out if Angela Degas was up to the task.

"I'll come for you, promise. I'll come save you—" Bran stopped as Mary's son reached out and cut the connection.

Jess didn't move. "This is not what we agreed on." She shook her head with a slow, threatening pace. "You are going into dangerous territory."

Mary stared at her. "This isn't Board business anymore. This is between us and him." She turned away from Jess and pointed at Bran. "You want her back, you give us Evan. Simple as that."

Jake looked behind him at Eddie with a "why didn't we think of that?" scowl.

Eddie said nothing and continued staring at the ground.

Jess snatched the picture up off the table and handed it to me. "Don't think I won't be taking this up with the rest of the Board. And the Grand Council." She turned back to Mary. "You've made a big mistake pulling this human into our business."

Mary got to her feet and placed her fingertips on the table. "You made a big mistake referring me to this outcast and her mate. And she made a big mistake underestimating how far I'll go to get my son back." She picked up the cell phone and handed it over to her son.

I stood there, frozen in place as Jake Middleston stood up.

He looked almost embarrassed. He shuffled his feet and avoided looking at me directly, addressing Jess with his head tucked into his chest.

"This doesn't involve us. When you've finished your other business I'd be willing to talk to you again." He strode out, Eddie and the unknown Felis in tow.

Mary beamed at Bran. "If you want your girlfriend back you'll either bring my son to me or give us the information on where to find him before sunrise." She looked at her watch. "I'm being generous with the amount of time. Don't make me regret it."

Jess made a sound, almost a hiss. "You are not going to get away with this." She pointed at Bran. "He's got nothing to do with this. You dragging him in is a violation of our laws."

"No. That mutant you've got tucked under your tail is the real violation. I'll take my chances with the Grand Council. But this'll be done one way or the other within the next twenty-four hours." She spun around, her ponytail whipping across her shoulders. Her bloodied son followed, grinning.

Nathan chuckled before taking up a spot behind Chandler and her son as they headed for the door.

Bran waited to react until the room was empty except for the three of us, his strained breathing echoing in my ears.

"McCallister," he snarled. "He took her, the bastard. He must have seen her with me, with us when we were tracking the kids." He shook his head, replaying the events in his mind. "When this started out we were looking for the teenagers, not for someone stalking us. That's how he chose Angie." He closed his eyes. "I handed her right over to them. I didn't even warn her to stay sharp, take some precautions."

I had to say something before he broke under the self-imposed guilt. "It wouldn't have stopped McCallister. It might have gotten people hurt, more than just me or you. He's a hunter, he would have gone over and through anything to achieve his goal. It's that bitch Chandler behind him, she let him loose on her." I flopped into one of the vacated chairs, my new-found strength ebbing away with the shock. "I didn't even consider this happening."

Jess came up beside me and touched my shoulder. "You shouldn't have. This isn't a case of life or death, it's about two kids wanting their freedom." She sighed. "I never thought either family would go so far. I'm partially responsible for this."

"For bringing me in?"

"No." She gestured toward the now-vacant parking lot. "For not taking this straight to the Grand Council as soon as I realized the two families were involved.

This shouldn't have ever landed in your lap, not with the way she's thinking." Jess swallowed hard. "I never thought Mary would take it to this extreme. I knew she took the feud seriously, been trying to destroy Middleston's business for as long as I can remember but this takes it to a whole new level."

"By grabbing a human hostage," I filled in the blanks.

"Yes." Jess snorted. "Damned fool. She's not going to be able to show her face in public after the Grand Council finishes with her." She curled her fingers into a fist. "After I finish with her. The Board's going to drop a ton of bricks on her head for this."

"But right now we have a problem." I directed her back to the present. "And the Grand Council isn't here, we are."

Bran hadn't moved from where he stood. "If they hurt her—"

"Leave that part to me," Jess warned. "Let's not cross that bridge until we get there." She looked at me. "Who is this woman?"

"An old friend," Bran said before I could respond.

She turned toward him. "Did I ask you?" The icy snap had Bran closing his mouth and waiting.

"She used to be one of the street kids from Bran's article," I interrupted before the argument could gain momentum. The last thing I needed right now was a split between any of us. "We ran into her while looking for the kids. She runs an outreach project and helped us get away from the hunters last night. Wouldn't be hard to track her down either at her home or at the drop-in center and grab her there." I closed my eyes for a second, trying to process what had just happened. "Mary's willing to pull an innocent human into danger for her family? That doesn't make sense."

"I know. She's put us all in danger." Jess cleared her throat, enough to bring us both around to look at her. "Feud or no feud that's not acceptable under any circumstances."

I flinched inside. Mary Chandler had crossed over a line. By pulling Angie into the mix she'd put the Felis in danger of being exposed and that was right at the top of Thou Shalt Nots for the family.

"How tough is Angie?" Jess asked Bran.

He gave her a blank look. I knew what was going on—he was going into shock at the idea of exposing Angie to the Felis. He'd had a rough enough entrance and couldn't imagine inflicting that on someone else.

"How tough is she?" Jess repeated. She strode over to stand in front of him, staring at him directly. "Look, they're not going to kill her but she's got to be terrified and wondering what the hell she's gotten herself into. Is she going to fold like a delicate flower or can she hold her own against them and stay strong until we can get to her?"

Bran licked his lips before pulling them into a straight line. "Are they going to beat her?"

"Maybe." Leave it to Jess to tell the harsh truth. "If we don't hand over Evan in time they might. It'd be a way to push your buttons, just like that phone call. It was pretty obvious to everyone that you care for her and wouldn't want to see her get hurt."

Bran didn't say anything. I imagined him turning the clock back and assessing how Angie had changed from the tough alley rat he'd originally befriended.

"She survived for years on the street," Bran finally answered. "She'll be good."

"I hope so." Jess turned back to me. "I've got to call the other Board members and then the Council, give them an update and start the wheels turning. Can you handle it from here?"

I heard the unspoken question. Could I figure out how to save Angie without giving in to Mary Chandler's demands and keep our family secret?

I levered myself out of the chair with a grunt. "We've got to get moving." My legs felt like wooden fence posts. "We're running the clock down."

Bran sighed. "I don't like it." He swept one hand in front of him, encompassing the room. "I brought you up here to keep you safe, give you a chance to heal. I can deal with this on my own." He took the picture from me and stared at the glossy image. "I can call Hank, I can get some professional help—"

Jess replied before I could. "No you can't."

It wasn't a question.

Jess continued. "They've got her someplace safe, surrounded by Chandler family and friends. You'd be tilting at windmills trying to find out where they are." She poked at the photograph. "They grabbed her to get you to pressure Rebecca to give up the information about where Evan is. They don't give a shit about you or Angie." Her tone sharpened. "And they sure as hell won't care about a SWAT team showing up on their doorstep. If you're looking to expose the family you couldn't pick a better way to do it. It'd be a bloodbath, pure and simple."

The unwanted image flashed in front of me. Felis fighting with the police; injured or dead on both sides and our secret out to the entire world. There'd be no containing such a disaster—it'd be impossible.

"Wait a minute." I drew a deep breath, banishing the bloody images. "They'd risk everyone finding out about us to keep Angie?" I asked. "Wouldn't they run and leave her behind?"

Jess fixed me in place with a piercing stare. "Maybe, maybe not. Depends on how psychopathic the guards are. They might start firing or attack instinctively and not even think about leaving. A clusterfuck all around. Do you want to take that risk?" She answered before I could. "No, you're not." She pointed at Bran. "And you're not. Period."

"So what do we do?" I asked.

"I don't know and I don't want to know. But whatever you do, remember you've got to keep our existence secret." Jess headed for the kitchen. "The Chandlers have kicked this up to a Code Red. I'm not happy and no one else is going to be when this is all finished."

"Can you force them to give Angie back?" Bran asked. "Get the Grand Council to issue some sort of edict, some sort of paperwork to turn her loose?"

Jess stopped in the doorway. "This sort of thing hasn't happened before. It's going to take hours to get through to all the members, the Board and the Council. Then they've got to consider some sort of action and all the politics involved."

"Politics?" Bran's voice rose. "This is a woman's life you're dealing with."

"This is something we've never had to deal with before." The stress in Jess's words scratched the inside of my eyelids. "Mary Chandler's gone off the deep edge and now we're talking damage control. We don't have a protocol in place for this, so it's going to take some time to put things in place, decide what the best move would be."

"There's not enough time," Bran replied. "You'll meet and talk and talk and by God do nothing and she'll end up—" The words caught in his throat.

He was imagining Angie under McCallister's claws, screaming as he ripped her face to shreds.

To start.

"Probably not. Chandler thought this out, she knew it'd take too long for us to get the higher-ups involved." Jess glared at him. "Whatever you're going to do, get to doing it and let me handle it from this end."

"Fuck." Bran shook his head. "I'll be in the car."

The screen door slammed shut, bouncing twice before coming to a full stop.

"She means a lot to him." Jess eyed me. "How does she fit into his life?"

"Whatever she was, that's in the past. Bran said it was a one-way love affair. She adored him and he did the right thing and stayed focused on his article."

"Doesn't mean it was all one-sided. The way he reacted to that photo tells me it's not."

My stomach twisted into knots. "He's upset because when he went back to save the kids, pull them off the street, they were all gone. Including Angie."

"Now he's got another chance to save her. I get that," Jess said. "As long as she knows he's yours and backs off when it's time."

"He knows. She knows. And I know."

"Yes, yes, you do. She means a lot to him. But don't forget he's wearing your marks on his skin."

I paused, one hand on the screen door. "He's wearing her marks as well—but they're on the inside."

Bran was standing by the side of my Jeep when I walked out, his arms crossed in front of him and scowling.

I wasn't the reason.

Eddie Longstrand stood a few feet away, watching Bran watch him. The parking lot was near-empty. There were three cars left—my Jeep, Jess's Taurus and a beat-up pickup truck I assumed belonged to my friendly neighborhood enforcer.

I stood on the porch and lifted my face toward the sun. The cool breeze brought me the news there was a new litter of barn cats. Out in the forest along the edge of the farm I caught the scent of a deer, springing away from any potential hunters.

I walked up to Eddie. "What are you doing here?"

"My job." He looked over my shoulder out into the forest. "Jake told me to help you."

"What?"

He rolled his shoulders back, the thick, toned muscles rippling under his shirt. "Jake told me to help you out. He don't like the way the Chandlers are acting and don't want to get caught up in the trouble coming down."

It took me a few seconds to decipher the silence between the words. Jake knew there'd be hell to pay at the end of all of this and didn't want his family pulled down when it hit the fan.

The chance to tweak the Chandlers' tail was a bonus.

"You going to behave yourself?" I asked.

Bran coughed, saying a curse in the middle of it.

Eddie ignored it. "I'm not a thug like McCallister." He turned his head to one side and spat on the gravel. "Hitting you was bad enough, but this, this kidnapping a human? He went too far. She went too far."

"You know the Chandlers better than I do. What's Mary thinking?" I leaned back on the hood of my car. The warm sun on my skin was wonderful and I sucked the sensation up, trying to store it away for what I knew was going to be a rough few hours. "She must have known this was going to start trouble, big trouble."

Eddie chuckled. "That she does. But she's worried that if she lets her youngest go off and ignore her legacy that others are going to follow, leave her dream. Her older son, her family associates who have already spent time and money trying to bring Middleston down." He spread his hands. "How can you have a feud if no one wants to feud?" A smile twitched at his lips. "And I'd be out of a part-time job."

"Works for me," Bran said. "If you weren't working for this jackhole we wouldn't be here."

I'd forgotten how fast Felis could move. Especially when pissed.

I blinked and Bran was flat against the driver's door, Eddie's forearm pressing on his windpipe.

Bran scrabbled to get a hold on him, trying to dig his fingers under the iron bar threatening to cut his air off.

"Do not disrespect Jake Middleston," Eddie said in a low rumbling voice. "You can get away with a lot 'cause of who you are and who you're with but you're not going to get away with that."

I slowly peeled myself off the hood, trying to look concerned but not threatening. He wouldn't hurt Bran and Bran knew it.

Didn't make the situation less ugly.

Bran's breathing was high and wheezy but he wasn't panicking. He glared at Eddie, the defiance in his brown eyes not waning.

"What sort of dirty work have you done for your boss? Covered up for a crime?" He coughed and drew a shallow breath. "Beaten on any women lately like your buddy Nathan? You get your rocks off pounding on girls?"

Eddie's arm shifted a fraction, allowing Bran more air. "I'm not like McCallister. I'm not a thug. I don't know what you think an enforcer is but we're not all punks."

"Could have fooled me," Bran rasped. "If it looks like a duck—"

Eddie pulled his arm away, letting Bran slide free. He didn't move away but kept deep inside Bran's personal space, close enough to renew the attack.

I tried to stay calm despite my pulse shooting into triple digits. This was not what I needed right now.

Eddie tipped his head toward the road and the departing Felis. “You have no idea what I do.” He gave me a sideways glance. “I coach a curling team every year made up of kids without fathers. I do a lot of work you’ll never see if you’re lucky.” He snorted. “If I were like McCallister I wouldn’t be here to help. I’d be tucking away a few beers at the bar and wondering who to take home tonight.” He locked eyes with Bran. “I don’t expect you to trust me without question but I do expect you to respect me as a family member.”

Bran didn’t say anything for a long, agonizing minute. He didn’t look away but kept the stare going, neither of them blinking first.

The lump in my throat grew, demanding attention. I couldn’t interfere with this but I needed to cough badly.

Bran dropped his gaze to the ground. “I apologize.” He stuck out his hand. “I was wrong in my comments about you and the Middleston family.”

Eddie studied Bran’s face for a second before grabbing the hand in a tight bone-crushing grip. Both men grimaced as they squeezed harder, each trying to top the other.

Men. Felis or not, they drove me nuts.

I cleared my throat with an almost-painful cough.

“Okay, break it up before I get seriously turned on.” The two men turned toward me, both red-faced. “Eddie, you know I’m going to have to go to where Evan and Lisa are. No disrespect intended, but what’s to stop you from grabbing Lisa and making a break for it?"

Eddie grinned, confirming my concerns. "You are a smart one."

"Not just a pretty face." I pointed at the farmhouse. "But I'm not going to turn down help when I can get it. You know the Chandlers. You've been brawling with them for years. Where would they take Angie?"

Eddie leaned against the Jeep. "Won't be their main farm. Be too risky to have her near all the kits. Mary might be angry but she's not stupid, she's not going to let this human find out 'bout the family." He tapped his chin. "They won't take her farther north, make it harder for them to bring her back. She's got to be somewhere within maybe fifty miles." His eyes narrowed as he did the mental math. "Still leaves a lot of options but not as many as before."

"Right. I need you to track down where she is. You know their farms, their businesses, where they could be stashing her."

Eddie chuckled. "Good idea. And it keeps me out of the way, right?"

"Yes. Nothing personal." I didn't have time to mince words. "I've got your phone number. Here's mine." I rattled off the digits. "Call me when you have their location. Don't move in until I arrive." I paused, choosing my next words carefully. "I'm assuming you'll be reporting back to Jake. Please don't call in any more *friends* until we get this sorted out."

Eddie nodded. The last thing we needed was a swarm of Middleston enforcers charging to Angie's rescue under the premise of "helping out." That was a fast way of moving the family feud up from the occasional brawl to all-out Felis war.

"I'll call." Eddie headed for his pickup truck, one of the few vehicles left in the lot.

Bran rubbed his throat. "Strong bastard."

"Yep." I opened the driver's door. "Give me the keys."

"What's the plan?" Bran asked as we pulled out of the parking lot, tires spewing gravel everywhere.

"No idea." I stomped on the gas pedal, taking some of my anger out on the car. "No fucking idea. Yet."

We pulled onto the highway just before rush hour—which was to say that the roads were three-quarters clogged with people racing to get back to Toronto instead of up to Northern Ontario. Bran had a death grip on the dashboard as I wove between tractor-trailers, tucking the Jeep into spaces technically not recommended for cars my size.

"So," he gasped as I narrowly swerved around a chemical tanker, "where are the kids?"

I put a finger to my lips and pointed at my feet. He caught on quickly enough.

I wouldn't have passed up the chance to put a bug in my car as it sat outside, unguarded.

I wouldn't put it past the Chandlers and McCallister to do the same. I'd have to wait until I got home to make a full sweep but I couldn't risk it.

"Let's get home first." I feigned a yawn. "I'll have to

make some phone calls and see how the bus schedule is. I don't remember when the next run is from Buffalo."

"Drop Trace a call." Bran ignored my glare. The last thing I needed was for the Chandlers or Middlestons to start brawling with the Penscotta Pride.

I aimed the Jeep between two large SUVs, brushing the paint on both bumpers and enjoying Bran's discomfort.

He'd earned it. Besides, it kept him from worrying about Angie.

That made one of us.

TWELVE

We made it back to Toronto just before six o'clock, my internal clock screwed five ways to Sunday thanks to all the disorientation I'd experienced in the last twenty-four hours. My throat was sore from making small talk about every sports team Toronto had and a few we thought should be added. I slipped the Jeep into the tiny parking lot at the back of the house and we headed inside.

Bran tugged at my sleeve as I fumbled with the lock.

"Think they've got bugs in here too?" he whispered.

"I doubt it. Still—" I locked the door behind us and went to my desk, ignoring Jazz's demanding trill.

Bran picked her up and stroked her white fur, muttering sweet nothings.

I opened the bottom drawer and pushed aside a stack of newspaper clippings and a very old package of Scotch mints.

It'd been an expensive purchase for a very nervous client who demanded his house be swept weekly while he dealt with a very angry ex-wife-to-be. His paranoia wasn't totally unfounded as I found not only a hidden camera but also two microphones, clumsily placed by the ex during one of her visits. The divorce had gone much smoother when I explained the illegality of what she'd attempted and her lawyer had given in to most of my client's demands to avoid getting the police involved.

I put the small electronic box on the desktop and turned it on. The answering *beeps* and *boops* told me all I needed to know.

"We're good." I let out a sigh of relief. The last thing I needed right now was to strip the house down looking for electronic bugs. The place was so old I'd be better off just setting it afire and claiming the insurance.

Bran walked into the kitchen, the cat still in his arms. The refrigerator door opened and closed with the familiar sound of cat food being dumped into a bowl. He re-appeared with two cans of soda.

He placed one on my desk before opening the second and drinking half of it in three gulps.

The man had excellent breath control. My heart gave a little flutter before calming down and remembering the current crisis.

"Okay. What's the plan?" he asked again.

"The kids are with a homeless man called Red. He's family." I popped the punch-tab on the can. "Down in a squat under the Gardiner Expressway."

Bran flopped down on the sofa. "A homeless Felis?"

"I got lucky. So did they." I sipped the carbonated drink. "I'm going to ask Evan to go home. I'll explain the situation to them."

"And if he says no?" Bran finished his drink. "You can't leave Angie out in the cold like this."

"I wasn't planning to." There was a bit more bite in my words than I'd planned.

Bran shook his head as he crushed the can in one hand. "He's a kid. He doesn't know what he wants to do. You can't leave this up to him, it's a lot bigger than just running away with his current love du jour. There's a woman's life at stake."

"He's going to be a man in a few days. He's a man now." I sloshed the drink around. "He's got to make adult decisions and this is the first one."

"And if Evan says no and decides to run? Are you going to stop him?"

"I don't know if I can." I took another sip. "He's an adult, not some little kid I can tuck under my arm and run with. I'm hoping he'll be honorable enough to realize he has to deal with this now. There's no putting it off any longer thanks to McCallister grabbing Angie."

"Tell me the truth. Will they kill her?" The sharpness in his voice cut deep. "If you don't get Evan to go home and we don't or can't drag his ass back—will they kill her?"

"No." I paused. "I think not."

I couldn't lie. Not to him, not even on this subject.

He shifted on the couch. "What do you mean, 'think not'? I thought it was illegal for a Felis to kill a human. We've seen that before."

I swallowed. This wasn't going to be pretty. "It's not illegal but severely frowned on. You remember Shaw."

The anger in his eyes ebbed a bit as he recalled Jess killing his half-brother's kidnapper.

"She had to answer to the Grand Council for that. It's not taken lightly. But it does happen." I didn't bring up our visit to Penscotta and the hard fact that the Pride down there had considered hiding Mike Hancock's death if I'd discovered he was poking his nose in family business.

If Angie died the family would close ranks and she'd disappear, another statistic in the thick file of missing people.

I knew Bran knew this.

I knew he didn't want to think about it.

"Look, I get that she means a lot to you." I got up from behind my desk and walked toward him. "But I'm not going to lie to you and say it's all going to be okay. I can't guarantee that. We're dealing with a mother who wants her son back and is willing to break all the rules to get him. I don't know how to handle that."

"I get that, I really do. I don't know why I'm not calling the cops right now and calling in the damned SWAT team to get her back." He rubbed his face with his hands, turning away from me. "I just don't know what to do. Or what not to do."

I pressed my hand on his back, his body heat searing my skin. "I'm sorry. All I can tell you is that I'll do my best to save her."

"That's supposed to be my job," he murmured through his fingers. "I'm supposed to be saving her. I fucked it up before—I'm supposed to be saving her."

I didn't know what to say.

I looked around the living room, imagining Nathan McCallister sitting not far from where Bran was, Eddie opposite him. The two enforcers invading our homes, our lives.

The options were narrowing and I wasn't sure if my

idealism, my belief in true love was going to carry us out of the storm this time.

Jazz curled around Bran's leg, her short stuttering strides winding her between his feet. He looked down and chuckled.

"Silly cat. Got more common sense than all of us I expect."

"At least she doesn't spill salsa on the bedspread."

"True. She barfs up hairballs instead." He stroked the white cat's back before looking up at me, the pain on his face ripping my heart open. "I can't lose her, Rebecca. I can't lose her again."

The words caught in my throat, keeping me from answering for a minute. "I won't let you." I reached out for him. "Let's go bring her back."

We went down to King Street to grab a cab. I wasn't sure if anyone was still following us, electronically or otherwise, but it never hurt to be careful.

We switched cabs twice until I felt comfortable with the third, instructing the cab driver to drop us off a few blocks from the camp.

It took me two passes to find the right opening in the fence, the bent and cut wire ready to catch and rip flesh if we entered the wrong way.

"Whew." Bran wrinkled his nose as he maneuvered his way in. "What a dump."

I sidestepped a mysterious puddle of liquid, trying not to inhale. "Tell me about it." I didn't want to insult Red by mentioning it before but the variety of smells coming from his fellow residents ran from nice and fresh soapy to rank and disgusting. Between the body odors and items in different stages of decay my stomach was doing flip-flops as we made our way toward Red's camp.

I wasn't sure how Red managed.

I'd be curious as to how the kids did.

No one gave us a second look, either due to having seen me before and assessing me as mostly harmless or not wanting to get in our way.

Lisa was the first to see me, leaping up from the piece of wood she'd been using as a seat by the small campfire. She rubbed her arms despite it being a warm evening.

"You're back. What's happening? Can we leave now?" The words tumbled out one after the other.

I didn't need to be Felis to know she was scared. Whatever love she had for Evan had been sorely tested over the past twenty-four hours. But she'd held on despite the changing and dangerous circumstances.

This had to be more than an infatuation.

Red appeared out from under the makeshift tarp tent. "Suz!" He tossed something back inside the tent and charged at me, letting out a rolling gurgle.

He grabbed me and swung me around like a sack of potatoes. On one of the passes I spotted Bran, caught between scowling and staring.

Finally my feet hit the ground again and I extracted myself with a laugh. "Thanks for the hearty welcome but I haven't been away that long."

Red shrugged. "Pretty girl like you should get

hugged every chance you get." He looked at Bran, squinting as he sized him up. "You her mate, then?"

Bran looked at him.

"Good." Red poked Bran in the arm, hard. "She deserves a strong man. Strong woman needs a strong man to stay balanced. Like daily fiber." He nodded toward Lisa. "Like that one. She's got herself a keeper as well."

Lisa didn't say anything but her cheeks went pink.

"Where's Evan?" I asked.

"He's over there putting a new wooden skeleton together for Ed. His tent fell down last storm and he hasn't gotten the knack yet of making somethin' that stays up." He motioned with me to follow him. "Young man's good with tools. That'll stand him for a lifetime if he stays in practice."

"'Suz'?" Bran whispered as we followed, Lisa in tow.

"It's a long story. Roll with it."

We made our way under a stack of rotting wooden crates into a larger part of the camp where Evan stood with an older man, wrestling with some misshapen boards. He swung the hammer and bashed in the nails one by one.

"He's got a knack for building," Red said. He lifted a hand. "Ed—gotta take your handyman away for a bit."

The white-haired man with a noticeable hump on his right shoulder patted Evan on the arm. "Thanks. I'll take it from here."

"Okay." Evan handed the hammer over. "Just be careful. Don't put the nail in too close to the edge of the wood or it'll split." He wiped the sweat from his forehead with the back of his hand. "What's happening?"

"We need to talk." I turned to Red. "Family business. You too."

Red said nothing and led us back to his camp.

Lisa went to her previous spot by the wooden stool and shuffled her feet back and forth over the well-trodden ground. "Are we going home?"

From the tone in her voice it was obvious she wasn't thrilled with the street life. I hadn't meant to make her miserable but I wanted her to realize there was more to living free than snuggling in trees at night.

"Maybe." I sat down and motioned for them all to do the same. Bran settled in beside me on the piece of driftwood, so close I might as well have been in his lap.

Evan crouched next to Lisa and put his arm across her shoulders. He pulled her close to whisper something in her ear. She whimpered and tucked her face into his neck for a second before sitting up again.

"We have a situation." I studied Evan's face. If he bolted or ran I'd have little chance of catching him.

Red and Bran, on the other hand, just might.

I spoke slowly and carefully, watching both Evan's and Lisa's expressions. "I met with both your families to plead for peace and to allow you to return and continue your relationship."

"Let me guess. My dad freaked," Lisa said with a crooked smile. "He's not very open to change." She covered her mouth and giggled. "Took him forever to decide on a new car color when the old truck blew up."

Evan didn't laugh. He watched me with a seasoned hunter's stare. "My mother did something, didn't she?"

"I tried to negotiate with her and she took action. Dangerous action." I licked my lips, not sure how to explain Mary Chandler's thinking to her son.

"How dangerous?" Red interrupted. "A mother, she's gonna go to the wall for her kit." He looked sideways at Evan. "Don't be holding it against her. It's a natural thing."

Evan nodded. "I understand." His attention returned to me. "What did she do?"

"She's kidnapped a friend of ours. A human friend."

Red sucked in his breath. "That's not right." He looked at Bran. "We ain't supposed to get too involved in human lives."

"I've noticed," Bran answered dryly.

"Your mother is demanding I either bring you back or tell her where you are so she can send someone to come get you." The still-fresh scar on my left arm throbbed. "I'm assuming you know Nathan McCallister."

Evan scowled. "He's a punk. Ever since my dad died he's been strutting around the farm playing cock of the walk, trying to get my mom's attention. She's not stupid enough to fall for that crap but he keeps chasing her tail hoping for a chance to make good."

"Well he's got it now," Bran said. "Either he came up with the idea of kidnapping Angie on his own or she put him up to it. No matter who thought of it he's grabbed her and taken her hostage."

"Angie? You mean the woman who runs the drop

in center? The one that drove us here?" Lisa dug her nails into Evan's arm. "Her?"

Evan's jaw tensed. "That's not right. Angie's got a good street rep. She doesn't deserve this. Not because of us."

"True," I agreed. "You know what sort of danger she's in when it comes to the family." I was trying to be delicate.

"They could kill her," Lisa whispered. Her nails twisted farther in Evan's skin.

So much for delicate.

Evan reached over and carefully pulled her hand free. The inflamed crescents on his tanned skin began to fade as he lifted her hand to his mouth and kissed it in a silent soothing motion.

"We'll make it right. Promise."

I cleared my throat, bringing their attention back. "I wanted to talk to you, give you the choice of what to do." I felt Bran's body tense beside me. "I could have told them where you are and let you deal with McCallister on your own but part of being an adult is making your own decisions and taking responsibility for them." I pointed at myself. "I wouldn't want someone to do that to me so I'm not going to do it to you. You've got the choice here."

"What if we run?" Lisa asked. "We can get out of here before you can get to McCallister, we can leave the city." She squeezed Evan's hand. "It's one option."

I rubbed my palms on my knees, trying to quell the sudden itching. "They'll track you down. You could get lucky and escape right now but then you'd have to always hide, stay underground. Never contact another Pride, never come in contact with any other Felis." I paused, letting my words sink in. "It won't be easy."

"And what happens to Angie?" Lisa whispered. "What happens to her if we run?"

I shook my head. "I don't honestly know. The Board's getting involved along with the Grand Council but that'll take time and I don't think it's on our side. They might just dump her at the side of the road and tell her to forget it ever happened."

"Or beat her," Bran interrupted. "As payment for helping you escape. Or claw her up, maim or mutilate her." His hand ran over my back. "I don't know what your mother is capable of. You do."

Evan chewed on his lower lip. "I knew she'd be pissed but this is beyond anything I thought." He looked at me. "Did you see Dale?"

"If Dale's your older brother, yes." I resisted the urge to gloat. "Tried to challenge me to get the information on where you were."

"And?" Lisa prompted.

"He's probably still walking bow-legged," Bran answered. "His nose might heal straight, if he's careful." He jabbed his thumb at me. "That's why I let her lead."

Lisa coughed back a laugh.

Evan grinned. "Dale's such an ass. He talks smack but never does well in challenges." He held up one arm and flexed. "I've beaten him enough times that he should know better."

"He picked the wrong woman this time," I said.

"But that's neither here or there right now." I leaned in. "What do you want to do?"

"We can't let an innocent suffer for our decision." Evan looked at Red. "What do you think?"

The older Felis scratched his chin. "Give me a minute."

We all watched the small campfire, the scraps of wood turning dark and falling away as the flames devoured them.

Red slapped his hands together. "Okay, I'm ready."

We waited.

I felt Bran chuckle beside me, the stifled emotion shaking his body.

"I think you're too pretty to be here." Red addressed Lisa. "You don't like being here much, do you?"

Lisa shook her head, her face flushed.

"This isn't a soft life. You walk this path you'll eat out of Dumpsters and wear rags, worry 'bout freezing overnight and roasting during the day." Red tugged at his own well-worn jacket. "Charities are good but they can't do everything."

"We can get work," Lisa said in a small voice.

"You finished high school?" He continued, seeing her shake her head. "You can't get a job flipping fries without that much. What you going to do to make money?"

"Evan plays guitar. I figured I'd get a sketchbook and do caricatures, get money that way."

"No one's going to come near you if you stink." Red sniffed the air. "So you gotta be clean and look good.

And that's all fine when you're young and healthy—what about when you're my age?"

Lisa's blank pale face said it all.

"I'm not going to throw you out of here," Red said. "But at some point you're going to be alone." He pointed at Evan. "One day he ain't going to be here, whether by choice or by the good Lord calling him home." A weariness came over his face, the deep crow's feet around his eyes darkening even more. "You don't know how much you appreciate family until you ain't got it." He scratched his chin, short stubby nails tearing through the salt-and-pepper beard. "I'm old enough to remember that."

Lisa's grip tightened on Evan.

Evan touched her cheek with one finger, turning her toward him. "I'm not going anywhere for a long, long time. But I can't let Angie suffer because of this damned feud. This crap has to stop and stop now. We've never dragged humans into this before. She doesn't deserve this."

"You can't go back." Lisa grabbed his arm again. "They'll kill you. They'll kill me." Her voice rose, verging on hysteria.

"No they won't," I said, as gently as I could. "They're not out for revenge. Felis don't kill Felis."

"They killed my grandmother," Lisa said quietly.

I resisted the urge to reach over and slap her. This wasn't helping the situation.

"They they they," Red repeated in a loud voice, startling all of us. "Your grandmother was your grandmother. She chose her own road." He leaned in, the light from the campfire giving him an eerie appearance. "What if she hadn't challenged Laura Chandler for that spot on the Board? What if she had just given up, let her have the position and gone home?"

Lisa sniffled. "She would have lived."

"And been miserable for the rest of her days wondering if she had the stuff in her to make good." Red scowled. "Don't go thinking you know what she felt, what she wanted. People do things and you never know what's behind it until you wear their skin, walk their tracks."

He turned and looked at Evan. "And your grandma Laura. She never walked good again. Lots of pain. You think she would have traded it all to have taken that day back, have Maureen alive again?"

"Maybe," Evan answered. He looked into the flames for a minute. "I don't know. I don't know if she would have." He gave Lisa a sideways glance. "We don't know. We can't know."

"Exactly. You don't. Neither do your mothers or your fathers, they don't know what really happened there in that field." He reached out and tapped Evan on the nose. "You gotta be yourself. Not Chandler, not Middleston. Be Felis. Be yourself."

Red sat back with a wide grin, obviously pleased with himself.

Evan let out a huff and stared at the ground.

Lisa said nothing, keeping her death grip on Evan's arm.

Bran reached for my hand and squeezed it.

The firewood crackled and popped, sending sparks into the air.

"What would you do?" This was from Evan to Bran.

Bran shifted on the log, not letting me go. "Why ask me?"

"I'm doing a survey," Evan said. The dry tone had me smiling despite the circumstances.

"Do you love her?" Bran asked.

Evan looked at Lisa and smiled. "Yes."

"Then you fight for her." Bran let go of my hand and pulled up his T-shirt. Carson's claw marks were faded but still visible.

I winced. I'd seen them numerous times since Penscotta and every time it scared me, remembering how close I'd come to losing him.

"I got these fighting for her," he said with a nod in my direction. "I almost died making sure she was safe and out of danger." Bran locked eyes with the young man. "How far would you go for your woman?"

"Far enough," Evan replied.

"No." Bran shook his head. "You have to go farther. Go where you're afraid to go, go the distance. Go all the way, not for you but for her."

We sat quietly for a minute.

Evan stood up.

We all followed, including Lisa, who released his arm.

"I'm going back." Evan turned to Red. "Will you come along and stand as my second?"

I almost fell backwards over the log in shock at his phrasing. Bran grabbed my arm and steadied me as

Red rubbed his chin again, his thick fingers brushing over the thin beard.

"Been a while since I was with family." He looked at Lisa. "If you'll have me along for this I'd be honored."

Lisa nodded, giving him a weak but honest smile.

Evan looked at me. "Now we go home."

The first cab sped by us without slowing down, spooked by Red's appearance. The Felis had taken a few minutes to clean himself up, using a bottle of water to wash his face and a dingy yellowing towel to dry. His salt-and-pepper beard became whiter, accentuating his dark shaggy hair. He pulled on a clean red T-shirt and smiled when we asked if he needed to bring anything along. He still looked pretty ragged, which is why the first driver didn't give us a chance.

The second took his foot off the gas long enough to study our little group and slowed to a stop, primarily due to Bran stepping out in front of the vehicle and waving a twenty-dollar bill.

Red jammed himself in the back with the two kids while Bran and I crushed ourselves into the front seat. Something was jabbing me in the ass but I said nothing, afraid of what I'd find if I started digging under me.

As we crept toward Parkdale, Bran leaned in. "So what's this 'second' business all about?"

I glanced behind me at the trio. Lisa sat on Evan's lap and Red was chortling at some joke Evan must have just told.

"A second is a ceremonial position used when you issue a challenge, much like in dueling."

Bran frowned. “Never heard you mention it. Never seen it, obviously.”

“Never seen it myself.” I shifted from side to side with no relief. “It was part of our history class. I’d guess it evolved at the same time as formal dueling, the idea of having a second.”

“Ah.”

“It dropped out of favor decades ago because there’s usually plenty of people around for a challenge. The goal is to have someone stand by to take care of you or your affairs if things go wrong, same as if you were using pistols in a duel.” I frowned. “There were seconds at the fight with Middleston and Chandler out in the field. Each supported their faction’s story, as if that’s a big surprise. So it’s still used but I have no idea how often.”

He grunted. “So how does Red fit in here?”

“I think he wants Red to take care of Lisa, or in other words if something goes badly with his challenge, to take her away.”

“I don’t know if he can take Jake Middleston,” Bran said.

I gasped as we hit a particularly nasty bump. “I’m not sure if he’s going to get to try. Jake’ll probably get Eddie to fight for him if it comes down to a challenge.” I wrinkled my nose. “I’d put money on it.”

“I don’t know if he can take Eddie,” Bran said as the cab turned down our street. “He’s a big fellow. Not to mention he’s sort of on our side helping out, right?”

“Can’t think about that right now.” I shook my head. “It’s been a long time since I worried about this sort of stuff. If Evan beats Middleston or his proxy that doesn't mean anything if his mother keeps Angie as a hostage. She wants him to come home, period. This business with Lisa is secondary to her."

"Not to him." Bran jabbed a thumb at the backseat.

My phone vibrated against my hip. Bran chuckled as I maneuvered my hand between us to extract the phone.

"A little more to the left," he murmured.

I answered him with a light elbow to the ribs. "Oh, sorry."

He sighed as I looked at the small screen. "Tease."

"It's Eddie." I put the phone up to my ear. "Yes?"

"She's being held at the Stepford farm. The old man kicked off a few months ago and it's been used for storage while up for sale by the surviving daughter."

I racked my memory trying to pull the name. "Who are they?"

Eddie chuckled. "You wouldn't know them. Family business is running a shuttle down to the airport, makes good money. Stepford's daughter went to school with Mary Chandler and let her use the barn, probably without asking too many questions."

"Of course. How far is it from the Pride's farm?"

The cab came to a stop as he rattled off instructions.

I slid out with a new set of aches and pains. "Text them to me, Eddie. I'm not sure I got all that."

"On the way. What do you want me to do?"

"Keep an eye on them until we get there. Don't get caught. I figure you know how to lie low."

He laughed. "That I can do. How long?"

“Within two hours, tops. I’ll call if we get caught up in anything. Just don’t tip your hand.”

“Roger that. Instructions on the way.” The phone went silent.

I watched the words scroll across my tiny screen as the rest of my group poured out of the taxi and onto the sidewalk.

Bran paid the driver, who made a show of cracking the wrapping on a new hanging air freshener and hanging it on the rearview mirror.

I ignored him and led the pack around to the back of my house and to the Jeep. It was another tight squeeze but we managed, Red continuing to stay in the back with the two young people and Bran riding beside me.

THIRTEEN

I flipped the headlights on and maneuvered down to Lakeshore before turning north on the 400 highway.

Evan was silent as we drove out of Toronto, the tension in his face evident. Lisa kept whispering to him and squeezing his hand. I didn't hear what she was saying but it had little effect on him as he stared out the window.

I figured he was mentally running through his upcoming challenge to Middleston. The old Felis wasn't going to be an easy fight and if he handed the job over to Eddie it'd be even tougher. It'd take all the kid's tricks to win and claim Lisa for his own.

I didn't even want to think about his mother. She'd get her boy back all right, just in time to issue a challenge to Middleston—something usually only a family head did. It wasn't against the rules, just highly unorthodox.

Seemed to be the trend these days.

I ran through the probable scenario in my mind.

Arrive, trade Evan for Angie and get her out of there. After the happy family reunion Evan waits for Jake Middleston and challenges him for Lisa's hand.

He wins, Lisa goes to the Chandlers. He loses—

I gave myself a shake, banishing the bloody images

in my mind's eye. If Mary Chandler thought her son was losing she could take McCallister off his leash and set him loose on the Middleston group, start a full-fledged brawl right there.

I just hoped it wouldn't come to that. The last thing I needed was to be in the middle of a Felis riot with my inability to Change leaving me at my most vulnerable. I wouldn't put it past McCallister or his friends to take some cheap shots at me in the heat of battle, even if they would have to answer to Jess later.

Red wouldn't stop babbling to Bran about the trees, the Jeep, the other cars, anything and everything we drove by. He kept away from family topics and didn't ask about Bran's connection to me and to the Pride.

I was grateful for that much. I really didn't want to get into a major discussion as to how Bran fit into my life and how he'd won the respect of two Prides along with my love and devotion.

Mostly because it was too full of awesome.

The highway ran into a smaller road and into a third one, wide enough for one car at a time. There might have been a faster way if I'd pulled out a map but I didn't want to risk getting lost.

The sun had set by the time we pulled into the long winding driveway, the ancient metal mailbox with the mismatched lettering of StePForD signaling we were in the right place.

Eddie's brown pickup sat on the side of the dirt road, not far beyond the mailbox. We pulled up beside it and Bran rolled down his window.

Eddie glared at Lisa. She let out a squeak and curled up into Evan's shoulder.

Red moved up, putting himself between the enforcer and his prey. "Hey." He waved from the backseat. "I'm Red."

Eddie's facial expression was priceless, something between being annoyed, curious and what I'd expect upon tripping over roadkill.

I brought Eddie's attention back to myself by snapping my fingers. "Time for small talk later. Details now. Where are they? How many? And where is Angie being kept?"

"She's in the old barn behind the house with McCallister and the Stepford brothers watching her. Mom Chandler's in the farmhouse with her boy and a few more friends. No more than two or three, grand total of ten at the max." He smiled. "Don't know if they scented me, don't care if they did. I figured their attention was more on the woman than on sniffing out trouble." He eyed me. "What's your plan and how do I fit into it?"

I rested my forearms on the steering wheel. "I'm not sure. Do they know we're here yet?"

Eddie gave me a noncommittal shrug. "I've been quiet enough. But I don't doubt that they've got lookouts."

I tilted my head and eyed Evan. "What do you want to do?"

Evan's face in my rearview mirror was that of a strong, mature Felis. "I'm tired of hiding. This is supposed to be my family, my people." His eyes met mine. "Please call my mother and tell her we're coming up the driveway to get Angie. Straight up, straight in and we'll get this over with."

I couldn't fault his approach. By initiating the meeting we'd have less chance of running into a mob scene if Chandler felt like calling in more family and friends.

It wasn't a perfect situation but I didn't think we could make it much better.

"Can't we just sneak in and take her?" Lisa said in a tiny voice.

Red shook his head. "Not a chance." There was a sudden shift in his voice, a strong seasoned warrior's tone taking over. "This isn't something you settle in the darkness. It's got to be up front and done in the light." He looked at Evan. "Something for men to do."

I resisted the urge to roll my eyes at the chauvinistic comment.

Instead I dialed Mary Chandler's number.

She answered on the first ring.

"I have Evan with me." I didn't feel obliged to mention Lisa, Red, Bran or Eddie. "Where do you want to meet?"

"Come up the road. We're waiting for you. Go to the barn, that's where we're keeping your friend." The phone went dead.

I looked at Evan again. "Are you ready for this?"

He looked over Bran's shoulder at Eddie. "Please call Mr. Middleston and tell him to come here. We'll be finished with family business by the time he arrives."

Eddie arched an eyebrow in return. He glanced at me.

I didn't say anything.

"This isn't exactly a great place for a talk." Eddie chose his words slowly and carefully. I could see him sizing Evan up, trying to figure out his strengths and weaknesses. You didn't get to be an enforcer by making rash decisions. "This is Chandler territory. Enemy ground."

"It won't be by the time he arrives," Evan replied. "Please ask him to come here. Thank you." He leaned back.

"Okay." I looked over Bran into the pickup truck. "Thanks for the help."

Eddie nodded, still eyeing Evan. "I'm done for now." He looked at Lisa. "Don't think this is over. Your father loves you a whole lot and won't hand you over without a fight."

"I'm not his to hand over," she shot back. "Welcome to the twenty-first century."

"And..." I drew the single syllable out as long as I could, raising my voice to cut them both out. "You can both deal with all that after we take care of this. One crisis at a time, 'kay?"

Eddie narrowed his eyes. "Could drag her out of your car right now."

"Could try." Evan Changed and showed his fangs, the bright teeth a sharp contrast to his black fur. "Won't work." The threatening growl echoed around the inside of the Jeep.

Eddie Changed as well, white stripes showing through his dark furred face. "Bring it, kit." He put one hand on the car door, claws exposed.

I closed my eyes and rested my forehead on the steering wheel, exhausted.

"Shut the fuck up," Bran snarled. I heard him bang on the dashboard.

I looked up to see him glaring at both Felis, switching his attention back and forth between the two men.

Evan and Eddie fell silent, surprised by Bran's interruption.

"There's an innocent woman inside there, a human who's got nothing to do with your goddamn feud and who might die because you can't get your shit together." Bran pointed at Eddie. "If you want to call Middleston and tell him his daughter is here, fine. If you want to bring down a whole damned posse to beat the Chandlers into snail snot, fine. Do whatever you want but you're not doing anything until I get Angie out of there."

Eddie didn't say anything for a minute, his black and white fur covering his facial features. His skin reappeared and he returned to full human form, showing his approval.

Bran's attention turned to Evan. "And you—" He paused, studying the young face. "I know you're pissed at your mother and I can't blame you. I know something about that. But the priority right now has to be saving Angie and keeping your family secret. You want to fight for Lisa and I hear that. But everything has to be done one step at a time and the first step's got to be mine."

The young man nodded. He didn't Change back.

Bran continued. "Now we're going to go in there

and I'm walking out with Angie. I don't care what you do afterward, tear each other to shreds. But I'm taking her home."

I felt a burning at the back of my throat. I swallowed hard, keeping the foul-tasting bile at bay.

Bran grabbed my hand off the steering wheel. "Then I'm coming back to take you to our home."

Tears pricked my eyes, daring me to blink and set them free.

"Okay." I put the car into drive. "Let's get this done."

We rolled away from Eddie's truck, past the farmhouse and up to the hay barn.

I looked in the rearview mirror. Eddie didn't move, his truck sitting on the shoulder in silence.

The small parking lot was nothing more than trampled soil, the spots carved out of good farmland. A variety of cars were already there, empty.

The barn was like a thousand others, the basic architecture unchanged over decades. The large double doors were closed along with the smaller, regularly-sized one.

I got out of the car and sniffed the air. Rabbits, deer, fresh manure, hay. A slight breeze brought me the scent of running water.

Felis. McCallister, Mary Chandler and her older son among others.

Along with one familiar human.

"Here." I tossed Bran the car keys. "You'll need these."

He pocketed them in silence.

Evan and Lisa stepped in front of us, holding hands.

"I'll lead," Evan said. He stood tall, his back ramrod straight and shoulders back, looking much older than when we'd first met. He flexed his fingers, claws fully extended and ready.

We trudged toward the closed door, Evan leading the way. Red was strangely silent, staying close to Lisa as Bran and I brought up the rear.

Evan pulled the door open and walked through.

It took a second for my eyes to adjust to the dim lighting, the dying sunbeams coming in through various cracks and bends in the old structure. It reminded me of the classic showdown from the spy movies where the hostage is tied to a chair and sitting under a spotlight, waiting to be rescued by the gallant hero.

I wasn't far off.

Angie Degas lay in the far corner of the first stall to our right, her hands tied behind her and blindfolded. She whimpered as she squirmed in the loose hay. Her long blond hair was all over the place, tangled in the duct tape covering her mouth. A black rag covered her eyes, tied at the back. Her hands were taped as well, tucked behind her.

"Angie." Bran went to her, ignoring anything and anyone else.

She thrashed around at hearing his voice, kicking out with her running shoes.

I smiled inside, suspecting she'd left her mark on McCallister and his buddies when they snatched her.

"Hold on, hold on." Bran kneeled down and put his hands on her shoulders. She stilled at his touch. "This is going to hurt."

He ripped the duct tape off in one smooth move, wincing at the reddened skin left behind.

He didn't remove her blindfold or untie her hands.

Angie coughed as he brought her up, unsteady on her feet. "Brandon." She leaned against him, breathing heavily. "What's going on? What's happening?" Her bound hands brushed against him. "Take this off."

"In a minute. We're leaving." He put one hand around her waist "Just follow my lead. I'll explain everything later."

Evan said nothing as Bran led Angie past him. His attention was on the shadows farther on.

He saw what I saw. A line of Felis standing there, just waiting. Some Changed, some still in human form.

Bran paused, shifting his weight to accommodate Angie's shuffling gait. "I'll be back for you," he whispered. He shambled off with Angie, shushing the woman's frantic questions.

Nobody moved until the door closed behind us, the slap of wood on wood like a rifle shot.

"Well done." Mary Chandler advanced out of the growing darkness. She wore a dark blue blouse and jeans, long dark hair loose on her shoulders. She spread her hands with a laugh. "You see? We can be reasonable about this."

My lips curled away from my teeth. "You risked exposing the family," I snapped back. "Not a good move."

She shrugged. "No harm done. Your boy gets his newest toy back and I get my son." Her gaze went to Evan. "Welcome home."

He let go of Lisa's hand, nudging her to stand beside Red. The older Felis took the hint and put his arm around the young woman's shoulders, drawing her into his protective space.

Evan moved forward. He stopped in the center of the aisle and crossed his arms. "Mother."

She cocked her head to one side. Behind her other Felis came out of the shadows in a semicircle. McCallister stepped into view, grinning like a hyena.

Chandler's older son moved to stand beside her, still wheezing through his swollen nose.

At least he was able to stand straight.

Evan looked at him. His mouth twitched and I could tell he was holding back a laugh. "Dude, what happened?"

The young man jerked a thumb at me, staying silent.

Evan glanced at me before turning back to his brother. "You're out of shape. Letting her beat your ass like that." He laughed. "But then I've done that enough times, eh?"

I heard the Jeep's engine start up. The tires ground into the dirt before getting traction and shoving the car down the road.

I let out an internal sigh of relief.

At least Angie and Bran were safe. This was no place for a human, even one like Bran.

Mary moved closer and glared over at Red and Lisa. "And I see you brought your little slut as well." She smirked. "Might be something we can use. Call up Daddy and see what he's willing to give us for her return."

Mentally I slapped myself. If Chandler would hold

a human hostage it wasn't a far leap to see her holding on to Lisa and using her as leverage.

This was turning into a whole new level of bad. If Jess was furious about bringing Angie into the fight she'd blow an artery if the Chandlers held Lisa for ransom. The repercussions would shake the Pride to the core and the Grand Council would be howling for blood.

I began to move and found Red's hand on my shoulder.

He looked at me and shook his head. This wasn't my fight, not yet.

I hesitated. His grip increased, fingers digging into my jacket.

I moved back into line with Red and Lisa, earning an approving grunt.

"No," Evan said in a loud, strong voice. "I love her. I'm going to marry her and you can't stop me."

Mary smiled. "You're not eighteen yet. And as your mother I still call the shots here."

"As my mother you have certain rights. And more as the head of the family," Evan conceded.

"Yes, of course."

"Then I challenge you," Evan said, "for the leadership of this family."

My knees went weak.

I'd thought he planned to make up with his mother and call out Middleston for Lisa's hand. If he'd defeated Jake or Eddie it'd have gone a long way for him to assert his adulthood and allow him to claim Lisa for his wife. Mary could object but the men in her circle would see Evan's move as that of an adult male taking charge of his life—something she couldn't deny.

I hadn't even guessed he'd try to take over the family. It was a fast shortcut to getting everything he wanted.

It was also a dangerous one.

Mary put her hands on her hips and laughed. "Silly boy. You're just head-over-heels in love. I've seen it before, sweet things wagging their tails in front of young boys and they fall in line begging for a chance to sniff her feet." Her tone shifted. "Seriously, don't be a fool. We'll work out something so you can see her, maybe in a few months. This isn't the time or place to do something stupid." She gestured toward the other Felis. "Don't make a fuss."

Evan didn't flinch. He looked past her at McCallister. "You heard my challenge?"

The tone wasn't that of a child.

It was that of an adult.

The thin man glanced at Mary then back at Evan. "Yes." The disbelief in his voice was clear. He hadn't seen this either.

Red stepped up behind Evan, leaving Lisa and me behind. His voice boomed out, clear and low.

"Seems to me you've got a decision to make." He pointed at Mary. "Either you accept the challenge and fight your son or you decline it and lose your position. Them's the rules."

Mary looked at Red as if he were roadkill. "And who the fuck are you?"

"His second." He puffed his chest out. "They call me Red."

"This is insane." Mary put her hands on her hips. "You can't challenge me. I'm your mother. Hell, you're not even an adult yet by law." She looked at her elder son. "Dale, go bring your brother to me."

The young man took a hesitant step forward. I could see the confusion in his eyes—obeying his mother or obeying Felis law. It wasn't an easy decision to make.

Red held up his hand, stopping the Chandler son in his tracks. "Unless I recall different it don't make no difference what age someone is if they want to challenge for leadership of the family." He eyed Dale. "You just need to be able to beat the leader."

I sucked in my breath. The idea of a younger kit taking out an older, more seasoned fighter was more an adolescent wish than reality. The family bond was too strong, the devotion of children to their parents part of the Felis legacy.

Most families never worried about this sort of thing anyway—at some point a parent would relinquish leadership anyway, handing it over to the next in line. The position was more ceremonial than practical, useless for most families and nothing more than a tradition. It had no home in present-day Felis business.

Except in a family feud that had lasted generations.

Dale's attention flickered from Evan to Red, from Red to Lisa and me standing behind them. The confusion in his eyes was evident, his mouth hanging slightly open as he wheezed through his broken nose.

Evan made the decision for him by striding forward with short, measured steps.

He strode up to his brother and stared at him.

Evan had maybe ten pounds more on him than Dale. Side by side I would have put my money on Evan—the ease with which I'd taken Dale out told me his older brother spent more time in front of the television set than exercising. He might be the eldest but Mary had done a piss-poor job in training him to deal with challenges both inside the family and out.

The standoff lasted less than a minute. Dale lowered his eyes and stepped to the side, submitting to Evan's authority.

One down.

Mary huffed. She Changed in a flash, her off-white fur obscuring her features. "I can't believe you want to do this. My flesh and blood." She pounded her chest, claws tearing at the thin blue fabric. "You dishonor not only me but your grandmother. The woman the Middlestons killed."

Evan rolled his shoulders back. "I can't change the past. What went on between Laura Chandler and Maureen Middleston was between them. But I can change our family's future." He assumed a general fighting stance, claws at the ready.

The other Felis moved around the two, forming a rough circle in the aisle. I spotted another young woman staying to the side, Mary's sister from the looks of it. Next to her was a young boy, maybe about ten, his eyes saucer-wide as he watched the proceedings. She clutched the kit to her.

The numbers were too small; this couldn't be the entire Chandler clan. I suspected Mary hadn't wanted many of her family to know the problem she was having with Evan. It'd start tongues wagging about her ability to lead. If she'd brought all of her family and supporters the barn would be full.

Small blessings. At least we weren't facing a large group of pissed-off Felis.

But there were just enough to make me nervous, given the way McCallister kept licking his lips and glancing at me. If the situation deteriorated into a full-fledged brawl he'd be charging at me first and hang the consequences.

Evan didn't move, frozen in place. His charcoal fur shone in the dim light as he waited.

Lisa bit down on her lower lip and gripped Red's arm.

Mary charged first.

She lowered her head and screeched as she ran at her son, claws out. It was a high shriek of a roar, tearing at my ears like nails on a blackboard.

There wasn't any room to maneuver so Evan met her head-on—literally. He ducked under her right-handed swing with ease and stepped in to slam his forehead into hers with a sickening thud.

The headbutt sent Mary staggering back out of range, the inch-long gash in her forehead spurting blood. She staggered to one side before straightening up. Her chest rose and fell, the pained panting from the initial rush filling the air.

Evan's head was bleeding as well but not with as much vigor, the trickle running down the side of his nose.

It wasn't a classic attack but a street fighter move, well-executed.

I wondered if he'd learned that from Red.

Mary shook her head and went at him again with both hands outstretched, claws out and swinging. It wasn't a focused attack, it was an angry swipe at someone who had betrayed her.

He easily sidestepped it and drove his left fist into her belly, his own claws pulled back to deliver the non-lethal attack.

I winced. She could have been disemboweled if he'd used his claws. In my mind's eye I remembered Carson charging at Bran, trying to tear his belly open.

Mary fell to her knees, gasping for air. Blood flowed freely down her face, staining her off-white fur and obscuring her vision. It dripped off her chin and splattered on the dirt floor, a few yellowed strands of hay soaking up the crimson spots.

Evan didn't waste any time; he moved behind her and grabbed her long black ponytail with his left hand. He yanked her head back and put his right hand, claws out, to her exposed neck.

I held my breath. Beside me Lisa let out something akin to a squeak.

Red cleared his throat.

Evan's lips drew back and he snarled, a dominant male growl that reverberated around the circle.

Mary sobbed, the tears running down her face to mix with the bloodied fur. She hadn't been ready for this fight and she'd practically conceded the minute she'd offered such feeble attacks.

She couldn't fight her son. She loved him too much.

Now she'd lost both her son and her legacy.

I didn't like her but I felt her pain. Her world had just collapsed around her.

"I surrender." Mary's rasped whisper echoed around the barn.

Evan released her and stepped back. He drew a deep breath and pulled back his claws. The blood had stopped and now there was a red line down the side of his face, the drying scarlet streak mixed in with his black fur.

"I am now the leader of the Chandler family. Does anyone challenge me?" He looked around the circle.

Dale shrank down, almost hiding behind McCallister. It was obvious Dale hadn't the stones, despite being the older brother.

Mary's sister clutched her son even tighter and shook her head. The boy looked up at his mother with a confused look, as if to ask why they were there.

McCallister looked like a lost kicked puppy. He stared at Mary, who was still on her knees, weeping, as if expecting her to tell him what to do.

"You." Evan pointed at McCallister. "Come here, please."

I smiled at the polite request. Given everything the enforcer had done it was a surprising courtesy.

McCallister approached Evan and stood at parade rest, hands tucked behind his back. He didn't look directly at Evan but at Mary where she still sat on the ground.

"You've worked for our family for years. Drawn a check as an enforcer for the Chandlers."

A respectful nod.

"You helped out when my father left. You stepped in and served my mother well for years, helped build the business."

A slower, more hesitant nod.

"I appreciate your time spent working for my mother but you're not what I need right now. I'm terminating your status with the family. You're on your own." Evan turned away from the unemployed enforcer and back to his mother, effectively dismissing the thin Felis.

McCallister stood there for a minute, looking confused. He watched Mary, who was getting to her feet with the slow, weary gait of an old woman.

Lisa moved into my field of vision, unChanged and taking slow steady steps. She approached Mary, who stood beside her son, both of them Changing back to human form.

The gash in Mary's head still oozed blood, albeit at a slower pace. She didn't move to wipe the fresh lines off her face.

Lisa stopped at a respectful distance and waited.

Mary looked up, her eyes red and ringed with tears.

"I know you don't care much for me," Lisa whispered, stretching out her hand. "But I think we can agree that we both love your son. I'd like to be at least friends, if that's possible."

Mary drew a staggered breath. “I think—” She swallowed hard and closed her eyes for a minute.

She lifted her right hand and waved Lisa away, staying silent.

Lisa pulled back. She wrapped her arms around herself and looked at Evan.

Evan dropped his head with a weary sigh. The one sound carried so much emotion in it I almost broke into tears. Exhaustion, sadness, the pain of losing one’s childhood.

McCallister moved in, coming to Mary’s side. He touched her arm and whispered something low and soft. The slimy thug I’d seen up to this point changed in front of my eyes, evolving into a concerned friend and possible lover, his concern for her showing in every move.

Mary opened her eyes, staring at the ground before taking his hand and allowed herself to be led away back into the shadows.

Evan reached out to Lisa. She touched his fingers and moved into his embrace with a loud stuttering sigh. He curled around her, enveloping her with every bit of himself.

I felt like an extra on a movie set.

Red nudged me with his elbow. He beamed like a proud poppa, white teeth glistening in the dim sunlight. “He’s a good kid. Tough. Going to be a good leader.”

I looked at him. “How can you tell?”

He smiled. “’Cause if you love someone that much you’re willing to do anything to keep ’em. And if you know that love you know how others feel, so you dunna want to hurt them too much." He tapped his head. "Good leaders know when to move forward and when to back off."

I rubbed my temples. "You need to write this down. The Felis Art of War."

Red made a smacking sound with his lips. "A writer. Sounds right up my alley. I do like happy endings." He nudged my ribs with a sharp elbow. "Love that Roberts woman. She writes some good stuff."

I nodded, unsure what I was supposed to do. For once I wasn't in the middle of things and either being threatened or beaten up or having Bran threatened or beaten up. In fact I was so off to the sidelines I could probably sneak out and wait for Bran to come get me without being noticed.

My heartbeat increased as I remembered him walking out with Angie. She'd grabbed onto him like a drowning woman and I wasn't sure how he'd be able to get her to let go.

Angie had told me she'd given up on Bran but—

I looked over to where Evan was holding court, talking quietly with his aunt and cousin. His aunt wasn't saying anything, her head bobbing up and down while her son stayed attached at the hip. I suspected Evan was reassuring her nothing bad was going to happen now that he was in charge. For all I knew it might be a blessing for the poor woman and her son, not having to worry about Mary Chandler's obsession with the feud.

I needed a drink.

Evan motioned at Red, waving him over. His aunt was smiling, signaling a good start to Evan's new role.

The older Felis glanced at me, unsure of whether to leave me or not.

I made the decision for him, jabbing my thumb toward the entrance. "I'm going outside for some fresh air. Call me if you need anything." A wave of nausea washed over me, a mixture of exhaustion and a hangover from my recent concussion. I staggered through the door, ignoring the stares coming from the other Felis. I wasn't in the mood for any questions or any opinions as to my status or what I was supposed to be doing there.

FOURTEEN

A cool breeze slapped my face as I rested my back against the wooden exterior wall. I closed my eyes and focused on the scents and smells, hoping to distract myself from the pain.

An old manure pile was nearby, acidic and still pretty potent. Faint gasoline fumes from the cars. A mixture of Felis scents, some unfamiliar and some—

I opened my eyes to see Jess standing a foot away, watching me with her one good eye. Behind her stood a small posse of Felis including Jake Middleston and Eddie Longstrand.

Jake wore jeans and a loose flannel shirt pulled over a black T-shirt. I wasn't sure if that was his usual outfit for facing a challenge or not. He took measured breaths as if preparing for a speech.

Or a fight.

He glanced at Jess, waiting for permission. She nodded and he moved past us, the rest of the Felis trailing behind. Eddie caught my eye long enough to give me a playful wink before following his boss. The three other men didn't look at me and kept their eyes on the ground in deference to Jess's status. They might be Middleston supporters but they were first and foremost Pride members and Jess was still a Board member.

"You okay? You look pale." She stepped to one side as Jake and his men went through the door. "Bran called me and said you were out here getting things done."

I choked back a laugh. "You could say that."

The parking lot was full with vehicles. I'd totally blanked out and missed their approach. At this rate the entire armed forces of any small country could have surrounded us and I wouldn't have noticed.

Not my best hour.

"You look like you're about to throw up." Jess pressed the back of her hand to my forehead, pressing her lips into a tight line. "You're not running a fever."

"Just a headache." I rubbed my eyes with the palms of my hands. "What are you doing here?"

"As I said, Bran called me. Told me where to find you and told me he'd be back. I told him to take care of his own business and I'd drive you home. Don't need him driving while distracted." The impatient tone in her voice made me feel better. Obviously I didn't look all that bad. "It didn't hurt that I got a call from Jake, asking me to come and see what this was all about. Man gets a call to come out here to enemy territory he's going to ask for Board backup, especially given the situation."

I looked around. "You're the backup?"

She glared at me. "Me and the twenty men just out of sight waiting for me to signal them to come in. You think I was born yesterday?" She ran a hand through her near-white long hair. "So what's going on?"

"Evan Chandler just took over leadership of his family." I enjoyed the shocked look on Jess's face. "Yeah, I didn't see that one coming either."

"Damn." There was a sense of wonder and respect in her voice. "How did Mary handle it?"

"Not." I swallowed hard. "She's broken, I think. She thought all she had to do is tell Evan to fall into line and he'd do so. Now he's stood up to her and taken charge not only of his life but also that of his family."

"The kit's become a man now, has he?" Jess said. "And he had Longstrand call up Jake Middleston and invite him here to—"

"I guess we should go in and look." I gestured toward the open door. "Because I'm not making any more guesses on anything."

"What about the hostage?"

I noticed Jess wasn't referring to her by name.

"Bran took her out. She didn't see anything and he'll give her a good cover story."

"Good." Jess moved toward the opening. "One less crisis to deal with."

I followed her in, feeling better for her presence.

My eyes took a second to adjust to the dim lighting again, the fledgling headache giving a sigh of relief at the darkness.

Mary Chandler had moved to the back of her group, supported by McCallister. The gash on her forehead had closed, leaving an ugly scarlet line.

Her sister stood nearby with a distinct air of shunning about her. The other Chandlers and their few supporters were busy muttering to each other but there was no evidence of anyone stepping up to challenge Evan's claim to leadership.

The Middlestons and their enforcers, including Eddie, stood just inside the door. They parted like the Red Sea upon seeing Jess, allowing us to move into the open space between the two parties.

In the neutral zone Evan was talking to Jake Middleston in a low voice, standing almost toe-to-toe with the patriarch. There was a lot of hand waving and gestures, frowns and smiles, but no clenched fists.

Jake took a step back. The wariness I'd seen before had been replaced with a look of relief, almost happiness. Whatever they'd been talking about had been good, at least on Jake's side.

Eddie came to my side. He nodded respectfully to Jess before speaking. "They're about ready."

"For what?" I asked. "He's going to challenge him for Lisa?"

I didn't think Evan could take on another challenge, not so soon after the last. It wasn't that he'd been physically exhausted by defeating his own mother; it was the emotional toll I worried about. It'd be worse if Jake used Eddie. I still wasn't sure Evan could take Eddie and didn't want to see if he could.

Evan had come a long way from hanging in the tree and strumming chords for spare change.

Jake cleared his throat, getting the attention of everyone in the barn. "First, I'd like to thank Jess Hammersmythe for coming here in her capacity as a Board member."

Jess stayed silent.

"Second, well—" He licked his lips. "As you all know this feud has been going on for years, generations. We've spilled plenty of blood over the years on both sides, Middleston and Chandler. A lot of bad blood spilling out into our businesses, deals cut that make us bleed money when we couldn't afford it just to keep a deal from the other side. Until my wife died it was all I thought about." He swallowed hard. "And when she left I looked around and found I had a family who needed me and a daughter who didn't want anything to do with me. Typical teenager."

This won a chuckle from the crowd, including Evan who gave a sheepish nod. Lisa didn't say anything but her flushed face spoke for her.

Jake looked over at Lisa, standing by Red. "When I heard my daughter had taken up with a Chandler, well—I was speechless. Which, for those of you who know me, is hard to accomplish."

Low laughs reverberated off the wooden walls. Lisa kept a firm grip on Red's arm, joining in with her own giggles. She hadn't moved from her position on the Chandler side.

"My first idea was to get her back and lock her up until she was at least thirty."

Another round of soft laughter.

"Then I thought things over, thanks in part to what Rebecca said at the meeting." He gestured at me.

I resisted the urge to hide behind Jess as a dozen curious eyes scanned me.

"I love Lisa, but I've got to let her grow up. Her mother, God bless her, would have wanted her to be happy even if it wasn't what we would have chosen for her." He looked at Lisa, his eyes watering. "But I see she's become a young woman. And she's got a man who's willing to stand up for not only what he believes but for their love. I respect that and I ask you all to do as well."

He tilted his head toward Evan who moved up beside the patriarch.

Evan cleared his throat. "I've asked for the privilege of courting Lisa Middleston." The nervous quaver in his voice had many of the men smiling on both sides. "With the goal of marrying her in the future, of course." He looked at Lisa. "If we're going to do this, we're going to do it right by both our families and our Pride."

Jake grinned, clapping a hand on Evan's shoulder. "Takes a brave man to come up to a father and ask for courting these days." He eyed Lisa. "Considering you both just up and ran away a few days ago against both families' wishes."

Lisa cringed. Evan looked at the packed earth at his feet and shrugged.

"But I'm willing to at least let you two date," he conceded. "I'm afraid of what'd happen if I don't."

Evan straightened up, giving Lisa a smile and a wink.

Jake took his hand off Evan's shoulder. "Jess, I think you should come up here for this."

Jess strolled toward the two men, her near-white hair loose around her shoulders.

She stopped in front of the two.

Evan visibly shrank under her concentrated gaze. Jake withered a bit but not as much, holding his own.

"As for the feud, we've discussed it as well. Family leader to family leader." Jake stuck out his hand toward the young man. "Evan Chandler, I'm willing to accept your agreement offered here to end the disagreement between our families. All's forgiven and done, says I as the head of the Middlestons."

Jess's eyes went wide. She hadn't seen this coming.

Neither had I.

Evan took Jake's hand. "As the head of the Chandler family I am pleased to put an end to this fight." He looked around the circle. "Too much blood's been split over this—Chandler, Middleston and those closest to us. Now humans have become entangled in this and it cannot continue. It would endanger the family."

Jess nodded. As soon as Mary Chandler kidnapped Angie the feud moved to a whole new level of concern.

Evan looked at Jake. "I say the feud is over." A mischievous look came into his eyes, a young man's playfulness. "Now we can talk about the wedding."

Jake chuckled as he shook Evan's hand. "Now we can talk about you dating. Especially when it comes to curfews." He wagged a finger at the young man. "And no sneaking out of windows. I know a bit 'bout that myself so don't be thinking you can put something over on me."

A round of spontaneous applause broke out.

Jess raised her arms and everyone fell silent. The powerful aura she cast was clear—no one wanted to get on the wrong side of this woman.

"I spoke to the Grand Council before coming here. To say they weren't happy would be an understatement." She zeroed in on Mary Chandler, half-hidden in the shadows. "You kidnapped a human, someone who had nothing to do with the family or with your feud. You could have exposed all of us and for what? Your precious son?"

Mary straightened up, pushing McCallister away. She snarled, showing her teeth.

Jess pointed at her. "Don't start with me, woman. You're lucky I'm willing to let you walk out of here in one piece. I'd be within my rights to challenge you right here and now and beat your ass into a bloody pulp." She glanced at Evan. "I'll let him handle you from here on. But know that our friendship is over and your bad decisions have been noted by the Council."

Mary opened her mouth as if to answer but hesitated thanks to McCallister's hand grabbing her forearm. He whispered something in her ear.

Jess's eyes narrowed as she watched the pair.

She turned back to Evan and Jake. "I'm glad things worked out this way. I'm sure the Board will be pleased, along with the Council." She shook both their hands before walking back to stand by me.

"Those two might be trouble in the future." I looked toward Mary and her new best friend.

"I can deal with that. New generation, new start." She zeroed in on Red, frowning. "Who is that?"

"Ah—" I wasn't sure how to even start explaining his presence.

The older Felis must have overheard Jess because

he left Lisa's side and strode on over with a wide grin. "I'm Red."

He grabbed Jess's hand and shook it, pumping it up and down. "You a friend of Suz's? Friend of hers is a friend of mine. 'Specially if you're on the Board, be good to have a friend in high places."

The confusion on her face was priceless. "Rebecca?"

Red released her hand. "Okay." He ran a thick calloused finger along her scarred cheek, a gentle caress. "You're cute. Call me sometime." He spun around and marched back to where Lisa stood, taking up his previous role as protector.

Jess blinked wildly, frozen in place. Her mouth fell open but nothing came out.

It was an effort not to laugh. I felt muscles straining, about to burst as I held in my reaction to her shocked expression.

"Where—where did you get him from?" She exhaled, something between a gasp and a sigh.

"He was in a homeless camp down by the lake. I have no idea who he is or where he came from. He thinks he's from the east, by the sea. He thinks my name is Susan." I tried to keep a straight face. "And now you know as much about him as I do."

"A rogue," Jess whispered. "Interesting."

I moved toward Evan and Jake before I said something that would get me smacked down by Jess. The two men smiled at my approach.

"So," I tucked my hands in my pockets. "All's well that ends well, then?"

Jake spoke first. "I have to confess I wasn't sure how

helpful you'd be. Figured I'd just send Eddie after you and bring my girl home whether she wanted to go or not." He smiled at Lisa, who was busy talking to Red. "I forgot she was turning into a woman."

"It's a father thing." I looked at Evan. "So no more sleeping in trees?"

He smiled. "Not for a bit. I've got lots of bridges to mend. We might lose a few friends but I suspect more of them will be relieved not to have this burden anymore, both financially and emotionally." He glanced at his mother who stood quietly in the corner with McCallister. "I know she wanted revenge for her mother and I can respect that. But we can't let one event determine our entire lives."

A shiver tore down my spine. "Yeah. I hear what you're saying." I looked at Mary Chandler. "Just watch your back."

"You bet. She is my mother, after all," Evan replied, a note of sadness in his voice.

"And Red?" I nodded toward the tall Felis standing by, waiting for orders. "What about him?"

"Geez." He shook his head. "I almost forgot." Evan waved Red forward, clearing his voice to get everyone's attention.

Jake eyed the large man with a mixture of curiosity and apprehension. I suspected he'd worried about having to face Red as an opponent when he first spotted him.

"Everyone, this is Red." Evan smiled at the older Felis. "I'd like you to be a part of my family, if you'll have us."

Red grinned. “I’m up for a change.” He threw a saucy wink Jess’s way, enough to startle most of the Felis in the barn. “Change is good.”

Evan laughed. “Then it’s settled.” He touched my shoulder. “I appreciate everything you’ve done, both Lisa and I do. Can I offer you a ride home?”

I snorted. “You got a driver’s license?”

Jess strode up. “I’ll take her.” She didn’t look at Red, tugging at my sleeve. “Let’s go.” Her gaze spun around the rough circle, marking each Felis in turn. “It’s all over.”

Jake and Evan lowered their heads, acknowledging Jess’s status. Red, after a second, followed suit.

I didn’t look around to see if Mary and her buddy did.

We headed for the door. I spotted the curious glances aimed at me on the way out, the muttered comments not meant for me to hear. I might be family but I was still a freak, outcast for my inability to Change.

“Don’t pay attention to them,” Jess ordered as she led me to her car. The Taurus sat diagonally across two parking spots. “It’s good.”

“No, it’s not.” I got in the passenger side and rested my head on the thin cushioned headrest. “It’s not good at all.” The throbbing had subsided into a dull thumping behind my eyes, threatening to pop my eyeballs out like marbles into my lap.

Jess stayed silent until we pulled onto the highway and for another half hour, driving in the growing darkness.

“That fellow—” she started, then stopped.

She was talking about Red.

"I'll have to poke around, contact the Pride out East. I'm sure they know who he is. Need to find out more about him."

Despite the pain I smiled, hoping she wouldn't see it.

She looked over. "You look like shit. When did you eat last?"

"When Bran fed us."

Jess snorted. "Let's get something before you pass out. Can you keep it down?"

"There's always room for donuts and coffee."

She pulled off at the next exit, the neon sign signaling both.

The rest stop consisted of a Tim Horton's donut shop and a gas station, one of which I needed bad. Jess nodded when I asked if she wanted a coffee and filled the car up as I went inside and picked up a box of Timbits the size of the Taurus and two large coffees, double-double.

She said nothing when I got back in, busy working on extracting her credit card from the greedy gas pump. I said nothing when she pulled into the parking lot instead of back onto the highway.

"Okay. What the fuck are you thinking about?" she rasped after taking her first sip of coffee. "I can see you're upset and that's what's causing the headache. It's not over Evan and Lisa, it's not over the feud. Are you thinking Bran's going to leave you for this woman?"

"She's not just a woman. Her name is Angie." I nibbled on a cinnamon donut hole, letting it soak up the hot coffee in my mouth. "She knew him before."

"And you know him now," Jess snapped back. "He's bled for you and almost died for you. What else can he do?" She smacked the steering wheel with the heel of her hand, startling me. "Dammit, Reb. Why don't you trust him?"

The coffee tasted bitter, despite the double helping of sugar. "I don't—it's not that I don't trust him. I don't trust her to not pull him into her orbit. She told me she wasn't interested, that she wouldn't make a play for him. But that was before she was kidnapped and he saved her like the white knight he wants to be." I ran my finger around the edge of the cup. "She's a part of his past he can't ever give up. I don't know if he wouldn't feel more comfortable in her world, her human world." I hesitated, trying to find the right words. "Her safer world."

"He already made that choice at your front door. So what if she makes a move on him 'cause she feels obligated? She can't take what's not hers." Jess shook her head. "In my day you'd just challenge her, beat the shit out of her and that'd be that. He'd fall into line like a good little boy and it'd be done."

I smiled. "You're assuming I could take her."

Jess snorted. "I've seen her. You could, Changed or not." She plucked out a dark chocolate Timbit, rolling it between her long slender fingers. "You're overthinking this and it's going to hurt your relationship with him."

"I guess."

"I know." She popped the whole donut hole into her mouth and chewed for a few minutes before speaking again. "You think it's because you're Felis and he's not."

I squirmed in the passenger seat. "Maybe. I don't know."

Jess sipped her coffee. "Bran is your first serious love, right?"

My cheeks felt hot. "Yes."

"And, God willing, your last."

I nodded.

Jess poked around in the box. "They never add enough chocolate ones. I think they do that on purpose." She looked at me. "Trace offered to marry you."

"It wasn't anything serious." I flashed back to the tall proud Felis from the Penscotta Pride. He'd been assigned as my babysitter by the local Board and ended up helping me find a killer. He'd also ended up facing Bran's wrath for daring to court me. Trace had backed down but the feelings he'd stirred up as a virile male Felis were hard to forget, despite my commitment to Bran.

"Serious enough." She came up with a white powdered hole. "I bet you thought for a second, a fraction of a second, about how nice it'd be to be part of a Pride again. Married to a Felis who wouldn't ask so many questions, wouldn't be curious about who you were. Accepted by not only him but by his family, by his Pride without question."

"It was because he felt sorry for me. A warped, mutant Felis who dared to love a human." I looked out into the darkness. My eyes burned.

"Maybe, maybe not. Ever think what prompted this?

He'd known you for a few hours and here he is proposing."

I shrugged. "I figured it was because his uncle wanted to distract me, toss something down in the road bright and shiny to throw me off the trail."

"I doubt that. I think Trace wanted you to become part of the family again, part of your clan," Jess said. "It was a kneejerk reaction but an honest one. He wanted to take you away from Bran not just because he was a human but because he knew you needed to be part of a group again. It failed because you told him no and went to your own family. You went to Bran." Powdered sugar fell on Jess's shirt. "Ever think this might be the same thing?"

I blinked away tears. "What?"

"Think about it." She held up a finger. "I'm going to spend a few moments here drinking some fine coffee. Don't answer, just drink and think."

The coffee was strong and hot, urging me to blow on it through the little opening on the lid before taking another sip.

We sat in the parking lot in near-darkness, the neon red sign reflecting off the windshield.

"Trace is to Angie what I am to Bran." I paused and frowned. "I think."

"Spell it out." Jess bit into a glazed Timbit. "Love these. Well worth adding a mile to my daily run."

I spoke slowly, choosing each word with care. "Angie is like Trace. She wants to offer Bran a chance to get back into their world, back into saving street kids. Back with her 'cause she never stopped loving him." I rubbed my eyes. "Their group, their family, their clan of street kids broke up when Bran left. If she gets him back she'll have pulled him away from the nasty outside world that drove him into writing trash articles, the world that hurt him and keeps on hurting him." I stopped, out of breath and befuddled. "And Bran's like me. He doesn't want to go back to her and to the streets because he knows he won't fit in but he's tempted because it's the familiar, the comfortable way to go. A simpler life with a simpler way of doing things." I couldn't help smiling. "Bran and I, we're our own Pride, our own little family. Fucked up, but we match up."

Jess plucked the last donut hole from the box. "Way to go, grasshopper." She waved it at me before taking a bite. "And now I can take you home without you screwing up a good thing."

"Since when did you get to be so wise?" I glanced at the inside of the box, hoping to find some crumbs.

"Since I got old. Now shut up and drink your coffee."

The rest of the drive back I sat quietly and did so, wondering whether age really brought wisdom or just bitchiness.

We pulled up in front of my Parkdale house an hour later, around dinnertime.

The windows were dark.

I peered down the alley running along the side of the house to my parking spot.

Empty.

"Don't." Jess put her hand over mine, squeezing it lightly. "Don't go there."

"He should have been home by now." I tried to keep the quiver out of my voice and failed.

"Maybe they went out for something to eat, same as us. Best place to debrief her would be in public, keep her from making a fuss if she didn't buy his cover story." Jess pulled out her cell and checked for messages.

"What's that for?"

She tapped something on the minute keyboard. "I would have gotten an alert if he'd been in an accident or anything like that."

I stared at her. "Since when do you keep tabs on that?"

She waggled the phone at me. "Do you think I do nothing all day but eat pie? I have eyes and ears everywhere to make sure my charges stay safe." Her eyes narrowed. "And that consists of the entire Pride plus you and your mate. When I said I put him under my protection I meant it, including having his name on our list to be flagged if it comes up at an emergency site." She put the phone into her hip pocket. "I knew you were at the hospital within an hour of you being admitted. I also knew you'd have that cop there because you hadn't updated your emergency contact and Bran was on his way, courtesy of the cop's voicemail."

I opened my mouth to speak and then thought better of it. It might be better for me not to know the extent of her connections into my world, past and present.

"And before you ask—the reason I didn't rush over

there was because your buddy was already there. No use muddying the waters with extra people, not to mention getting that cop's attention."

"Then why didn't you pull the trigger on McCallister there and then?" I was too tired to keep the anger hidden. "You knew all this and did nothing until Bran called and brought me up to the farm?"

"You were handling it well enough." She checked the phone again. "No use getting involved until I had to. Besides, Bran had it under control."

I didn't have a response to that.

"Might as well go inside and rest." Jess unlocked the car doors with a flick of her finger. "You've had a long day."

"That makes two of us." I stifled a yawn, watching her do the same. "Would you like to come in for a drink?"

I might be exhausted but I was still my mother's daughter, polite to the end.

I was also Canadian.

She shook her head. "I've got a stack of paperwork and plenty of calls to make. The Board's got to be updated and the Grand Council as well. If I'm lucky I'll finish up by morning." She paused and I saw an uncharacteristic look, curiosity mixed with something else. "And I want to find out a bit more about this Red."

I resisted the urge to smile. "Thank you for the help."

She looked at the dark house and then at me. "Don't underestimate Bran or his love for you, kit." One finger tapped the scar on her cheek. "I know how far a man will go for a woman. He's gone as far and farther, in my book."

The car drove off with a roar and skidded around the corner before disappearing. I winced, smelling the burned rubber.

FIFTEEN

I walked up the short path to the front door, fumbling with my house keys. My left arm ached and my head was on the verge of exploding. The coffee and donut holes had helped but I was exhausted and just plain worn out.

Jazz wove between my legs before I had a chance to hit the main lights, merping her annoyance with my prolonged absence. I made my way to the kitchen and replenished her food bowl.

I didn't feel like food but I needed something more in my belly than fried bits of dough if I wanted to take some pain relievers.

The toaster hummed as it moved toward burning the toast. I poured a glass of milk, not daring to add tea atop the coffee. My stomach was already twitching, between my nerves and the coffee.

I forced down the milk and toast before staggering upstairs to the bathroom and various over-the-counter drugs. The extra-strength pain meds caught in my throat on the way down just long enough to send me into a coughing fit, making the headache worse.

All I needed now was for Jazz to throw up on the bedspread.

I checked, just in case.

The salsa-stained bedspread was still on the floor in a pile, a fat lump at the foot of the bed. I should have tossed it to the corner stack of dirty laundry but I was too tired to do anything.

The sheets were cool as I stripped down to just my panties and a ragged old T-shirt and climbed in, not caring much right now what happened or was going to happen. I was dog-tired and sore and more than a little heartsick.

Jazz leaped up beside me with a grunt. She head-butted my hip as I lay on my back and stared at the ceiling. Upset and ignored, she settled down beside me and purred.

Waiting for the drugs to kick in I took inventory of the past few days.

I'd gotten two young people off the streets and back into their homes, safe and sound. I'd helped end a family feud and I'd helped a lost Felis find a new family.

Not a bad day's work. And I'd even gotten some money out of it.

I still felt like shit. My stomach rolled, tossing around the toast and meds.

I closed my eyes and tried to relax, the white furry bundle at my side providing both heat and purr therapy.

The forest was dark and deep, a warped version of the one I'd run through in my youth up on the farm. Black gnarled roots jabbed out of the ground at odd angles, ready to trip me as I ran through the shadows.

The trail wasn't wide but it was well worn, the tracks of hundreds, maybe thousands of Felis before me clawing a way through the wilderness. I was barefoot, wearing a shirt and shorts as I sprang over a fallen tree trunk blocking the trail. A mossy rock threatened to send me flying but I regained my balance and kept going, relishing the challenge.

There was a full moon providing enough light to run by and I could scent the other animals around me—predators and prey keeping their distance from me, from the other Felis who surrounded me. We were masters and mistresses of the world and we were on the hunt.

Problem was I didn't know what I was hunting for.

Other Felis around me growled and hissed as they found their mates. I imagined them falling to the ground and wrestling in fiery foreplay, each trying to top the other in a never-ending battle of dominance.

Felis may not have invented BDSM but we sure could embrace it wholeheartedly.

A wind whipped around me, bringing me familiar scents. Trace, Jess, Evan and Lisa—I caught a whiff of Red that flashed through, his laughter a sparkling flash in my mind's eye.

A new scent crashed into my nostrils, wiping everything else away.

Bran.

I stopped still, trying to figure out where he was. The distinctive odor was everywhere I turned as I spun frantically, toes digging into the dirt.

I couldn't find him. It was like trying to pick out a single raindrop in a storm, the overwhelming strength of his scent flooding my senses to the point of overload. Goosebumps scrambled over my bare arms and legs as I kept turning, trying to see something, anything in the moonlight.

A haunting roar went up from nearby, a Felis declaring his love for his mate.

Bran.

It was echoed almost immediately by other Felis; males joining in to add their voices to the group song.

I turned again as his distinct voice emerged from the chorus, growing in intensity and volume.

The howling stopped.

Bran came crashing out of the shadows and knocked me to the ground.

I rolled onto my back in time for him to straddle me, both of us panting.

His hands grabbed my wrists and locked them over my head, the weight of his body pinning me to the ground.

I thrust upwards with my hips to dislodge him but he wasn't having any of that. He snarled and pressed down, rocking against me as he let out another possessive growl. One hand reached down to rip my shirt open at the shoulder, exposing my collarbone and neck.

His eyes locked with mine, freezing me in place.

Wild, feral.

Felis.

"Only you," he whispered as he moved in on my exposed skin, showing his teeth. "Only you."

"Only you."

I snapped awake to feel Bran's weight on my hips,

his face just above mine. My hands were free and I grabbed at his arms, anchoring myself on his bare skin as I tried to center myself.

He stared at me, not flinching as my nails dug into his forearms. He was wearing what I'd seen him in last when he'd walked out of the barn with Angie, and while it stunk of the farm it didn't smell like sex.

I relaxed, willing myself to take deep slow breaths and come out of my half-sleep.

Bran's shoes thumped on the floor at the bottom of the bed as he toed them off, not moving from his dominant position.

"Are you okay?" he said. "You were thrashing around when I came upstairs. I thought you were having some sort of a seizure, a nightmare—" He gasped and I saw the sweat on his face, heard his heart pounding frantically against his chest. "I didn't know what else to do. I didn't want you to fall out of bed or hurt yourself."

I glanced at my hands, grateful my claws hadn't come out. The damage was done, though, blood already welling up in the small crescent-shaped cuts on his skin.

"Are you okay?" he repeated. His hands went to my face, cradling it. "Rebecca? Do you want to go back to the hospital? Are you sick? Is it your head, the concussion?" He studied my eyes. "Do you know who I am?"

"You're that punk ass reporter I'm madly in love with."

Bran shook his head. "Brain damage. Horrible stuff."

I chuckled. “I’m fine, I’m fine. Just a dream.”

“Okay. Just a dream.” He didn’t sound convinced. “So what happened after I left? Anything interesting?”

“Nah, nothing much.” I smiled, willing my heartbeat to slow. “Evan challenged his mother, won, and took over as leader of his family. He asked Jake Middleston for a truce and for the right to date his daughter. Feud’s over and our lovebirds are together.”

Bran let out a low whistle. “Wow. Didn’t expect that.”

“Neither did I. And Red seems to be fascinated with Jess.”

“Oh, no.” He shook his head. “I am not going to be in bed with you and have that image in my mind. No, no, no.” Another enthusiastic shake. “I’m sort of sorry I missed all the fun.”

I stroked the fresh wounds, remembering why he’d missed all the fun.

Angie.

“She’s gone,” Bran said as if reading my mind. “We went to the shelter so she could check that it was locked up and then I took her home. That’s why it took me so long to get back here.” One edge of his mouth tipped up in a smile. “Seems there’s good money in helping the homeless. She’s got a nice spot at Yonge and Lawrence, renting a semi-detached house that costs easily a grand a month. A long way from sleeping in the park and scrounging for food.”

I blinked, feeling the tears begin running down my cheeks.

Bran kissed me. “What? What’s wrong?”

I shook my head, not sure where to start or even if I could explain the confusion running through my mind.

Bran sat up again, rubbing his arms where I'd scratched him. "It's Angie, isn't it?"

I nodded.

"She's gone for good." Bran licked his dry lips. "I won't lie and tell you she didn't make an offer to me regarding carnal knowledge of her body. I put it down to emotional distress at first, giving her an easy out." He paused. "She declined the opportunity and tried to press her advantage, having me all to herself without you around to claw her eyes out." His cheeks puffed out as he crossed his eyes.

I sniffled my way through a chuckle at his expression.

"But I pointed out, and quite firmly I might add, that I had someone waiting for me at home. Someone I loved and cared about." He kissed away a tear. "Silly little Felis."

I snorted, trying to regain my composure. "Not silly or little."

"Hmm." Bran shifted his hips, rocking forward with a snarky grin. "Me neither." He looked from side to side. "Who brought you home?"

"Jess."

"You didn't ask her to stay for tea?"

"No." I took a deep breath, inhaling his natural musk and wallowing in it. "She's got things to do, people to terrorize." I paused before asking the million dollar question. "Will Angie keep quiet?"

"I told her it was some sort of family feud—that

much wasn't a lie. She won't go to the cops, she's still wary of law enforcement from her time on the streets. And she never saw anyone Changed so that's not a problem and no one reported her as missing."

I frowned. "No one?"

A bit of a smirk emerged as he continued. "McCallister grabbed her without anyone noticing. Her staff figured she went off on an errand without telling them and then went home or out. I also pointed out it wouldn't look good for her charity to get bad press about harboring runaways involved in gang fights and so forth, so keeping quiet about the past few days would be a very good decision." He bent down and licked away a wet streak on my cheek. "She's got nothing to say and that's the last of it. I don't plan to see her again."

"Ever?" There was more of a lilt in my voice than I'd planned.

"Ever," he said. "She's doing quite well for herself and I don't think there's anything to be gained by dwelling on the past."

"Good." I gulped.

He studied my face. His forehead furrowed with a mixture of concern and worry. "Did you think I'd choose her over you?"

"No."

Bran touched my chin with one finger. "Liar. Now tell me why you thought I'd walk out on you."

I gulped. "You've got it easy with her. She's human and I'm Felis and we're so damned complicated and you have to keep fighting for every inch of respect and I'm so much trouble—" I broke off, at a loss for words.

"I won't say that being with you isn't a hell of a lot of hard work." He tapped the tip of my nose. "And yes, I get tired of having to prove myself every time we meet family. But it's no worse than having a human girlfriend with her in-laws, brothers and sisters and pissy girlfriends and ex-boyfriends who'd want to take me on." He rolled over to lie beside me, taking my left hand in his right. "But I understand why you'd feel that way."

I turned my head to look at him. "I'm sorry."

"You should be." His free hand pulled up his shirt, showing the fading scars. "I didn't get these for loving her. I got them for loving you." He tugged on my fingers. "Only you."

"Okay." It was all I could say without dissolving into a puddle of tears.

"Now." Bran pulled me to my side with a devilish grin. "Let me say it again without words. But still using my tongue."

SIXTEEN

I awoke to hear Jazz hissing in my ear.

In all the years I'd had Jazz as a roommate I'd never heard her hiss. Yawn, fart and trill—yes.

Never hiss.

She screamed again and launched herself into the air at something, someone standing at the bottom of the bed, the shadowy silhouette a fuzzy imprint on my mind. Stunned and still half-asleep from our lovemaking, I didn't understand what was going on until Bran leaped from the bed with a yell.

The thick masculine smell stung my nostrils as I rolled to the side and hit the floor, dropping the sheets and now as naked as the day I was born.

Nathan McCallister.

Changed and flailing around, fangs bared and screeching as he clawed at the cat attached to his shoulder.

Jazz yowled and dug her nails farther into the right side of his face, a white-hot furball of fury.

She screeched again as McCallister pulled her free and tossed her at the wall. She smashed into the pale green drywall and slid down to the floor.

Jazz didn't move.

Bran launched himself at the Felis enforcer, the brief

delay from her attack giving him a momentary advantage. He sidestepped McCallister's weak swing and laid down a series of jabs into the man's right side, slamming his fist into the dark sweater like a jackhammer.

I jumped across the edge of the bed at McCallister's left, snarling as I smashed my right hand into his face.

With claws.

Unbidden, they'd sprung out and now ripped at his already-scratched skin, slicing across his face from right to left, across his nose and barely missing his eyes.

It wasn't for a lack of targeting.

He roared and moved back a step into the doorway, giving ground. Jazz's attack had given us the edge but if we flinched or fell back we could still lose.

McCallister was a Felis, an enforcer trained to fight.

We weren't.

McCallister screamed again and swung his left hand upward, his claws narrowly missing Bran's vital parts. The sharp edges scored Bran's torso, dragging upwards toward his face.

Bran leaped back as I moved in, following up my facial attack with a jab at McCallister's belly.

My claws caught on the thin black T-shirt he wore, tugging on the fabric before coming free—just long enough to let McCallister counterattack with his right.

His claws skidded across my ribs, breaking the skin. I gasped at the pain. It hurt like a son of a bitch but at least he hadn't disemboweled me.

Yet.

Bran grabbed the comforter from the floor and

tossed it over the enraged man's face. As McCallister flailed for a second Bran charged, shoulder out and head down, slamming into McCallister's left side and sending him back out into the hall.

Dangerously close to the stairs.

I followed close behind just in time to see the quilt explode in flying strips of shredded fabric, McCallister's claws making swift work of the distraction. The cheap, white stuffing whirled around us as Bran grabbed McCallister's wrists and yanked up. Bran's right knee shot up and nailed him in the balls, a straight-on crash that would have brought lesser men to their knees.

McCallister let out a yell but he didn't crumple. His hands twisted around to break free of Bran's, seizing Bran's wrists in a reverse grab for domination.

I skidded to a stop as McCallister wobbled on the top step, his sneakered feet trying to keep purchase on the varnished floor. He snarled as he fell backward, keeping his death grip on Bran.

I'd rolled down these steps once before in a fight with a Felis, a rogue half-breed male who had tossed my world upside down.

Now my world was about to be twisted bass-ackward once again.

I grabbed for Bran as he arched away from me, trapped in McCallister's grip and falling down the stairs, tumbling head-over-heels to the bottom floor.

The sickening thud spun my stomach into knots, the sight of the two unmoving men sending my pulse into overdrive.

I scampered down the stairs, bracing my hands on the walls for support. The remains of the comforter fluttered down around us like a white tickertape parade. The two bodies lay on the floor, motionless in the faint light drifting in through the windows.

"Bran." I kneeled down by him, panting for air. My claws had vanished, retreating back into my hands and leaving behind bloody gashes between my knuckles.

He lay on his stomach atop McCallister, his bare back covered with fresh scratches from our recent lovemaking. His hands, now free, were pressed to the ground as if trying to break his fall.

I couldn't see his face.

I could see McCallister.

His face was contorted in pain, blood streaming from his nose and from the nasty gouges courtesy of the double attacks from Jazz and me. He'd Changed back sometime during the fall and now looked like a slimy burglar.

One who'd just fallen down the stairs and broken something.

Bran let out a gasp and levered himself off the semiconscious man's body with a grunt.

"Damn. I was too tall to ride that ride." He scowled as he got to his feet, still naked. Fresh blood stained the side of his head and I mentally freaked for a second before placing it as McCallister's.

"Are you okay?" I took hold of his forearms and steadied him as he wobbled for a second. "Are you hurt?"

He sucked in his breath. "A bit dizzy. Been a long

time since I did a somersault. Like, decades." He shook his head. "Wow."

"Can you stand?" I lessened my grip.

"Yeah. Go." He waved me off, a slight wheeze in his words. "Get help." Bran looked down at the unconscious man. "Damn."

I hit the main set of lights and grabbed up the phone. It took a second to dial 911, my heart still racing. I stammered out the details. Intruder and ambulance needed. I hung up before the operator could ask more—I knew what they needed and I didn't want to get caught flatfooted chatting on the phone if there were more attackers on the way.

Felis tended to travel in packs.

"Get up there and get dressed. Toss something down the stairs for me." I glanced around the ground floor. "Bastard might have brought friends."

For all I knew we were about to be under siege.

Bran dashed out of sight as I put one hand to my forehead, trying to push away the start of a migraine.

Felis didn't kill Felis.

I had no idea what was going on and I didn't like it.

McCallister moaned and twisted his head to one side, letting the blood trickle down his clean cheek onto the floor. I headed for the desk and grabbed the taser out of the bottom drawer. Without my claws I had nothing. Unless the sight of my naked ta-tas would strike him blind, and I really didn't want to count on that.

Bran thundered down the steps wearing only gray sweat pants, leaping the last few feet to land beside me. He tossed me a matching pair of pants and a red T-shirt before kneeling by McCallister.

"You," Bran wheezed, "better be alone. If not I'm going to bring your entire Felis world down around your ears for pulling this stunt."

McCallister didn't say anything, blowing out bloody bubbles through his nose and mouth.

Tugging on the shirt I drew in deep breaths—both to settle my pulse and do a quick search for more Felis.

Nothing.

No one but McCallister.

Sirens split the air as I walked over to stand by the enforcer, holding the stun gun at my side. He was wearing a black T-shirt and jeans, ideal to sneak around in.

The jimmied front door told the story. He'd forced his way in and come upstairs to kill us. And in my exhausted state I'd slept right through his initial approach, letting him get close enough to take us both out in our sleep if we hadn't woken in time.

"Jazz," I gasped. I tossed the taser at Bran and sprinted up the stairs, taking them two at a time.

I skidded into the bedroom, tears blurring my vision.

The old white cat lay on the floor where she'd fallen, eyes closed.

I fell to my knees, unsure what to do. What I knew about cats could be put on a business card in Times New Roman 20 pt font.

I reached out with a trembling hand and stroked her back, watching her belly for movement.

"Jazz," I whispered. "Jazz."

Her eyelids fluttered for a second before opening. She blinked and started up a gravelly purr that sounded like an engine in dire need of a tuneup.

"Oh sweetie," I whispered. "Thank you so much."

I could hear voices downstairs, a familiar one rising over the others.

Hank.

Bastard probably had a special alert set up to inform him every time an emergency call came in from my address.

I wasn't going to complain. Right now I needed all the friends I could get.

Jazz got to her feet, wobbling like she'd been on a day-long catnip binge. I picked her up gingerly, watching for any sign she was in pain. She curled up in my arms and kept purring as I descended the stairs.

Bran looked up from where the paramedics were working on McCallister, discarded white wrappings from their treatments spread across the floor. His gaze settled on Jazz.

"Good kitty," he whispered, choking up.

McCallister glared at me with bleary eyes as they maneuvered him onto a backboard. The two men working on him muttered to each other and to the uniformed cop standing nearby, too low for most people to hear.

For humans to hear. As a Felis I could hear it just fine.

Back injury...he can't feel his legs...possible paralysis...

I didn't flinch, returning McCallister's glare with

interest. He'd come here to kill us and would have done so if Jazz hadn't attacked, giving us time to respond.

Hank came to my side, face flushed with worry. "Are you okay?"

"I'm fine." I nudged Jazz. "She woke us up in time."

"Who is he?" Hank looked toward McCallister, who was being carefully bundled onto a stretcher. "Is he part of that runaway case?"

"Yes." There was no way to keep this separate. "He's a friend of the mother of the young man. I found him and he went home, had a fight with mom. Guess her boyfriend didn't like the way things turned out."

That was an understatement.

Hank shook his head. "According to the medics the bastard might never walk again. We'll run him through the system but he's going down for assault, breaking and entering and whatever else I can think of between here and booking." He glanced toward the front door. "You'll need a new lock."

"What else is new?" I replied.

Hank handed me a business card. "He'll give you a discount if you mention me. Does a lot of work for the police."

"Thanks. Do you know a good vet?" I lifted Jazz, still purring like an engine on overdrive. "I need her checked out."

A familiar voice broke in. "I'll take care of that."

Jess walked in the open door, waving away the uniform on guard. "I know a local who'll take good care of her. Family friend."

Hank's eyebrows rose. "You again." There was a

hint of a smile. He'd first met Jess here in my living room during the Hanover case and I knew he was curious as all get-out about her friendship with me.

"Me again." Jess came to my side and spread her hands. "I was in the area and heard the ruckus on the police scanner. Thought I'd come by and see if you needed any help."

Protecting the Pride, the underlying message said. Protecting my own.

I leveraged Jazz into her arms, the old cat not resisting. She licked Jess's hand once before settling down in her arms, still purring.

"I'll call Amy from the car, take her right over. She's got a clinic not far from here." Jess looked over at Bran. "I'll see you both at the hospital."

"St. Joe's." Hank offered, being helpful.

"We're not—" That was as far as I got before withering under Jess's lethal glare.

Hank nodded his approval. "Tumble down the stairs like that's not good for anyone, much less someone who got bashed about not so long ago."

"I agree. Get checked out. Both of you." She watched McCallister being wheeled by. "I'll meet you there to see how things are turning out."

McCallister didn't say anything and Jess didn't offer. This was a clusterfuck of the first degree, a direct attack of Felis on Felis.

This was not going to end well for McCallister, paralysis or not.

"She sure did a job on his face. Damned impressive work." Hank gestured toward the cat.

Jess chuckled and rocked the white cat gently. "She's a fighter."

Hank looked at me, his eyes searching mine. "She sure is."

I cleared my throat before addressing Jess. "Thanks for the help."

"I'll be in touch." Jess gave Hank a polite nod before retreating, the white cat still purring in her arms.

Hank let out a sigh. "You've got the most interesting friends, Reb."

I smiled, feeling the first bruises start to rise on my skin. "Tell me about it."

We rode in a separate ambulance than McCallister, Hank assuring me that he'd leave a uniform at the front door until we returned. The paramedics were impressed that Bran'd survived a tumble down the stairs with nothing more than what appeared to be a concussion, given McCallister's injuries.

"Cushioned my fall," Bran deadpanned as the emergency room doctor flashed a light into his eyes. "No regrets on my end. You come into our house and attack us, you take the consequences."

The doctor hummed and continued his examination.

I paced the length of the hospital room, my mind spinning through various scenarios. Had Mary Chandler been behind this? Had she taken control back from Evan and now declared a feud with me, with Bran? Or had McCallister gone out on his own, upset that he'd been dethroned as an enforcer and following a private grudge against us.

I rubbed the tip of my nose. This was far beyond anything I could deal with. I hoped Jess would have some answers.

"Looks good." The doctor scribbled on his clipboard. "Let me just get some paperwork done and we'll get you two out of here and home in time for breakfast." He gave me a sly wink. "I bet you'd rather be home in your own bed than hanging around here waiting for cold oatmeal."

I nodded with as thankful a smile as I could muster, given the circumstances.

"Bastard," Bran said seconds after the doctor left. "He would have killed us where we slept. Trash the house, make it look like druggies knifed us up looking for cash. With your neighborhood's rep it'd get by the cops without too much noise." He went to scratch his bandaged torso and stopped, holding himself back. "Maybe a rumbling or two, courtesy of Hank, but it'd go under as a cold case soon enough with the way they keep secrets."

"They" being the Felis.

I wrapped my arms around myself, trying to hold in the shivering.

I was getting too old for this crap.

"Think Jazz is okay?" Bran asked.

I shrugged. "She's a tough old broad. Hopefully she just got rattled by the entire thing."

He chuckled. "Did a good job on his face. Wonder how many stitches he'll need for that."

I gestured at the thin scratches on his torso. "Not enough for doing that to you."

We'd both accepted antiseptic ointment and bandages on our wounds.

Bran poked at them again, drawing his fingers over the itchy skin. "More love scars. At this rate I'm going to look like Frankenstein if we make it to old age." He reached out and took my hand. "That wasn't all Jazz's claws on his face, if I recall correctly." His fingertips traced my knuckles and he grinned. "You brought it, girl."

"Damned unreliable." I flexed my fingers, feeling the already-healing skin twitch with pain. "Damned freak."

"Don't say that." Bran hopped off the examination table and pulled me into a hug. "Jazz might have started it but you finished it and saved us both. If you hadn't clawed him he wouldn't have stepped back and fallen."

I tucked my head under his chin with a weary sigh. "I hope she's okay."

"She's fine." Jess said from the doorway.

Bran rolled his eyes. "How do you do that?"

"Do what?" She strolled in. "Jazz is out in the car, safe and sound. Amy gave her a clean bill of health but says she should take it easy for a few days."

I snorted as I pulled away from Bran. "Be lazier? That's not going to be possible."

Jess smiled. "Tough little kitty." Her eyes narrowed as she spotted the fresh bandages through Bran's half-open shirt. "McCallister do that?"

"Yep." Bran fastened the buttons. "Told them McCallister scratched us with his fingernails, psycho attacker. Figure it's as good as anything else to put on the report."

"Well done." Jess turned to me. "This is one hell of a mess."

"Is Evan okay?" I asked.

"He's fine. Pissed off to the max, but fine. Everyone's pissed off." Jess shook her head. "McCallister was acting on his own, so he says. Mary's denying everything and there's no way to prove she put him up to it."

I thought about asking how Jess'd managed to talk to McCallister, considering he was supposedly under arrest and isolated from everyone.

I reconsidered when I heard the anger in her words. Jess had her ways with humans and Felis alike—she got what she wanted.

"What was 'it,' actually?" Bran asked.

"Kill you, kill Rebecca and then burn the house down to hide the trail. Straight-out revenge for Mary losing leadership of her family and his demotion."

"Bad ass." Bran let out a low whistle. "What happens now?"

"Prelim report says he's got a broken back, possible paralysis. There'll be discussions on farther medical treatment but I think he's paid a pretty price up front for trying to take you both out."

Bran shifted from one foot to the other. "Going to be a hard life for him. Wasn't what I wanted to happen."

Jess fixed her one good eye on him. "From what I understand he dragged you down the stairs after him, seconds after he tried to kill both of you in bed. I wouldn't spare any tears for the bastard."

"I wasn't," Bran said. "Just don't like it being my fault."

"It's not your fault," Jess replied. "It was his for being a fool. Killing you and Reb would start a shit-storm and he was okay taking that road. His choice, his results." She turned back to me. "I can take the two of you home if you'd like. Save the cost of a cab."

I rubbed my eyes. "I'm not sure what I'd like right now."

Bran took charge. "That'd be nice, thanks." He tilted his chin toward Jess with the right amount of submission.

She eyed him. "You're getting quite the rep, kit. Taking out Carson and now McCallister." There was a twinkle in her eye. "You sure there isn't any Felis blood in your family line?"

Bran grinned. "Nope. Just good old red-blooded human male. You'd be surprised at how much we can do once we put our mind to it."

She arched one eyebrow, raking him with her gaze. "I'll make a note."

I took Bran's arm. "Enough. Let's go home."

Jazz was lying on the passenger seat as I opened the door. She merped as I got into the front seat and climbed into my lap with a slow weariness I could sympathize with. Bran sat in the back and said nothing.

The sun was breaking over the horizon, dodging between the houses as we drove. Jess said nothing until she stopped behind the police car sitting in front of my house.

I waved at the uniform, who seemed grateful to be released from guard duty. He pulled away from the curb at a fast clip, leaving Jess's car alone on the street.

Bran inspected the broken lock.

"Idiot didn't even try to pick it." He ran his finger over the shattered wood. "Dug in with something and pulled it out."

"His claws," Jess offered. "Had the gall to stand out here and dig the lock out with his claws." She sighed. "If he weren't hurt enough already I'd challenge him. This is beyond stupid."

I walked in, carrying Jazz in my arms. "Do you want to stay for tea and toast? I don't think I'll be able to call the locksmith before eight and—"

Jess put up her hand. "I've got work to do, least of which is making sure Mary Chandler and Nathan McCallister are held responsible for their actions."

I put Jazz down and watched her limp toward her food dish in the kitchen.

"What can you do?" Bran followed her, kneeling down and adding a handful of soft cat treats to Jazz's bowl. "Carson got away with killing Hancock and you did nothing. What can you do to them for trying to kill us?"

Jess's lips pressed together into a tight line and I knew Bran was walking the tightrope.

I didn't care.

I lowered myself onto the couch with a grunt, feeling my muscles ache with the effort. The last few days had pushed me to my limits mentally and physically.

"When family is the most important thing in your life it's also your biggest vulnerability." Jess crossed her arms, waiting for Bran's response. "You should know that."

His eyebrow rose but he stayed silent.

"They'll be dealt with," Jess said. "That's all you need for now."

Bran nodded. It wasn't a promise but it'd have to do.

I sighed, glad he'd chosen not to pursue the argument. I wasn't in any shape to deal with it and I suspected he was just as tired.

Time to shift things elsewhere.

"Thanks for the referrals but I think I'll try to stick to non-Felis clients in the future." I blinked, trying to clear the cobwebs from my mind. "There's got to be other family members who can handle these things. Lawyers, cops, other investigators looking for work."

Jess walked to the door and paused.

"There are."

"Then why me?"

She glanced at Bran, a knowing smile on her lips. "Because you've got a strong family here. And I wouldn't put my faith in anyone else to get the job done and done right with honesty and pride."

Then she was gone, sweeping out into the early morning light before I could respond.

Bran sat down beside me, rubbing his head in a mixture of exhaustion and confusion. "I'm too worn out to think that one over. Can we just barricade the door and snuggle here on the couch until things get real again?"

I yawned and tugged on a yellow and brown afghan lying on the back of the couch. "Definitely."

Bran pushed a table in front of the smashed door and returned to the sofa. He pulled me into his arms and I laid back, thoughts flitting through my mind like hummingbirds.

Jazz padded over to sit in front of us. She tilted her head to one side and let out a pathetic meow.

Bran scooped her up with one hand and laid her on my front where she spread out like a long white furry blanket, her rumbling purr vibrating through me and by default, through him.

"Damn we're a strange bunch," I murmured, feeling myself slipping into sleep.

"Yeah." Bran's arms tightened around me as Jazz purred even louder. "But I wouldn't have it any other way."

* * * * *